MW01632323

Books by April Wilson

McIntyre Security Bodyguard Series:

Vulnerable

Fearless

Shane–a novella

Broken

Shattered

Imperfect

Ruined

Hostage

Redeemed

Marry Me–a novella

Snowbound–a novella

Regret

With This Ring–a novella

Collateral Damage

Special Delivery

Vanished–a novella

Baby Makes 3–a novella

The Engagement–a novella

Wrecked

Under His Protection

McIntyre Security Bodyguard Series Box Sets:

Box Set 1

Box Set 2

Box Set 3

Box Set 4

McIntyre Security Protectors:

Finding Layla

Damaged Goods

Freeing Ruby

McIntyre Search and Rescue:

Search and Rescue

Lost and Found

Tattered and Torn

Dark and Dangerous

Locked and Loaded

Serve and Protect

Tyler Jamison Novels:

Somebody to Love

Somebody to Hold

Somebody to Cherish

Daddy Detectives Series:

Daddy Detectives Episode 1

Daddy Detectives Episode 2

A British Billionaire Romance Series:

Charmed

Captivated

Miscellaneous Books:

Falling for His Bodyguard

* * *

Audiobooks:

To purchase my audiobooks at a great discount, visit my online shop: www.aprilwilsonshop.com

Serve and Protect

McIntyre Search and Rescue Series

Book 6

by

April Wilson

Cover by Steamy Designs
Photography by Wander Aguiar
Model: Lachy and Ivenize Ruiz
Proofread by Michelle Fewer, Lori Holmes, Adelle Mery

Published by
April E. Barnswell
Wilson Publishing LLC
P.O. Box 292913
Dayton, OH 45429
www.aprilwilsonauthor.com

ISBN: 978-1-7372204-1-1

1

Jennie

I wake up in the middle of the night, my pulse racing. I'm drowning in sorrow. My throat is tight and clogged with unshed tears. It takes me a frantic minute to orient myself.

It's just a dream.

One that I have often. I cherish it even as it shatters my heart into a million tiny pieces.

It's my wedding day, and I'm wearing a beautiful white gown. All my friends are here—Maggie, Ruth, Hannah, Maya, Gabrielle, Robyn—as well as Granny and Grandpa, and of course my parents. Everything's perfect.

My dad walks me down the aisle, and Mom, Granny, and Grandpa wave from the front row of pews.

And standing at the front of the church, looking so handsome in a black tuxedo, is the love of my life—the guy I've loved since I was eight years old. The way he looks at me—his smile, the intensity of his gaze—takes my breath away. Even from this distance, I can see the sparkle of tears pooling in his eyes.

Beside him stands his best man—our best friend—Micah Jackson, who squeezes Chris's shoulder in a show of support.

Everything is so perfect, I could cry.

And I don't mean shed a few ladylike tears. I mean I could release a torrent of breath-stealing, heart-pounding, soul-shredding sobs.

Because it didn't happen.

It never will.

And it's all my fault.

It will never be anything more than a dream because my parents died when I was eight years old, my granddad passed nearly a decade ago, and the love of my life is beyond my reach. I missed my chance with him long ago because I was young and afraid and stupid. I let other people's opinions control my life, and I tossed away my chance for real happiness.

Out of loneliness and desperation, I ended up settling—and that turned out to be a colossal mistake.

I must fall back to sleep because the next thing I know, my 6 AM alarm is going off, dashing the cold water of reality in my face. I hit the snooze button, giving myself nine precious minutes of alone time before I have to get up and face the world and all my responsibilities—most importantly, Granny. And, of course, the diner.

The birds perched in the blossoming tree outside my bedroom window sing loudly and joyfully, welcoming this Wednesday morning in early May. Spring in Colorado is well under way.

Our male orange tabby, Pumpkin, saunters through my open bedroom door and jumps up on the bed. His squeaky purr is energetic as always.

"Good morning, Punky." I scratch behind his ears, and he eagerly headbutts my hand. "Yes, I know. You want your breakfast. Give me a minute."

My big, chunky boy walks across my belly, his feet somehow knowing exactly where my bladder is located.

"Not the bladder, Pumpkin!" I gasp as I gently relocate him onto the mattress. "I need to pee."

My alarm goes off once more, indicating my snoozing window is over.

With a groan, I shove the covers off, sit up, and swing my feet to the floor. I linger at the side of the bed for a full minute, giving myself a chance to wake up and gain my equilibrium. My mom always did this when I was little, and I thought it was a funny thing to do—something only *old people* did. But I'm just twenty-eight, and I don't consider myself old. Not yet, at least. Ironically, Granny is eighty-four-years old, and a spry little thing. When she wakes up, she's out of bed and on her feet in seconds.

I walk barefoot down the hall to the bathroom to pee and brush the tangles from my dark, chin-length hair. Pumpkin, my little shadow, rubs against my shins, purring loud enough to wake the neighbors.

I reach down to scratch behind his ears. "Shh, buddy. You'll wake Granny."

After taking a quick shower and drying my hair, I return to my room and dress in a nice pair of jeans and a pink T-shirt bearing the white *Jennie's Diner* logo. By the time I make it to the kitchen, I find Granny seated at the small table for four.

As Pumpkin races over to greet my grandmother, I switch on the kitchen light. "Good morning, Granny." I make my voice as chipper as possible because she takes her cues from the people around her. I stop to kiss her soft, wrinkled cheek. "Did you sleep well?"

She glances up at me, her blue eyes wide with surprise. "Hello, dear." She smiles. "My, aren't you pretty? I like your T-shirt. I used to own a diner."

"Thank you, Granny." I go check on the programmed coffee maker. "Would you like some coffee? It's ready."

Her brow knits in confusion. "Are you Sandra, my daughter?" she asks in her soft, sweet voice.

Hearing her say my mom's name causes a knot to form in my throat. "No, Granny. I'm Jennie, your granddaughter. Sandra is my mom." Or, rather, she *was*.

There's no point in reminding Granny about the loved ones she has lost, like her husband and her daughter. If I tell her, she'll experience the heartbreak all over again. She'll be devastated. And ten minutes later, she'll forget entirely. If I can spare her that heartbreak, I will.

"Oh!" She smiles. "I'm so glad you could come visit me. I hope you can stay a while."

"I would love to," I say as I pour myself a cup of coffee and add French vanilla creamer from the fridge. "Thank you."

There's no point in reminding her that we've lived together for the past two decades, since I was eight years old. That was the year I became an orphan. The year she and Grandpa took me into their home and into their lives.

"Would you like a cup of coffee?" I ask.

"Yes, please, dear." She smiles at me. "You're so kind to ask. I'm sure George would love some, too." She glances around the kitchen. "I haven't seen him this morning. Have you?"

My throat tightens like it always does when she mentions Grandpa. A heart attack took him from us ten years ago, and yet she asks about him every day. "I believe he went to the store to pick up a few things."

Granny smiles. "Of course." She reaches down to pet Pumpkin. "Good morning, my sweet boy." Then she turns her attention back to me. "He probably went to buy cat food. You know how much he loves Pumpkin."

At the sound of a quiet knock at the kitchen door, I unlock the door knob and both deadbolts to let Dawn Keller in. "Good morning, Dawn."

"Morning, Jennie." Dawn shuts the door behind her and secures all three locks. The extra deadbolt is so high up, Dawn has to rise up on her tippy toes to turn it. Granny can't reach that lock.

Dawn takes a seat at the kitchen table. "Good morning, Ms. Rosie." When she sees the empty placemat in front of Granny, she asks, “Have you had breakfast yet?”

Granny looks at Dawn, studies her a moment, and then smiles. “Are you my daughter?” And then, speaking to no one in particular, she says, “I have a daughter, you know.”

Dawn doesn’t miss a beat as she smiles at Granny. “I’m Dawn, your neighbor. I’m here to visit with you today while Jennie goes to work.”

“That’s a pretty name,” Granny says.

“How about a cup of coffee, Ms. Rosie?” Dawn asks. “I’ll even put some of that yummy French vanilla creamer you like in it.”

“That sounds nice,” Granny says. “I think I will.”

While I pour a cup for Granny, Dawn asks her, “Would you like some toast to go with your coffee? That sounds good, doesn’t it?”

“Oh, yes, it does.” Granny nods. “Thank you.”

After setting Granny’s French vanilla coffee in front of her, I pop a slice of bread in the toaster.

Dawn reaches out to gently squeeze Granny’s hand. “Eggs go really well with toast, don’t they?”

Granny nods emphatically. “Yes, they do.”

Dawn rises from the table and heads to the refrigerator to pull out a carton of eggs. “Would you prefer your eggs scrambled or over easy?”

“Over easy, I think,” Granny says as she takes a sip of her coffee. “This is good.”

Thank you, I mouth to Dawn. She has such a way with Granny. I don’t know what I’d do without her.

Dawn winks at me as she mouths back, *no problem*.

Dawn Keller has lived next door to my grandparents since before I came to live here. I hired her about five years ago, when it became clear Granny couldn't stay home alone. She watches Granny on weekdays while I'm at the diner. I come home for two-hour breaks between the meal rushes to spell Dawn for a bit, giving her a chance to go home and relax or run errands. Fortunately, we live only two blocks from the restaurant, so it's easy for me to come and go as needed.

Dawn gives me a side hug. "I've got this, young lady. You get going or you'll be late."

I finish getting ready, and then, on my way out the kitchen door, I slip on my work shoes and grab a sweater. I head out on foot for the five-minute trek to the diner.

As I pass my next-door neighbor, Mrs. Robinson, who's outside planting pansies in the front garden of her Victorian home, I say good morning. Mrs. Robinson watches Granny on Saturdays while I'm at the diner for half a day. I take Sundays off so I can spend a quiet day at home.

Next door to the Robinsons are the Andersons. Years ago, I babysat their kids. I say good morning to Mr. Anderson as he gets into his car to leave for work.

With its population a little over eight hundred, Bryce, Colorado, is a small town at the base of the Rocky Mountains. Everybody pretty much knows everybody. Sometimes that's a good thing, and sometimes it's not. News certainly travels fast.

I walk past two more houses on my street before I cross at the corner, turning west toward Main Street. There is one more block of old Victorian homes until I come up behind the strip mall where my diner is located.

I walk inside, flipping on all the lights as I go. I pass my office on the left, and the storage room on the right.

As I approach the kitchen where my head cook, Robert, is hard at work prepping for breakfast, I can smell the biscuits in the oven. "Good morning, Robert!" I say as I pass by the open kitchen door and continue into the dining room.

"Mornin', Ms. Jennie," he calls after me in his deep, baritone voice.

Robert has worked here for years, and he's the backbone of my staff. He's a big man with a broad, barrel chest, and a voice like warm molasses. His skin is dark brown, and he keeps his graying hair cut short. At over six-four, he's physically intimidating, but he's a gentle giant. As a former Army sergeant, he has a knack for keeping the kitchen running like a well-oiled machine.

We have two full-time cooks, plus a couple of part-timers. Their schedules are staggered a bit. Robert comes in at six and leaves at three, and Diego comes in at ten and stays until we close at seven. The part-timers are semi-retired and only come in as we need the extra help.

I love these quiet, early morning moments before we're flooded with hungry customers. This is when I make time for my favorite activities—starting on the cake donuts and slicing the pies I baked the day before. I've got a system worked out. I can make several batches of cake donuts fresh every morning and slice the pies—cherry, apple, blueberry, and pecan. I'm sort of known around these parts for my baked goods.

I learned everything I know about running the diner from Granny.

It's six-forty-five now, and the first shift of servers will be here any moment. When we switch on the OPEN sign at seven, the breakfast crowd will flood through the doors, and this place will be a madhouse for a good three hours. But I can't complain. Business is good.

The diner is open from seven to seven. It's a long day, but I run back home for two-hour breaks between breakfast and lunch, and between lunch and dinner, to spend time with Granny and give Dawn a break. Dawn stays with Granny until I get home for the day a little after seven.

The back door opens and my two full-time servers, Cara and Michelle, shuffle in, along with Chad, our resident dishwasher and general cleaning crew of one.

Cara readies the cash register and starts making coffee, while Michelle puts down all the chairs and lays out the place settings. Chad makes sure all the trashcans are empty and the bathrooms and floors are clean.

Right at seven, I switch on the neon OPEN sign and unlock the front door. There's already a line halfway down the block. Of course, it doesn't hurt that I'm one of the few places in our small town where you can get a fresh-cooked hot breakfast. The only other place that serves breakfast is the restaurant at The Wilderness Lodge. Ruth's Tavern, which is right next door to us, doesn't open until three. So, if folks want a hot breakfast, their choices are my diner, the restaurant at The Lodge, or the gas station on the south edge of town, which sells premade breakfast sandwiches and burritos hot out of the microwave.

I do a good business here in Bryce. Our small town is about half-an-hour north of Estes Park, so we get a lot of tourist traffic along our main road. I make enough to keep the business afloat, pay my bills, and hire two caregivers for my grandma. The house is paid off—has been for years. It was my grandparents' house, and when my parents were killed in a car accident in Texas, I came here to Bryce to live with them. I was just nineteen when Grandpa died. It was shortly after he passed that Granny was first diagnosed with dementia. She added my name to the deed on the house, and she handed responsibility of the diner over to me. *Rosie's Diner* quickly became *Jennie's Diner.*

As breakfast gets underway, I finish slicing the pies and put them and some donuts in the bakery display case. People drive a fair distance for my pies.

A few minutes before eight, I box up a dozen iced cake donuts to take next door to Emerson's Grocery Store, owned and run by one of my best friends, Maggie Emerson. Well, she's Maggie *Ramsey* now since getting married to Owen.

"Good morning," I say as I walk through the door that connects the diner to the grocery store.

"Good morning," Maggie says. As always, she's got a smile on her pretty, freckled face. "Perfect timing. I'm just about to open." She lifts the dome lid of her glass display stand while I arrange the donuts on the silver platter underneath.

"How's the family?" I ask as she lowers the lid.

"Good. Owen's renovating the barn. Claire is *not* teething at the moment, which is a miracle. And the boys are busy with part-time jobs, schoolwork, and sports. Riley has a girlfriend now, and Brendan just got his driver's license. All's well in the Emerson-Ramsey household. How about you? How's Granny?"

"She's living her best life watching reruns of *Little House on the Prairie* and loving on Pumpkin."

Suddenly, we hear a crash coming from the diner, followed by raised voices. I glance through the connecting glass door and see an unfamiliar female customer going toe-to-toe with Cara, my head server. The woman is shouting at the top of her lungs.

"Oh, dear," I say. "I'd better go deal with that."

Before I even reach the adjoining door, the irate customer hurls a coffee cup across the counter. She follows that up with throwing a plate against the half-wall behind the counter. There's an uproar in the diner as customers shoot to their feet. Cara starts yelling at the woman.

Robert comes barreling around the corner holding a metal spatula like it's a weapon. He looks ready to rumble.

I rush back into the diner just as the woman says, "I demand to speak to the manager!"

"I'm the manager," I say as I head straight for the commotion.

The woman is definitely not a local, or I would recognize her. About half our clientele are locals, and half are tourists passing through.

When Robert sees me coming, he rolls his eyes at me. "I'll let you handle this," he says as he heads back to the kitchen.

I finally reach the woman's side. "What seems to be the problem, ma'am?" I ask in my most professional voice.

She glares at me. "I'll tell you what the problem is! I ordered *white* toast, not wheat! And what did I get? Wheat! I'm allergic to wheat!"

I have to bite my tongue to refrain from telling her that white toast is made from wheat, too. Somehow I don't think she'd appreciate the clarification.

"And my eggs are overcooked!" she continues. "I said I wanted *soft* scrambled, and instead I got *hard* scrambled. I want a full refund!"

"But she ate it *all*!" Cara yells indignantly, her hands propped on her hips. "Every last bite. She's a freeloader!"

Unfortunately, this happens a lot in the hospitality business. Some people feel entitled to free meals.

The woman's face turns bright red. "I ate it all because I have hypoglycemia, and I was starving! Do you want me to pass out from low blood sugar?"

"No, of course not, ma'am," I say with a smile pasted on my face. Anything to de-escalate the situation. "I—"

"Don't listen to her, Jennie," Cara says, obviously still infuriated. "She's a scammer!"

The customer attempts to lunge past me to get to Cara. "You little bitch! How dare you speak to me like that?"

When I jump between them, my arms outstretched to prevent the woman from touching Cara, the customer screeches in frustration. She sweeps her arm over the counter, sending several place settings—plates with food, coffee mugs, silverware, and salt and pepper shakers—crashing to the floor. Everything made of glass or porcelain shatters.

My patience is wearing thin. "That's enough! Cara, call the sheriff's office."

"With pleasure," Cara says, gloating as she reaches for the phone.

My day is off to a bad start, but at least I'll get to see my best friend this morning. It pays to have the sheriff on speed dial. I have no doubt Chris will be the one responding to our call for help.

2

Sheriff Chris Nelson

I'm sitting at my desk at the police station, checking my e-mail, when our office administrative assistant, Darlene, pops her head through my open office door. "Hey, boss. Sorry to bother you, but Ricky just brought in Ted Monroe for DUI. He ran his pickup into the ditch."

"Again? It's the second time this week." I shake my head. "That old fool is going to kill himself one of these days." I check the time. "It's not even eight-thirty yet."

"They're in booking right now. Thought you'd want to know."

"Yeah, all right." I sigh. "Tell Ricky I'll be right there."

When I walk into the booking room, Deputy Ricky Stephens has Ted Monroe handcuffed to a bench as he takes the scowling man's photo for the booking report.

"He's too drunk to stand," Ricky says with a shrug. "And he wouldn't sit still, so I had to cuff him to the bench."

"Ted, I told you if we caught you driving drunk again, I'd take away your keys."

"You can't do that, Sheriff!" Ted yells. He's slurring his words so badly I can barely understand him. "I know my rights!"

"Watch me." I hold out my hand, and Ricky places Ted's car key on my palm. "This is mine now until you can prove to me you can stay sober."

"You're an asshole!" Ted sneers. "I'll never understand how you got elected to sheriff in this county."

"Well, Ted, it's a small county, off the beaten path, and apparently competition was thin. Looks like you're stuck with me."

The old man scowls. "It's cause you went away to that fancy university in Phoenix and came back puttin' on airs. You're no better than your whore of a mother."

Any time someone mentions my mother, I feel an inevitable sharp, stabbing pain in my chest. She's been gone almost a decade now—victim of a drug overdose when I was away at college—but folks around here still remember her. Hell, half the men in this town probably slept with her at some point, including old Ted Monroe. I ignore the possibility that Ted could be my father. It's certainly not out of the question. Of course, just about any Tom, Dick, or Harry in this town could be my daddy as well. I'll never know.

"Finish booking him and lock him up," I tell Ricky. "We'll let him sleep it off today. He'll get his chance in front of a judge tomorrow down at the courthouse."

"You can't do this!" Ted yells as I walk away. "Give me back my keys! That's my personal property! I know my rights, Sheriff!"

Ignoring Ted, I keep walking back to the administrative offices. My morning started off with a headache, and now it's gotten worse.

As I return to the front of the station, Darlene catches me. "We just got a call from the diner. A customer is causing a disturbance and throwing things. Do you want me to have someone—"

"No, I'll go." I head straight for my office, strap on my duty belt, and shove my hat on. I'm out the door and in my SUV in less than a minute. Fortunately, the station is only four blocks away from the diner.

When I arrive at the restaurant, I double-park behind a Jeep and a pickup truck parked out front and run inside just in time to see Jennie standing her ground between an irate middle-aged woman and the baked goods display case.

Just like it does every other time, my chest tightens at the sight of Jennie Lopez, and my breath catches. She's always beautiful, but right now she's nothing sort of magnificent as she fends off what looks to be an irate, belligerent customer. Her soft brown skin is flushed from exertion, and her dark eyes are lit up.

The woman grabs Jennie's arm and attempts to pull her away.

Well, there's a charge—*simple battery*—which I can add to *disorderly conduct* and *disturbing the peace*. Already I can tell this one is going to be fun.

"That's enough!" I yell, using what Jennie refers to as my *cop voice*.

As soon as she realizes I'm here, Jennie's entire demeanor changes, going from fierce mama bear to interested bystander. Her gaze locks on mine, and she gives me a smile, complete with dimples in her soft, round cheeks.

Curious to find out what will happen next, everyone in the diner goes silent. Even the perpetrator stops what she's doing and turns to face me.

"Thank goodness you're here," the indignant woman says with a huff.

I start mentally cataloging the suspect—white female, five-five, approximately 160 pounds, mid-fifties, white or blond hair (can't tell), wearing a pair of navy trousers, white high heels, and a silky white blouse with an obscenely low neckline. And lots of gold jewelry.

As I approach the counter, I'm resting my left hand on the butt of my service piece. It's a habit.

First things first. I glance at Jennie. "Are you okay?" If this woman hurt Jennie, I'll throw the book at her.

Jennie nods as she nervously tucks her chin-length, straight black hair behind her perfect shell of an ear.

Before Jennie can reply, the woman says, "Why are you asking *her* if she's okay? *I'm* the victim here! You should be asking *me*!"

"I'll get to you in a minute, ma'am. Right now, I'm talking to Ms. Lopez."

"I'm fine, Sheriff," Jennie says. "She—"

"Forget about her!" the woman screeches. "*I'm* the wronged party here. I want to press charges."

"She's wrecking the place," Jennie says to me, nodding behind her.

I step closer and peer over the counter at the mess of shattered glass and spilled food on the floor.

"She was unhappy with her meal," Jennie says, as if that justifies disorderly conduct.

"Yes!" the woman yells. "I want a full refund right now!"

Cara comes around the corner, spitting like a cat who got her tail stepped on. "Don't listen to her, Sheriff. She ate every single bite. If she didn't like her food, then she shouldn't have eaten all of it and *then* complained."

Jennie sighs. "Cara, it's okay. Let us handle this."

"I told you, I had low blood sugar!" the woman yells. "You stupid—"

"She's just trying to get free food!" Cara yells.

"Ma'am, calm down, please," I say to the woman. She's not a local, and I'd hate to arrest a tourist for being an ass, but if she keeps on being belligerent and wrecking the diner, I will.

And that's when the woman grabs another customer's coffee cup from a nearby table and lobs it over the counter. It hits the wall, shattering, and falls to the floor. Coffee drips down the wall.

"That's enough." I grab one of the woman's wrists and pull it behind her back. "You're under arrest."

"What for?" she shrieks. "I didn't do anything."

I grab her other arm, pulling it behind her so that I'm holding both of her wrists in one hand. I retrieve my handcuffs and secure her.

"On what charges?" she demands.

"Well, for starters, how about disorderly conduct, public nuisance, and simple battery."

"Battery?" she says, nearly spitting the word. "What are you talking about?"

"I saw you grab Ms. Lopez's arm."

"So what if I did? It's a free country." The woman tries to jerk out of my hold.

"Would you like to add *resisting arrest* to your list of charges? Now, where's your ID?"

"In my purse." The woman scowls at me. "On my table."

Jennie retrieves the woman's purse and hands it to me. "I'm sorry about all the commotion," she says, smiling apologetically. "I'm sure this isn't how you wanted to start your day."

"Are you sure you're all right?" I ask her quietly. "I saw her grab you."

Jennie flexes her arm, rubbing it and wincing slightly. "It's just sore."

When I ask the woman for permission to obtain her ID, she gives it, and I pull out her wallet and locate her driver's license—Bianca Hayes from Helena, Montana.

"All right, Mrs. Hayes, let's go," I say as I direct the woman toward the exit.

"Go where?" she shrieks. "Where are you taking me?"

"To jail. Where do you think?" It's all I can do not to laugh at her indignation.

She sputters in shock. "Do you know who I am? You can't take me to jail!"

"Actually, I can."

"I want to call my husband right now! And my attorney!"

"Relax. You'll get your chance to make phone calls after you're booked."

I pause a moment to glance back at Jennie. She looks a little flustered after her ordeal, but otherwise she seems fine. I allow myself a full second to take her in. If I weren't here on business, I'd stay long enough to eat a slice of her famous pecan pie. Anything that would give me an excuse to stick around a little while longer.

I try not to dwell on the notion she might have gotten hurt here today. When she smiles at me, my heart rate kicks into overdrive. Even after all these years of pining for her, I still feel gut punched when she looks my way.

"Call me if you need anything," I tell Jennie as I nudge the Hayes woman toward the exit.

Before I'm out the door, Jennie calls after me, "Will I see you at lunch?"

I nod. Barring a schedule conflict, I have lunch here every day. Sometimes alone, sometimes with Micah. I often come for dinner, too. I say it's because I hate cooking, but the truth is I just want to see Jennie.

When we were kids, I thought she was the prettiest, kindest, and smartest girl around. I still do.

I doff my hat to her. "I'll be here."

* * *

I ignore the constant bitching coming from the backseat of my cruiser as I drive Mrs. Hayes to the station. After taking her inside, I leave her in the capable hands of Deputy Stephens to book her and lock her up. It's early enough she's likely to get to see a judge today. I imagine she'll be out on bond before dinner time. Based on all the jewelry she's wearing, I don't think paying the bond will be a hardship for her.

"How'd it go?" Darlene asks when I finally make it back to my office.

"I arrested a tourist for disrupting the peace and simple battery. She's cooling her entitled ass in jail as we speak."

"Jennie's okay?"

"She was manhandled a bit, but she's okay. I'm off to do rounds now. See you later."

I climb back into my SUV and head down Main Street through the tiny town of Bryce. We have three whole blocks of a downtown. Blink and you'll miss it. As I pass the diner, I glance through the plate glass windows hoping I'll catch a glimpse of Jennie. I spot her standing behind the counter, laughing as she pours coffee for our friends Ruth Jackson and Jack Merchant. They probably heard about the commotion this morning and came to check on Jennie. It's a small town, and word travels fast. Maggie, who surely heard the commotion, undoubtedly called Ruth.

As I drive past the diner, I feel better knowing Jennie's got friends visiting her. She's not alone. There are a lot of people in town who would gladly jump to her aid, including me. I'll always be at the front of the line.

* * *

I fell in love with Jennie Lopez when we were in the third grade. I was eight years old when I first laid eyes on the brown-skinned, black-haired beauty. She took my breath away the minute she walked into my classroom, and I haven't breathed easy since. She was the new kid in town—the Mexican-American orphan who'd come to live with her white grandparents, Rosie and George Johnson, after her parents were killed in an automobile accident in Texas. A drunk driver had crossed the center line and hit Jennie's parents' car head-on. Jennie was not in the car at the time, or else she might not be here today.

Jennie's arrival caused a bit of a firestorm at the time. While things are a lot better now, Bryce was pretty racially insulated back in those days. Jennie was one of the few Latinas in our town. Unfortunately for her, the local kids looked at her with a lot of distrust. Not only was she *new* here, but she was *different*—Mexican-American. She was *other*.

But I didn't care.

I thought she was the prettiest girl I'd ever seen in my life. And probably the smartest. And when I got to know her, I thought she was the nicest girl I'd ever met.

Later that same year, Micah Jackson showed up out of the

blue—another new kid who was *other*—this one part Native American, part White. He was an outcast from the very first day, openly snubbed by the White kids.

And as for me—I was already a loner. I was the bastard kid of the town tramp, and everyone not only knew it, but they never let me forget it. I came from the wrong side of town, from a rundown trailer park filled with drug addicts and other unsavory sorts. The other kids shunned me for it.

I guess it's not surprising that the three of us glommed together like sticky rice—me, Jennie, and Micah. We just fit. And at the age of eight, we became best friends. *The three amigos*, Rosie used to call us when we'd gather at her diner every day after school for milkshakes and French fries. Rosie treated us all like we were her own kids. The diner was our safe place. We had each other, and that was all we needed.

In middle school, puberty struck, and that messed me up big time. Little Miss Jennie Lopez started developing like teenage girls do, and when that happened, she rocked my world.

I asked her to the eighth grade dance.

She said no.

I asked her to the Homecoming Dance our sophomore year of high school.

She said no.

I asked her to Prom our junior year of high school.

She said no.

So I stopped asking.

I finally took the hint and gave up because I didn't want to risk our friendship over my stupid adolescent crush.

Being her friend was better than not having her in my life *at all.*

* * *

When I drive past Jackson's Auto Repair Shop on the north end of town, I spot Micah standing out front, his head underneath the hood of a gray sedan. I park beside the car he's working on and walk up to him. "Hey."

Micah pops his head out from underneath the hood and nods. "Hey, man. How's Jennie? She okay?"

Of course he already heard about the incident at the diner this morning. Micah's older sister, Ruth, would have told him. "She's fine. A female customer threw a tantrum and broke stuff."

"I heard you arrested the woman."

"Yeah. She was aggressive. Yelling, screaming, threatening the diner employees. She also broke a bunch of plates and mugs." I peer at the engine he's fiddling with. "What's up?"

"I'm just replacing a headlight." Micah reaches deep into the engine compartment with a wrench in his hand, straining to grasp something. His long black braid falls over his shoulder. "This model is a bitch when it comes to headlights."

Micah is the mechanic who can fix anything. He's also a damn good helicopter pilot. After a career in the Army as a medevac pilot, he returned to Bryce to his auto repair shop. Now, in his spare time, he flies rescue missions for McIntyre Search and Rescue.

"Are you eating lunch at the diner today?" he asks.

I nod. "Unless something comes up." I can never predict how my day is going to go.

"Cool. We'll join you. I think Robyn's free this afternoon. I'll ask her."

We often eat lunch together—Jennie, Micah, and I. And now Robyn O'Neil, Micah's girlfriend, frequently joins us when she's not in class or working at Ruth's Tavern. She works part-time and takes classes at a university in Estes Park.

My radio squawks with an incoming message from the station. "See you at lunch," I say as I head back to my vehicle to answer the call.

Micah waves absently as he continues fighting to remove a recalcitrant headlight.

3

Jennie

During the lull between the breakfast rush and lunch, I run home for a quick visit with Granny, and to give Dawn a short break so she can go home and relax for a while. When I walk in through the side kitchen door at ten, I find Dawn loading dirty dishes into the dishwasher. Granny is seated at the kitchen table, wearing her favorite floral bathrobe over a blue denim dress and her fuzzy pink bunny slippers. Her purse is slung over her shoulder.

"Hi, Granny." I give her a kiss on the cheek. "Are you going somewhere?"

She nods. "I'm going to work." She points at the old kitchen clock on the wall that's been in this house for probably fifty years. "I have to get ready for the lunch rush."

"Well, you know, I just came from the diner, and everything is under control. Why don't you stay here and help me?" I wink at Dawn as she closes the dishwasher door and turns it on. "I could really use your help."

"Oh, sure, honey," Granny says. "I'd be happy to. What do you need help with?"

"Can you help me fold the laundry? There's a load of towels in the dryer." I nod to the side door, and Dawn takes the cue and slips out of the kitchen as I lead Granny to the laundry room.

I pull a load of washcloths and hand towels out of the dryer and carry them to the living room, where I dump them in the middle of the sofa. Granny and I sit on either side of the pile. Folding laundry is the perfect diversion, as it's something easy that Granny can do. It keeps her occupied and feeling useful, which is important for her mental health.

Pumpkin jumps up on the back of the sofa and walks back and forth, purring and rubbing against the backs of our heads.

"Where's that husband of yours?" she asks as she folds a washcloth in half once, then again.

My heart skips a beat. "He's gone, Granny. We got a divorce."

"When's he coming home?"

"He isn't. We're not married anymore."

Granny frowns. "Really? Are you sure?"

"Yes." *Thank God. I hope I never see David's face again.*

"That's funny because he was here just this morning."

My blood turns to ice. "What do you mean, he was here? You saw him?" That's impossible. David moved to Las Vegas right after our divorce. As far as I know, he hasn't stepped foot back in town in ten years.

She nods toward the front picture window. "I saw him outside, looking around. I thought he'd surely want to come in, but he didn't. Soon as he spotted me, he walked away."

My pulse starts racing, and my chest tightens. Surely, Granny is confused about who she saw. Sadly, her memory isn't reliable anymore. It couldn't have been my ex-husband.

As a distraction, I turn the TV on so we can watch reruns of *Little House on the Prairie* on DVD. Granny loves that show, I think because it reminds her of happy times. I remember watching reruns of the series with her and Grandpa when I first came to live with them. And before that, I watched them with my mom when I was little. It's a familiar comfort for both of us.

We fold washcloths and hand towels for half an hour, until we have two stacks of them. Granny helps me carry them to the linen closet and lay them on the shelf. Later tonight, after Granny is in bed for the night, I'll retrieve them from the linen closet and put them back in the dryer so we can do it all over again tomorrow.

"Would you like something to drink? Or a snack?" I ask her.

"No, thank you." She gives me the sweetest smile, and the corners of her blue eyes crinkle. "I think I'll just rest in my chair for a bit, if you don't mind."

"Of course, I don't mind. Let me get your blanket."

After she settles comfortably in her rocking recliner, I cover her with her favorite fleece blanket. This is Pumpkin's cue to jump into her lap and curl up. I turn off the TV and the light so she can nap peacefully.

She'll sleep for about an hour, and I'll have her lunch ready when she wakes up. She'll eat around 11:30, and then Dawn will return a few minutes before noon. That's when I'll run back to the diner to help out with the lunch crowd.

I walk over to the big front window to close the curtains and catch sight of a man walking away, down the street. I stare at him, unable to look away. He's the right height, and the right build. He's wearing the same type of cowboy hat David always wore. The same boots. He's got the same king-of-the-world swagger.

It can't be David. It just can't.

His parents are away for the summer on a European cruise. To my knowledge, I don't think he has any friends left in town. There's no reason for him to be here.

A chill runs down my spine.

It can't be him.

* * *

On my way back to the diner, I stop in first at Emerson's Grocery Store and find Maggie in the produce department unboxing a shipment of apples. "Hey."

She glances up from her work. "Hey, you. How's it going? Calmer now, I hope, after the drama this morning."

"Yes, much calmer, thank you."

"What's up? Do you need something?"

"No. I just wanted to ask you—I know it's stupid, and surely you'd tell me if you'd seen him—"

"Jennie, please, spit it out."

"Have you seen David in town lately?"

"David?" Maggie looks horrified. She never did like him, not even when I was dating him, and especially not after I married him. She wasn't stupid. She saw all the signs. "No! If I had, believe me, you'd be the first to know. Why are you even asking?"

"Granny told me she saw him this morning outside our house. I thought for sure she was confused. But then, a little while ago, I saw someone walking down our street, heading away from our house, and I could have sworn it was David. I mean, it looked just like him."

"Did you see his face?"

"No. I only saw him from behind."

Maggie looks worried. "No, I haven't seen him. And if he were in town, he'd need groceries, and I'm pretty much the only game in town. If he were here, I think I would have seen him. Granny must have been confused, and her confusion has rubbed off on you. She put the thought in your head."

"I know. You're right. I just thought I'd ask. I figured if anyone came across him, it would be you or Ruth."

She nods. "Yeah, he did like to drink, didn't he? He was his most abusive when he was drunk."

"You're right. I'm just being silly. Forget I said anything."

"Have you mentioned any of this to Chris? Maybe it wouldn't hurt to give him a heads up. He could ask the deputies to keep an eye out for David, just in case."

"Chris? No." *God, no.* "I wouldn't want to bother him with this. I'm sure it's all in my head."

Chris knows very little about my disastrous marriage right out of high school, but it's not something we've ever talked about. I was married and divorced while he was at school in Arizona. By the time he returned to Bryce, my relationship with David was old news. There was no reason to bring it up. Plus, I was ashamed to talk about it. I let myself get suckered in by an abusive asshole.

After saying goodbye to Maggie, I walk through the connecting door into the diner. Speaking of Chris, I spot him immediately, seated with Micah and Robyn at one of the booths near the front windows. My first thought when I see them is *Thank God.* The guys always looked out for me when we were kids. And now they've grown into formidable men. Just knowing I have them in my life makes me feel safer.

Micah and Robyn are seated on one side of the booth. His arm is across her shoulders, and she's leaning her head on him. He says something, and she laughs. They make such a striking couple. The contrast between his midnight black, long braided hair and warm brown skin and her auburn hair, blue eyes, and pale, freckled complexion is stunning.

Chris sits alone opposite them, looking so handsome in his tan sheriff's uniform. His hair has darkened a lot since he was a kid. He was so blond back then, practically a towhead, but now his hair is more of a darker blond. His trim beard, too.

His hair isn't the only thing about him that's changed over the years. Of the three of us, he was always the runt, but apparently he had a growth spurt in college. By the time he came back to town, he'd nearly caught up to Micah. The way Chris's shoulders and arms fill out that uniform shirt is enough to give a girl fantasies.

When Robyn catches sight of me, she straightens in her seat and waves. I return her smile and wave back. I'm so happy Micah has her in his life now. They recently purchased a home here in town, just two streets over from mine. They were living in Micah's one-room log cabin located behind the auto repair shop, but they needed more space. For an engagement gift, Micah asked Robyn to pick out a house in town. She was over the moon at the prospect of them having their own house because she spent most of her adolescence in foster care, moving from placement to placement, and it had been years since she felt like she had a real home.

"Hi, guys!" I say as I stop at their table. They already have drinks—milkshakes, to be exact. Not a surprise. "Sorry I'm late. I stopped in to speak to Maggie for a minute. Have you ordered yet?"

Just as I ask, Cara brings a tray to their table and delivers their lunches. Burgers and fries for the guys. Robyn has a turkey melt and mashed potatoes with gravy.

"Do you have time to join us?" Chris asks. He scoots closer to the window to make room for me and pats the bench seat beside him. "Sit."

"Sure, for a few minutes." I slide in next to Chris. God, he smells good. I detect a hint of cologne and the smell of fresh laundry.

When I steal a fry off his plate, he smiles. I swear, that man would let me get away with murder.

When I finish chewing, he holds out another fry. I open my mouth, and he pops it in.

"Let me go check on things in the kitchen first," I say. "I'll grab some lunch and come join you as soon as I can."

After I check in with Cara and Michelle, just to make sure everything's going smoothly, I pop into the kitchen and catch up with Robert and Diego.

Diego shows me a shopping list of the items we're running low on. "I'll stop next door later today and pick up what we need."

Chad's busy rinsing off dishes to put into the industrial dishwasher.

As usual, everything's running like clockwork. "I don't know what I'd do without you guys. You don't even need me."

Robert gives me a friendly side hug. "Don't be silly. Of course we need you. It's called *Jennie's Diner*, after all."

"Besides," Diego says, "who would bake the pies and donuts? Don't look at me." He shakes his head. "I'm a *cook*, not a baker."

I scoop some mashed potatoes into an oversized bowl and top it with homemade chicken noodle soup made with thick egg noodles Diego makes from scratch. I grab a warm dinner roll off the baking sheet, mix up a vanilla shake, and carry my food out on a tray to join Chris and the others.

When he sees me coming, Chris jumps up to take my tray from me and set it on the table. "Your public disturbance case this morning is cooling her heels in the county jail cell right now, waiting for her attorney to fly down here from Helena to get the ball rolling."

"That's going to cost her. Couldn't she just hire a local attorney? Imagine being that entitled." I take a sip of my shake. "I feel bad for her husband."

Chris nods toward his plate. "Help yourself to my fries. You know you want to."

Grinning, I grab another one, dunk it in my shake, and pop it into my mouth. "Mmm. Thank you."

Sitting here like this, sneaking his fries and dipping them in my shake, reminds me of the good old days when we'd come here every day after school. We'd sit at the counter where Granny would have milkshakes and French fries waiting for us. Vanilla for me. Chocolate for the boys. Apparently, not much has changed. We're just older now, and hopefully wiser.

No matter how rough school was, we looked forward to coming to the diner every day. This was our happy place. Our safe space. No one talked down to us in here—Granny would never stand for it. No one bullied us when we were in here.

Granny called us the three *amigos*, but really we were more like the three misfits. But at least we weren't alone. We had each other.

"How are your classes coming, Robyn?" I ask.

She gives me a thumbs-up sign as she finishes chewing. "So far, so good. The term is about half over, and I have A's in both of my classes." She crosses her fingers.

Robyn is majoring in social work. She wants to help kids in foster care—kids like she once was. She and I have a lot in common. We both lost our parents young. I had Granny and Grandpa to come live with, though. Robyn had no one. She drifted in the system for years collecting one bad experience after another until she aged out and ended up here in Bryce.

The bell over the door rings as two women—tourists, from the looks of them—walk into the diner. The sign at the entrance says *SEAT YOURSELVES*. As they approach our booth, they slow so they can let their gazes linger on Micah and Chris. I certainly don't blame them. Both guys are good looking. But Micah's obviously taken. As for Chris—well, actually, he's not. He's single. But I resent the idea of them thinking that means he's available. This isn't Tinder.

As the women pass our table, one of them—a tall, curvy brunette dressed in a pair of skinny black jeans, a tight-fitting magenta workout top, and shiny new hiking boots—nods at Chris. "Good afternoon, officer." She notices the badge on his shirt and corrects herself. "I mean *sheriff*."

Chris returns her nod. "Ma'am."

Faker. Those shiny new boots have never spent a minute hiking these trails. I may not be the most experienced outdoorswoman, but I know a poser when I spot one. The two women sit at the table beside ours.

"Excuse me, Sheriff," the brunette says as she leans in our direction.

He gives her a polite smile. "Yes?"

"My friend and I were wondering if you could recommend a good hiking trail nearby. Nothing too strenuous, of course." She chuckles. *Faker.* "We're newbies."

"Eagle Ridge is popular," he says. "If you're lucky, you'll catch a sighting of our local nesting pair of bald eagles. And then there's East Ridge Trail. That one's popular with families. It's an easier trail, more suited for beginners."

"I'll bet you do a lot of hiking in these mountains, don't you?" the woman asks. "Oh, where are my manners? I'm Aria, and this is my friend Bristol."

Chris's gaze darts to mine for a split second, and he has an almost panicked look on his face, as if to say, *What do I do now?* "Nice to meet you, ladies."

"Please, call me Aria," the brunette says.

"Yes, ma'am," he replies automatically.

"So, you're the actual sheriff in this town?"

"In the county, yes," he says.

I've had enough of watching this woman preen in front of Chris. I rise from the table and collect my half-eaten lunch. "If you guys will excuse me, I need to get back to work."

Chris reaches out and snags my hand. "Don't go." He gazes up at me with pleading eyes.

I notice Aria giving me the once over. Out of spite, I'm tempted to stay longer just to derail her flirting. But I really do need to get to work. When I made a visit to the kitchen earlier, I noticed our display case was running low on pies. I need to plate up more slices.

"Sorry," I murmur to Chris. "Gotta work. Later?"

He nods. "All right. See you later."

As I head toward the counter, I glance back once. Aria is talking to Chris again, but his gaze is on me. When he catches me watching, he turns his attention to Micah and Robyn. Micah says something under his breath, and Robyn elbows him.

I admit I struggle with jealousy any time a woman pays attention to Chris. I honestly can't blame them because he's a great guy. He's not just good looking, but he's kind and brave. But the idea of him with someone else makes me crazy because he's *my* friend.

No, he's... *mine.* He has been since the third grade.

When I was young, and Chris had a crush on me, I always declined his overtures. I was afraid. And stupid. Now, I'm not afraid. And I'd like to think I'm a lot wiser. And things really have changed over the years here in Bryce. I'm not bullied anymore. Neither are Micah and Chris. The guys have made their mark on this town, and they've earned the respect and admiration of the townsfolk. As for me—well, the townsfolk like the diner, and they love my pies, so I don't get dirty looks any more. And I no longer hear their whispered racial slurs.

But I made my bed years ago, and now I have to sleep in it. I turned Chris down so many times he eventually stopped asking.

I guess marrying David was the *second* worst mistake I ever made.

I'm pretty sure saying no to Chris all those years ago counts as the worst.

4

Chris

After we finish lunch, Micah, Robyn, and I wave goodbye to Jennie, who's busy ringing up a customer's order. I walk outside to my vehicle and climb into the driver's seat. Micah appears at my window and motions for me to roll it down.

"Just tell her, will you?" he asks. "Come on, man. You saw how she acted when that woman was hitting on you. *Tell her.*"

"I'll think about it." That's my pat answer to get Micah off my back. I'm not going to put Jennie in the position of having to say *no* to me ever again. I won't do that to her. That would make me no better than a creep, and from what I've heard, she's had to deal with enough creeps in her life.

Micah shakes his head. "I think you're making a big mistake, man. I think she'd say yes if you asked again."

"I said I'll think about it." But I can tell from the expression on Micah's face he doesn't believe me.

I head back to the station to check in with my staff and find out what else is going on in Bryce today.

"Not much," Darlene says. "There was a minor fender bender out on the highway at Phelps Rd., someone shoplifted at the hardware store, and someone broke into Mrs. Stauffer's garage and stole her brand-new e-bike. That last one, it turned out to be her grandson had *borrowed* the e-bike to take it for a joyride. She dropped the charges. Oh, and Jace burned the microwave popcorn this morning, so now the break room stinks to high heaven. Other than that, it's been a quiet day so far."

"I didn't burn it," Jace says as he walks out of the break room. "Don't listen to her, Chris. She ate more than half the bag, so that tells you something."

Jason Carver is my newest deputy, hired just three months ago after finishing the police academy at a small college in Denver. He's technically still on probation, but I'd say he's a keeper. He learns fast, and he's a hard worker. He's also a good team player, which is important when it comes to law enforcement. We need to be able to count on each other in times of crisis.

"The break room still stinks," Darlene mutters as she picks up a ringing telephone. "Sheriff's office. How may I direct your call?" She glances up at me as she listens to whoever's on the line. "Yes, ma'am. I'll tell him." As she hangs up the phone, she says, "That was Mrs. McPherson. She said her neighbor's goats are out again, and they're in her front yard trampling her flower garden. She wants you to call in a SWAT team."

"I'm pretty sure the Larimer Country Regional SWAT Team has more important things to do than come wrangle goats here in Bryce."

"That's life in a small town," Jace says with a grin. "I never once saw a runaway goat in downtown Denver." He thinks he's so smart, having come from the big city. He said he wanted to experience life in a small town. Well, that's exactly what he's getting.

I sigh as I shove my hat back on my head. "Come on, Jace. Let's go round up some wayward goats. Grab a few ropes from the supply closet, will ya?"

"How many?"

"Just bring 'em all."

I laugh when I hear his dumbfounded question. "We keep ropes in the supply closet?"

After Jace and I round up six escaped goats and return them to their rightful owner, Mrs. McPherson gives us a tin filled with her famous homemade chocolate chip cookies as a thank-you. We take them back to the station and set the container on Darlene's desk. The cookies are gone within an hour. Between us, three more deputies, housekeeping, and the evidence locker technician, the cookies didn't stand a chance.

I head back out in the afternoon to do my rounds, patrolling around Bryce and the surrounding areas. I bring Jace with me. It's all part of his training, teaching him the area and the folks who live here. Policing is as much about building relationships in the community as it is about chasing criminals.

A call comes in on my radio. It's Darlene letting me know some kid is doing donuts in the United Methodist church parking lot again. I head over there just in time to see Stevie Henderson burning up the rubber with his mom's twenty-year-old Honda Civic. The kid's only had his license for six months, and he's nearly lost it several times already.

Stevie stops on a dime when I pull into the church parking lot with my lights flashing and siren on. I park my SUV, and Jace and I walk over to Stevie's driver's door.

Stevie rolls down his window. "Hello, Sheriff, Deputy."

I sigh. "Stevie, did your mother say you could do donuts with her car?"

"No, sir."

"Where is your mother?"

"She's at home, sir. Sleeping one off. She had a late night."

I know exactly where Stevie and his mama live. They reside in the same run-down trailer park I grew up in. In fact, their trailer is two doors down from the one I spent the first eighteen years of my life in—up until the day I left for Phoenix. Stevie's mom is an alcoholic, just like mine was. She's also known for bringing strange men home for the night. Just like mine did.

At least Stevie knows who his father is. That's more than I can say.

"We got a complaint at the station," I explain. "Can you find someplace else to do this? Preferably where no one can hear you—or smell the burning rubber?"

"I could go out on Mitchell Road, to the old abandoned paper mill. I doubt I'd bother anyone out there."

"Thank you. Just be careful, will you? And don't talk to strangers."

"Yes, sir. Thank you, sir."

Jace and I walk back to my SUV and climb in.

"You're just giving him a warning?" Jace asks. "Isn't this the third time we've been called out here for the same thing?"

"Yeah. Stevie's a good kid, and I'd rather have him doing donuts in a parking lot than doing drugs."

"True."

I pull out of the parking lot and head back toward town.

* * *

After my shift ends, I head home to shower and change into civilian clothes—a pair of blue jeans and a dark green Henley. I live in a small, one-bedroom cottage on the edge of town, just four blocks from Jennie's house. It's nothing fancy, but it's clean. I don't own much in the way of stuff, so it's easy to keep tidy.

At six, I comb my damp hair—making sure there's no remnant sign of hat hair—and put on a bit of cologne before I head to the diner to catch Jennie before her shift ends. I know it'll be busy this time of the evening, but that's okay. I just want to see her one last time before I call it a night.

Does this make me a stalker? I don't think so. I prefer to think of myself as her protector. I just want to make sure she's all right.

5

Jennie

On Friday nights, I meet my girlfriends—Ruth, Maggie, Hannah, Maya, and Gabrielle—at Ruth's Tavern for dinner and drinks. They're my girl posse. *My family.*

Hannah McIntyre and her husband, Killian Devereaux, own McIntyre Wilderness Excursion Lodge, located on the outskirts of town. The Lodge offers outdoor activities for tourists who come from all around the world to ride horses, camp outdoors, fly fish, hike, learn how to climb rocks, and flirt with the local men. Proceeds from running the Lodge fund their true passion—McIntyre Search and Rescue.

Maya McKendrick works as a rock climbing instructor at the Lodge. She's also a member of the search and rescue team. Gabrielle Hunter is manager of the Lodge restaurant.

When I walk into the tavern tonight, I spot Robyn working as a server. Ruth and her significant other, Jack Merchant, are manning the bar. The guys—Micah, along with Maggie's husband, Owen, and Hannah's husband, Killian—are seated at a booth. John Burke, Gabrielle's grumpier half, is there, too, along with Travis Hicks, who also teaches rock climbing at the Lodge.

I wonder if we can legitimately call it Girls Night Out when all the significant others are sitting just a few yards away.

The only person missing at the moment is Chris, but I'm sure he'll be along soon.

"Jennie!" Maggie waves me over to an available seat next to her.

We're at one of the big tables that seats six. It looks like I'm the last to arrive.

As soon as I'm seated, Maggie puts her arm across my shoulders for a one-armed hug. "How's it going?"

"Good."

"Any more sightings of your ex?" she whispers.

"No, thank God."

There's already a pitcher of beer on our table, so I pour myself a glass. I notice Maggie is drinking a Coke tonight instead of beer. "What's with the soft drink?"

Her expression transforms instantly into a huge grin, dimples flashing as her cheeks deepen in color. "Why do you think?"

"Oh, my God! Are you serious?"

She nods. "We just found out this morning. I think I'm about six weeks along."

I lean in to hug her. "Owen must be over the moon!"

"He is." Maggie and Owen have one child between them, a one-year-old daughter named Claire. Maggie has two teenage sons, Riley and Brendan, from a previous abusive marriage. "He's been hoping we'd have another one. I told him not to hold his breath. Not at my age anyway. I told him we were lucky to have conceived Claire. I certainly didn't expect to luck out twice."

I bump shoulders with her. "Forty-three is not too old."

Ruth joins us then, bringing a party platter filled with all sorts of hot appetizers—boneless wings, mozzarella sticks, potato skins, fried pickles, pretzel bites with cheddar cheese sauce for dipping. The works. "I guess Maggie told you the news," she says, noticing my smile. "I just found out a few minutes ago. Tonight, we're celebrating."

We all raise our glasses and toast to Maggie and her new bundle of joy. The guys notice what we're doing, and they raise their glasses, too.

A few minutes later, Chris walks into the tavern. Clearly, he's off duty as he's dressed in blue jeans and a dark gray plaid shirt, open at the neck. He's got a white T-shirt on underneath. It's not often I see him out of uniform. My pulse speeds up at the sight of him, and for a moment, I allow myself to look my fill. His sleeves are rolled up, and I can see quite a bit of the tattoos decorating his right arm, as well as his sexy forearms.

Chris immediately scans our table, and when he spots me, he

smiles and waves. As I return the gesture, I do my best to ignore the butterflies in my belly. I watch as he joins the guys at their table.

Maggie leans close to whisper, "All that boy needs is a little encouragement from you, missy."

I snap my attention back to our table, to Maya who's telling us about one of the guests she took rock climbing this morning.

"Or, rather I tried to," she says. "Turns out this woman's afraid of heights and hadn't bothered to tell us. When she was about ten feet off the ground, she totally panicked and practically threw herself off the wall. If Travis hadn't been belaying her, she could have hit the ground and broken her neck." Maya raises her glass toward the guys' table. "Kudos to Travis, the tourist wrangler!" she calls out loud enough to be heard over the music.

Upon hearing his name, Travis turns his attention our way. I doubt he heard exactly what Maya said, but he raises his glass anyway.

The night progresses like it always does, with lots of conversation and laughter. We play pool and throw darts. We're on our second pitcher of beer when the door opens and two women walk in. I'm facing the entrance, so of course I spot them immediately. It's not hard to recognize Aria, the curvy brunette who was flirting with Chris at the diner the other day and her red-haired friend.

As soon as the two women walk into the tavern, they scan the interior. They start walking toward the bar, but as they pass the guys' table, Aria stops short as she notices Chris.

"Sheriff!" Aria says loudly enough we can hear her from our table. "What a surprise, running into you again."

Chris nods to her. He says something, but I can't hear what.

"Oh, my God, that's her!" Maya says as she nods toward Aria. "The lady who's afraid of heights." Her dark eyes narrow as she observes Aria fawning over Chris. "What the hell is she doing?"

Aria says something to Chris. He smiles politely and shakes his head.

"Probably asking him to dance," I say, trying not to sound petty and snarky.

"No way," Maya says. "Chris has better taste than that. She's such a drama queen."

When it's clear Aria bombed with Chris, she turns her attention to Travis.

Maya shoots out of her seat. "Oh, hell, no! She's not getting her claws in that boy!" She stalks over to the guys' table.

"This should be good," Maggie says as she reaches for a mozzarella stick.

The rest of us watch to see what's about to happen. There's no telling with Maya. She's a twenty-six-year-old Korean-American pistol with no filter. When she reaches their table, Maya grabs Travis's collar and literally pulls him out of his seat. He's laughing as she hauls him to the dance floor.

The remaining guys seated at the table—Owen, Micah, Killian, and John—quickly shut Aria and her friend down. They're all happily taken.

With a frown on her pretty face, Aria and her friend head to the bar. Heaven help them if they try to flirt with Jack. Ruth will read them the riot act and kick them out of her tavern.

Owen walks up behind Maggie's chair and puts his hands on her shoulders. "Do you feel up to a dance, babe?" he asks as he bends down to kiss her cheek.

Maggie pops the last of her cheese stick into her mouth, wipes her hands on a napkin, and rises. "I'd love to."

A moment later, Killian and John approach our table to claim their partners for a dance. That leaves just me seated at the girls' table. I glance over at the guys' table to see Chris looking at me. He smiles as he rises and walks my way.

"Looks like it's just you and me," he says as he takes the empty seat beside mine.

"Did that woman ask you to dance?"

He nods.

"What did you say?"

"I said, 'No, thank you, ma'am.'"

"Why didn't you dance with her? I mean, she's pretty. And she's obviously into you."

He shrugs. "She's not my type."

That doesn't make much sense to me because, if I'm being honest, Aria is probably every man's type. She's gorgeous and curvy in all the right places. I want to ask him what his type is, but I don't see how it's any of my business. I lost that right a long time ago.

Chris nods toward the dance floor, where all of our friends are partnered up, swaying to a nice, sedate slow song. "We might as well join them." He offers me his hand. "What do you say?"

I look at his hand—long fingers, clean blunt nails, no rings. There are sexy veins visible beneath his tanned skin and a light dusting of brown hair on his forearm. My belly quivers at the thought of those fingers touching me in a non-platonic way, those strong arms around me.

"Jennie?"

I realize I'm still staring at his hand.

He gives me a gentle smile. "Come on. It's not right that the prettiest girl in the place is sitting this one out."

I think about all those dances he asked me to when we were in school. All the times I told him *no*. But, I never told anyone else *yes*. Instead, I stayed home and watched TV with my grandparents. I didn't say no to him because I didn't want him. I was trying to protect him from all the bullying that came my way.

I rarely dance, so why is he asking me now?

He squeezes my hand gently. "There's nothing wrong with friends dancing, is there? Look at Maya and Travis."

I'm too old to have butterflies in my belly just because a cute boy asks me to dance, so I ignore them and chalk the sensation up to the little bit of alcohol I've had tonight. I nod and try to sound nonchalant. "Sure, okay."

The next minute, I'm on my feet, and he's leading me to the dance floor.

It's a Friday night, so of course the tavern is crowded with both locals and tourists, like Aria and her friend. That means the dance floor is packed. Chris pulls me close and settles one hand on my waist. His other hand holds mine. Not knowing where to place my other hand, I end up resting it on his broad shoulder. That seems like the safest option. Around his neck would feel too intimate.

We're standing only inches apart when he starts to move.

"It's busy tonight," he says as he scans the dance floor.

I nod, not trusting myself to speak.

We sway easily to the slow song, Chris moving us effortlessly. I feel his shoulder muscles flex as we change direction. He's taller than I am, so I end up staring at the strong column of his throat. His skin is tanned from exposure, and I see a hint of dark chest hair.

His Adam's apple moves as he talks. "I heard the big news."

"What?" I force myself to focus on what he's saying.

"Maggie and Owen, expecting again. Owen is thrilled. It's all he can talk about tonight. He wants Claire to have a sibling close to her own age. Maggie's boys love her, but they're practically adults, and Claire's still a baby."

I nod. "Maggie's happy, too. I think she's genuinely surprised she was able to conceive."

"I don't think forty-three is that old to be having a baby, is it?"

I'm not sure how to answer. I really wouldn't know. My mom was just twenty when she got pregnant with me.

I glance at Chris and find him watching me, and suddenly I'm hyper aware of the fact his arm is around me. We're standing close enough that I can feel the heat of his body and smell his scent—a mix of man, faint cologne, and fresh laundry. My belly quivers in response, and I want so much more.

The hair tucked behind my ear falls forward into my face, and Chris reaches out to fix it. Automatically, I flinch and pull away, out of his reach.

He frowns, obviously confused. "Jennie? What's wrong?"

Embarrassed by my knee-jerk reaction, I freeze. It's been *years*. Surely, I'd stop reacting to every little thing.

My heart lodges in my throat. "I'm sorry. It's nothing." But I feel stupid. I thought I was past this. But sometimes the memories return unexpectedly, and like a tsunami, they are wild and beyond my control.

"Excuse me. I need to—" I take a few steps back until I reach the edge of the dance floor before I turn and head for the ladies room so I can hide my shame in private.

Even after all these years, David still impacts my life like a malignant shadow that won't go away.

6

Chris

I stand rooted to the spot as I watch Jennie disappear down the back hallway. It leads to the restrooms, as well as out the back door. I have no idea what just happened. All I did was reach out to tuck her hair behind her ear, and she flinched like she thought I was going to hit her.

What in the hell? I know a fucking red flag when I see one.

I move quickly, heading down the hall hoping to catch her, but the hallway is empty. She's either in the women's restroom, or she actually made it out the back door into the dark of night. I certainly hope it's not the latter. It's not safe for a woman to walk home alone in the dark.

My pulse starts pounding at the idea of Jennie being outside on her own, especially in the frame of mind she's in right now.

I turn and head back toward the dance floor. The two women who would best know Jennie's past history would be Maggie and Ruth. Maggie's the closest, so I wave her over. She comes right away, Owen behind her.

"Hey, Chris." Maggie is a bit breathless from dancing. "What's up?"

"Something just happened with Jennie. One minute we were dancing, and the next she raced off in a panic. She seemed utterly spooked."

Maggie glances around the room as if she's looking for someone. "Tell me exactly what happened."

"Absolutely nothing, I swear. All I did was fix her hair, and she flinched. The look on her face—God, Maggie, please. See if she's in the ladies' room, and if she is, make sure she's okay."

Maggie heads for the back hallway with me and Owen right behind her. The two of us wait while Maggie slips into the ladies' room. Less than a minute later, she returns.

"She's okay. She's just a bit tired after a long day. She said she's ready to head home."

"Okay." I nod. "That's fine. I'll walk her."

Maggie shares a look with Owen before she smiles at me apologetically. "Actually, she asked if Owen and I would take her home tonight."

I open my mouth to argue—I *always* walk Jennie home from the tavern—but the look on Maggie's face shuts me down quick.

Jennie's *not* fine, and Maggie knows it. And now, so do I. And yet no one's telling me a damn thing.

I feel like shit knowing this is somehow my fault. "Maggie—"

She shakes her head. "Just let it be, Chris." Her voice is gentle and filled with understanding. "She's tired, and we're taking her home. That's it. Don't make this into anything more. She said to tell you she's sorry for the way she reacted, and that she'll see you tomorrow."

I stand here frustrated and confused and feeling guilty as hell. Somehow I hurt my best friend, and I don't know how.

Jennie finally comes out of the restroom, her eyes red, her cheeks damp. She's obviously been crying.

My heart sinks because I did this to her. "Jennie—"

She gives me a teary smile. "Hey, Chris." She does her best to sound upbeat. "Thanks for the dance. That was fun. I'm not feeling so hot, so I think I'll head home now. Maggie and Owen offered to drive me as they're heading home now, too."

We all know that's a lie.

Jennie reaches out and squeezes my hand in what feels like a conciliatory gesture. Her bright smile looks forced. "I'll see you tomorrow, okay?"

I squeeze her hand in return. It feels so slight in mine, her skin so incredibly soft. "Sure. Get some rest. I hope you're feeling better soon."

"I will. Please say goodnight to everyone for me, will you?"

Reluctantly, I release her hand. "I will."

Jennie heads for the back door, Maggie and Owen close on her heels. I know she's in good hands, but I can't help worrying. Something happened to her tonight, out on that dance floor. Something bad. I know fear when I see it.

The problem is, Jennie has nothing to be afraid of. At least, not that I know of. And certainly she has no reason to fear *me*. I'd die before I ever laid a finger on her.

Obviously, there's something going on I don't know about.

I head back to join the others. All of the guys are now seated with the women at their table. Everyone but Jennie, Maggie, and Owen, who are conspicuously absent.

"Where did the others go?" Ruth asks as she scans the crowded room.

"They just left," I say. "Maggie was tired, and Jennie wasn't feeling well. Owen and Maggie offered to take Jennie home." *Or at least that's the story.*

"Pregnancy will do that to you," Maya says as she refills her beer glass. "It knocks the wind right out of your sails." She takes a big swig. "At least that's what I hear."

Everyone easily accepts the excuses why the three of them left so early. Everyone but me. Micah gives me a questioning look, but I shrug it off.

I'm too restless to stay any longer. What I really want to do is drive over to Jennie's house and check on her myself, but I can't get past the fact that I'm the one who set her off in the first place. Maybe she doesn't want to see me right now. So instead, I say goodnight to everyone and head home.

Five minutes later, I pull into my driveway and park the SUV in the detached garage. I walk into the house through the back door.

My house is nothing fancy, but it's clean and tidy. It's a veritable palace compared to the filthy, moldy, bug-infested trailer I spent the first eighteen years of my life in. The trailer had only one bedroom, which my mom took. I slept in the living room on a threadbare, brown plaid sofa mom and I picked up off the side of the road. It was destined for the trash, but it was actually better than the sofa we had at the time. At least this one didn't smell like booze and piss.

There was only one bathroom in our trailer, and half the time the toilet didn't work. I often had to use the public outhouse.

The back door of my house leads right into a small galley kitchen. There's not enough room for a table, so I eat off a folding tray in the living room in front of the TV. There is a little dining nook, but it's been taken up by my treadmill and free weights.

I've got a decent chunk of money saved up to purchase something nicer, but since it's just me, and I'm hardly ever home, what's the point? It's not like I have a family to provide for. I might as well keep the money in the bank until I have need of it.

I remove my boots inside the door and grab a cold beer from the fridge. As I carry it to the living room, I pop the cap and plop down on the sofa. Out of habit, I turn on the TV for background noise and nurse my beer.

The image of Jennie flinching keeps playing in my head, over and over, and I wrack my brain trying to figure out what the hell I did wrong. I've danced with her before and never had an issue. We laugh, we joke, we touch each other casually all the time. We're affectionate with each other like close friends are. We hug a lot.

So what was different about tonight? All I did was reach out to fix her hair. It was perfectly innocent. I relive the moment in slow motion, over and over, searching for a clue. There's got to be something.

All I did was—

reach out,

with my hand,

toward her face.

Fuck!

My blood turns to ice. I've seen enough domestic violence cases to recognize an abuse victim when I see one. I come across them a lot in my line of work.

The question is—who in the fucking hell hurt Jennie Lopez? And why don't I know about it?

7

Chris

The next day, just like I do every Saturday, I'm sitting across the table from Micah in Jennie's Diner. I called him earlier this morning and asked him to meet me here so we could discuss what happened last night with Jennie.

He's as clueless as I am.

"I have no idea," he says, as baffled as I am. "She's never said a word about anyone hurting her. Ruth has never mentioned it, either. If anyone knows everything that's happened to Jennie, it's Ruth and Maggie. They've been friends for years. Whatever it is, it must have happened when you and I were away."

Micah left Bryce right after high school for a six-year stint in the Army. I left that summer, too, for Phoenix. What the hell happened to her during those four years I was gone?

"Here she comes," I murmur, keeping my voice down when I spot Jennie walking our way.

"Hey, guys," she says when she stops at our table. She automatically fills our coffee cups. "What can I get you?" She smiles at the both of us, acting as if last night never happened.

"The usual for me," Micah says.

Jennie murmurs "scrambled eggs, sausage, and toast" as she jots his order down on her pad. Then she meets my gaze, calm as can be. "And for you?" she asks me, her gaze darting away as if she's afraid to face me after what happened at the Tavern. "The same?"

My chest tightens at the knowledge she feels uncomfortable around me. That's the last thing I'd ever want. "I'll have the same. Except can I have a biscuit with sausage gravy instead of the toast?"

"Sure." Jennie scribbles another note down. "How's Robyn?" she asks Micah, turning her attention back to him. "She was so busy working last night I didn't get much of a chance to talk to her."

Micah's dark eyes light up at the mention of his girlfriend. "She's good. She's at home this morning working on a paper for her lit class. It's something to do with Jane Austen." He rolls his eyes.

Jennie has a soft spot for Robyn, who worked for Jennie for a short while right after she arrived in Bryce with a broken-down car and no money. Micah secretly arranged for Jennie to hire Robyn to work at the diner so Robyn could ostensibly earn enough money to cover the repairs on her old Honda Civic, but when Robyn found out Micah had put Jennie up to it—and that he was actually the one paying her salary—she bounced. She ended up working next door at Ruth's Tavern, instead. Ruth actually had a legit job opening, and Robyn took it.

"Tell her I said hi." Jennie tucks her order pad into the pocket of her apron. "I'll go put your orders in."

Just as she turns to walk away, the bell over the front door rings as the door opens. When Jennie looks to see who's coming into the restaurant, her expression goes slack as she stares. She looks like she's seeing a ghost.

My gaze snaps to the entrance so I can see who she's staring at.

Micah turns in his seat to see what all the excitement is about. "Isn't that Dave Braggart?" he asks after he turns back to face me.

"Yeah," I say.

Dave Braggart is one of the kids we went to school with. He was—probably still is—a rich asshole who never missed an opportunity to rub our faces in the fact he had everything, and we three had next to nothing. He was lead pitcher on our high school baseball team even though he couldn't throw a strike if his life depended on it. He didn't have to—his dad donated a ton of money to the school athletic program. It's fair to say Dave is the reason we hardly ever won a game.

He was also the main point guard on the basketball team, even though he couldn't run and dribble at the same time.

Braggart was an all-around douchebag.

"I haven't seen him since high school," Micah says dismissively.

"Me neither. I heard he moved to Vegas and took up gambling

like it was an Olympic sport."

Jennie storms over to Dave like an irate hornet defending her nest. "What the hell are you doing here?" she hisses, loud enough we can hear her without problem. "We have an agreement!"

Dave gives her a cocky smile. "Well, hello to you, too, babe."

She points at the door. "Get out!"

Dave gives her a smarmy grin. "Can't a guy stop in to say hi to the love of his life?"

"What the fuck!" I shoot to my feet, but Micah grabs my wrist and tugs me back down. "Why is he talking to her like that?"

Micah shrugs, as clueless as I am.

"I said, get out!" Clearly, Jennie's fuming. She's trying to keep her voice down, but half the diner is paying rapt attention to the scene at the entrance.

I've heard enough to know this guy is harassing her. Just as I rise, Braggart makes a grab for Jennie's hand. She pulls it back, out of his reach.

"Come on, baby," Braggert says to her in a low, cajoling tone. "Is that any way to treat your long-lost husband?"

"You are *not* my husband!"

"Husband, ex-husband. What difference does one little prefix make? It's just a matter of semantics, Jennie-bean."

"I told you not to call me that," she hisses.

"Is there a problem?" I ask when I reach Jennie's side. I lay my hand on her lower back. *I'm here.*

She actually leans into my touch.

Dave grins at me. "No, officer. No problem at all. I'm just here to see my wife." The man narrows his dark eyes as he studies my face. "Holy shit! You're that kid—what's your name? Chris Nelson, the whore's son!"

"David!" Jennie snaps. "Don't call him that."

"Well, it's true, isn't it?" Braggert asks. "Half the men in this town diddled Kitty Nelson at one time or other."

Hearing my mother's name hits me like a bucket of cold water. I can't argue with his claim, though. He's right. And I'm sure his dad was one of those who bought what my mother was selling.

"Do you want me to trespass him?" I ask Jennie. I'm proud of myself for maintaining my calm. All Jennie has to do is say the word and I'll escort this asshole out of her diner, forcibly if necessary. He won't be welcome back.

Dave's smile vanishes as he glares at me. "Who the fuck are you to tell me where I can and can't go? Go fuck off, *officer*."

"Actually, it's *Sheriff* Nelson to you, asshole."

Braggart purses his lips as he chuckles. "Oooo, I'm so scared."

"I don't know what you're doing here, David," Jennie says, "but you need to leave. Now. We have an *agreement*."

"Our *agreement* is expired, babe. I have every right to be here."

She takes a shaky breath and lowers her voice and says, "Just go, David. *Please!*"

Braggart's grin widens. "Oh, baby, you know I like it when you beg. You beg so sweetly, don't you?"

"That's enough!" I grab the front of Braggart's shirt and push him back toward the doors. "You're not welcome here."

"Bullshit!" he says. "Half of this diner belongs to *me*."

That announcement shocks the shit out of me.

Red-faced, Jennie turns and storms off, heading down the hallway that leads to the kitchen and her office.

Honestly, I'm so in shock that Braggart is able to break free of my hold and chase after her.

As I race down the hall, I can hear them shouting at each other. Her office door is shut, but I shove it open wide and step inside. He's got her pinned up against the back of her desk, his hands gripping her arms as he shakes her.

"Get your hands off her!" I yell. I grasp his shoulder and yank him off.

Jennie slips around to the opposite side of her desk, well beyond Braggart's reach. She's breathing hard, her face flushed. She looks... *scared*. Not pissed or irritated, but downright frightened. Suddenly, her reaction to me last night at the tavern is starting to make sense. I'm pretty sure I know who hurt her.

Braggart turns on me, sneering. "You think I'm afraid of you? The town bastard? Hell no!"

I grab my handcuffs. "You're under arrest. Turn around and put your hands behind your back."

Dave stares at me, dumbfounded. "Me? What the fuck for? What did I do?"

"Assault and battery for starters," I say. "Would you like to add on more charges, starting with *resisting arrest*? Please feel free. I'd be happy to oblige."

He has the audacity to laugh. "It's not assault and battery if she *likes* it, Sheriff." Braggart turns his gaze on Jennie. "Tell him, baby.

Tell him you like it rough. This is just foreplay for us, man. We're just getting started."

When I hear a choked sob, I glance over at Jennie. Her hands cover her mouth as tears flood her dark eyes. She looks utterly wrecked. Humiliated.

Her pained eyes meet mine. "Let him go, Chris." Her voice is barely audible. "Please. I just want him gone. I don't want to complicate things."

I stare Jennie in the eye, taking in her apparent fear. I want to arrest this asshole and charge him with everything in the book, but the pleading in her eyes stops me. "Stay here," I tell her. "I'll be right back."

I twist Braggart's right arm behind his back and march him out of her office and to the back door. I open it and toss him outside, hard, shoving him so he has to scramble to keep from faceplanting on the pavement.

"Consider yourself banned from this establishment," I say. "If you come back, you'll be arrested and charged with trespassing."

"You can't keep me away from my own damn property, asshole!"

I have no idea if he's telling the truth or not, but before he can say another word, I shut the door in his face and turn the deadbolt.

When I return to the office, I find Jennie standing right where I left her. I've never seen her like this. She's almost always so calm and collected, but right now she's devastated. Tears are streaming down her cheeks.

"Jennie." On impulse, I open my arms, and she rushes to me, throwing herself against me.

I have so many questions, but now's not the time. First things first. "What did he mean when he said he owns this diner? Is that true?"

Jennie shakes her head vehemently. "No, that's a lie. The diner is still in Granny's name. I'll inherit it one day, but for now, she's technically still the owner. And when I do inherit it, David won't have any claim to it. Our divorce was finalized years ago."

"Sit down," I tell her, taking her hands and guiding her to sit on her desk chair. I crouch down in front of her and take her ice cold hands in mine. "I know you're upset, and I don't want to pry, but honey, you've got to fill me in. What's Dave Braggart doing here, and why is he calling himself your husband?"

"We married when we were eighteen and divorced a year later. It was a terrible, stupid mistake."

She married him at eighteen? She must have married him not long after I left town. "Why didn't you tell me this?"

"It was a nightmare experience, and I didn't want to talk about it. Honestly, not many people in town knew. Maggie and Ruth did, of course. And Granny. But not many others."

It's hard for me to wrap my mind around the notion she was married once and never told me. I guess part of the blame falls on me. I wasn't a good friend to her those four years I was in Phoenix. I didn't come home to visit during that time because it was just too painful.

I was trying to get over Jennie. I was hoping I'd meet someone at school who could take my mind off of her, but I never did. No matter how many girls I dated, none of them could make me forget

Jennie.

My mom passed when I was away at school, and Micah was off in the Army. My only friend—my only connection to Bryce—was Jennie, and I was avoiding her.

I didn't return to Bryce until I'd completed my degree in criminal justice and was ready to start my career in law enforcement. According to Jennie, she and Dave were already divorced well before that time.

"You never once mentioned you'd been married." I try to keep the hurt out of my voice, but it's hard.

When she begins to tear up again, I pull her to her feet and wrap my arms around her. "It's okay, Jennie. I've got you." As she sobs against my chest, she slips her arms around my waist and grips the back of my shirt.

I cup the back of her head with one hand, while the other rubs gently up and down her back. I've never seen her this upset before. "Hey, sweetheart, everything's okay. He's gone. If he shows up again, call me and I'll gladly arrest his ass for trespassing."

She shudders in my arms. "You don't know him, Chris. Nothing is ever easy with him. He's here because he wants something from me, and he won't stop until he gets it. He's relentless."

"What does he want?"

She shrugs. "What does he always want? Money. I imagine he's broke, and he thinks he can get ahold of the inheritance Grandpa left me."

I pull back a step, just far enough so I can see her face. I cup her hot cheeks. Last night is starting to make more sense. The way she flinched when she saw my hand coming at her. "Jennie, did he hurt you?"

My gut tightens as I watch the myriad of emotions that flit across her face—fear, anxiety, shame. "Jennie?" I brush her tears away with my thumbs. "Answer me."

"Chris, please, don't." Her voice comes out as an agonized cry. She breaks then, and it rips me apart to see her like this.

Realization hits me hard. That bastard *hurt* her, and I wasn't here when she fucking needed me.

I failed her.

She's close to hyperventilating, obviously having a panic attack.

"Just breathe, sweetheart." My hands are still cradling her face. "I want you to breathe for me. Take slow, even breaths."

I demonstrate, hoping she'll copy me. She struggles to comply, but eventually her breathing eases.

I stare directly into her eyes, willing her to hear me and believe me. "I will not let him hurt you ever again. You hear me?"

Nodding weakly, she presses her palms on my chest, her right hand over my heart. As we stare into each other's eyes, I swear I feel the ground shake.

"Why didn't you tell me?" I ask.

Her expression crumples. "I couldn't bear for you to know. I felt so stupid and ashamed. By the time you returned to Bryce, he was long gone. It was over, or so I thought. I wanted to put it behind me and pretend it never happened."

"He abused you?"

She nods.

"Tell me how?"

There is so much pain in her eyes. "In every way imaginable. He's a monster, Chris. A sadistic, narcissistic monster."

My blood runs cold. *He hurt her.* That son-of-a-bitch hurt her! I'm tempted to go after him, but I can't leave Jennie like this. "Tell me."

She shakes her head. "I don't want to think about it, let alone talk about it."

"Honey, you have to—"

The office door opens, and Micah walks in. He takes one look at Jennie and envelops the both of us in his arms for a bear hug.

When he finally steps back, he eyes me first, and then Jennie. "What the hell just happened?"

"I'm going to kill Dave Braggart," I say.

Micah rolls his eyes at me. "You're a cop, Chris. You can't go around threatening to kill people. Please tell me you meant that in a metaphorical way."

"Don't be so sure," I mutter. He's right, of course. But I can't let this stand.

8

Jennie

I can't stop shaking, and I'm cold all over, all the way to my core. I think I'm in shock. I had thought—had hoped anyway—I'd never see David again.

Chris sits me back down on my office chair and begins to pace. Micah stands off to the side, leaning against a filing cabinet, his arms crossed over his broad chest.

"Who initiated the divorce?" Chris asks.

"I did."

"You said he hurt you," he says gently.

I shake my head. "I don't want to talk about it. If this was something I wanted you to know, I would have told you long before now."

"I understand that, sweetheart, but if I'm going to help you, I need to know everything. How did he hurt you? Was it physical? Emotional?"

"Both. And more."

Chris's eyes close hard and his breathing deepens. "Jennie, I need to know what we're dealing with."

He says *we* like this is about both of us. *We* like we're *together*. The waterworks start again. I haven't cried this much in a long time. My eyes flood with tears, and they quickly spill over onto my cheeks.

Chris muffles a curse as he locates the box of tissues on my desk. He pulls out several and hands them to me.

I dab my cheeks. "I really need to go home for a while. Just to get my head on straight." I need to process. *David's back in town, and my restraining order expired a long time ago.*

"All right," Chris says with a reluctant sigh. Apparently, he's willing to put the interrogation on hold for the time being. "I'll drive you home."

"Thanks, but I'd rather walk. The exercise will help me clear my head."

"Fine. Then I'll walk you home." And before I can say a word, he says, "I'm not letting you take a step outside of this diner by yourself. In fact, you shouldn't go anywhere alone until this is under control."

"You'd better listen to him, Jens," Micah says. "I don't think the sheriff is going to take no for an answer. And I'm with him on this, so it's two against one. We win, you lose."

I laugh. When we were kids, we solved disagreements using majority rules. I guess some things haven't changed.

"Fine." I open my side desk drawer and grab my purse. "Just let me tell the staff I'm leaving."

Chris waits for me while I tell my employees goodbye for the day. When I'm ready, he walks with me to the back exit and out into the rear parking lot. As I notice him scanning the parking lot, I realize he's looking for David.

We cross the parking lot to the sidewalk that leads back into the residential part of town. He knows the way to my house like the back of his hand. We walked this route literally hundreds of times when we were in school. Micah, Chris, and I often walked back to my place to watch TV after school or play Tomb Raider or Grand Theft Auto on my PlayStation. We played a lot of video games in those days. That's what I got for having two guys as my best friends.

Chris is pretty quiet as he slows his pace to match mine. When we reach my house, we head for the side door. I pull out my key and unlock the doorknob and both deadbolts. The upper deadbolt is a bit of a stretch for me.

Because Granny has an unfortunate tendency to wander off, we keep the doors locked at all times so there's no risk of her getting out. In the five years since her dementia worsened, she's gotten out only twice—but that was too enough for me.

The first time she got out, I found her talking to one of our neighbors, Mrs. Cochran, in her front yard.

The second time was a bit scarier. She made it all the way to the diner. Now I don't take any chances.

The house is quiet when we step inside. Mrs. Patterson is seated at the kitchen table crocheting a bright yellow trim on a hand towel.

"Hi, Mrs. P," I say.

She glances up at me. "You're home early."

"I thought I'd take the rest of the day off."

Mrs. Patterson eyes Chris with more than a little curiosity. I guess she's surprised to find him here in my house. "Is there a problem, Sheriff?"

"No, ma'am. I just thought I'd walk Jennie home."

Mrs. Patterson rises from the table, tucks her crochet project into a quilted bag, and collects her purse. "I guess I'll be going now. Rosie's asleep on the sofa in the living room. I'll see you next Saturday, Jennie."

After she's gone, I lock the doorknob and turn both deadbolts. "Thanks for walking me home," I tell Chris.

There's a loud thud in the living room, and we both scurry down the hall to see what's up. Naturally, my first thought is Granny rolled off the sofa. It's happened before, but no matter what, that's one of her favorite places to nap during the day. She thinks beds are only for nighttime sleeping.

Turns out it was just Pumpkin, who's walking across the desk. He likely jumped down from the top of the bookcase. Granny is still sound asleep on the sofa, curled up with her fleece blanket.

"It was just the cat," I say, relieved. One of my biggest fears is that she'll fall and break her hip.

Chris nods back toward the way we came, silently asking me to follow him.

When I walk into the kitchen, he gestures to one of the chairs at the table. "Please sit."

He's in cop mode, sounding like he's ready to interrogate me again. But to my surprise, he doesn't ask me a single question. Instead, he picks up the stainless steel kettle off the stove, fills it with water, and sets it on the stove to heat. "Still drink peppermint tea?" He opens the pantry door and starts searching.

"I can't believe you remember that." It's always been my go-to stress relief. "It's on the second shelf down from the top, right-hand side."

He finds the box of tea bags, grabs a mug, and sets it on the counter near the stove. "I remember everything about you," he says quietly as he places a tea bag in the cup.

Chris grabs the kettle off the stove just as it's about to begin screeching, pours hot water into the mug, and brings it to the table. While I'm dunking my tea bag, as if that will make it steep quicker, he goes to the fridge for the milk. He brings that, plus a spoon, to the table.

It seems he does remember everything.

As he sits and watches me take my first sip, I realize I love him every bit as much today as I ever did. "You don't have to stay. I'll be all right. I appreciate you walking me home, though. Thank you."

I set down my cup and stir my tea unnecessarily. For some reason, I can't bring myself to look at him. He wants answers I don't want to give him.

I think it's because of the shame. I never told him about David. I never told Micah. My two best friends know practically nothing about the most traumatic period of my life. Some friend I am.

"You weren't dating anyone the summer after we graduated from high school." Chris chuckles bitterly. "I think I would have noticed."

He's right, because we spent nearly every free moment we had together that summer, the three of us, until Chris and Micah left.

We graduated from high school in early June. Chris and Micah both left town in August. After a whirlwind courtship, I married David at the county courthouse in November.

The silence grows heavy as he waits for me to explain.

"I didn't start dating David until after you and Micah left town. We got married on November 14th."

Chris freezes. I'm not even sure if he's breathing. Finally, with a gust of breath, he asks, "You dated him for only *three months* before you married him?"

"I don't expect you to understand." I understand why I said yes. I was lonely, and my two best friends had just left me. And then David shows up, day after day at the diner, love bombing me until I couldn't see straight. I was swept off my feet by a handsome, charismatic guy whose parents owned half of the property surrounding Bryce. He wined and dined me, and he showered me with gifts and compliments. He gave me everything I thought I needed.

Chris drops his head into his hand. "How could I have been so blind?"

"You didn't do anything wrong, Chris." My voice is shaking. I can handle my own insecurities and recriminations, but not his. He's never done anything wrong.

He lifts his face so he can look me in the eye. "I need you to tell me what he did to you."

I shake my head. "It's old history. I don't want to rehash it."

"You may not have a choice, Jennie. He's back in town. Who knows for how long or what he intends to do."

"Hopefully, he'll get tired of pestering me and leave me alone."

"And if he doesn't?"

"Then I'll get another restraining order."

"*Another one?*" Chris shoots to his feet and starts pacing. "You had to get a fucking restraining order against him?"

I wince. "Yes."

He carefully pushes his chair up to the table. We're both trying to be quiet so we don't wake Granny. Even after all this time, he remembers the little things like that.

"Will you be okay here alone?" he asks, abruptly changing the subject.

"Of course."

"I need to go to the station. I want to review the police records pertaining to your *ex-husband*." That last word has a bite to it. "I'll stop by later to make sure you're okay."

"Chris, please, don't go digging into the past. It was nearly ten years ago. It's water under the bridge."

"Is it really? I haven't seen Dave Braggart step one foot into Bryce since I've been back here—that's six years. So, why's he here now?

And why did he show up in your diner?"

I don't have an answer to that, so I don't even try to guess. "Please, Chris, leave it alone."

He shakes his head. "I'm sorry, Jennie. I can't."

And then he surprises the daylights out of me by leaning in and kissing my cheek. It's a chaste kiss, similar to the dozens of kisses he's given me over the years. Brotherly kisses. Friendly kisses. But this time, my cheek feels warm where his lips touched my skin.

As he lets himself out the side door, he says, "Be sure to lock up after me."

I get up to lock the door and find myself touching my face. I can still feel his lips on my cheek.

9

Chris

After leaving Jennie's place, I head straight to the station to see what I can dig up on Dave Braggart. When I walk in, I check the roster to see who's working today. I'm hoping there might be someone on duty who worked the year Jennie and Dave were married.

I figure one of them is Nigel Henderson. He's a detective now, but ten years ago, he was a beat cop. Fortunately, he's in the office. I pop my head through his open doorway. "Nigel, you got a minute?"

He glances up from a report he's writing on his laptop. "Sure, Chris. Come on in and have a seat. What can I help you with?"

I take a seat in the chair facing his desk. "I'm looking into a past case, and I wondered if you had any knowledge of it. Do you remember some trouble with Dave Braggart back in the day? It would have been right after he graduated from high school."

Nigel scowls. "Yeah. He'd be hard to forget."

"He showed up back in town today, at the diner."

Nigel leans back in his creaky office chair and purses his lips. "Really?"

"He caused quite a scene in Jennie's office."

"I'm not surprised," Nigel says. "I lost track of how many times we got called to their house for domestic disturbances. Finally, she got wise and divorced him."

"She mentioned she had a restraining order against him."

He nods. "She sure did."

"Do you remember why?"

The old guy nods. "This was before you were with the force, wasn't it?"

"Right. Well, he's back in town, and I need to get up to speed quick. So, let's have it."

Nigel crosses his arms over his chest as he gets comfortable in his chair. "Well, domestic violence for starters. Physical abuse. Emotional abuse. And well, you know—she accused him of sexual abuse. It was ugly. One of the worst cases of domestic abuse I'd ever seen. She had bruises everywhere, cuts and abrasions, too. After the divorce was final, Braggart left town with his tail tucked between his legs, and to my knowledge he hasn't been back since. Not until today, anyway. You're gonna need to keep a close eye on that SOB."

Hearing him rattle off all of Braggart's offences against Jennie makes me sick. I had no idea how bad things had been between them. It guts me to know she suffered through this when I wasn't here to protect her.

"Thanks, Nigel." Feeling numb, I stand and head for the door. "If you think of anything else I should know, give me a call."

He salutes me. "Will do, Sheriff."

It's only two, and Ruth's Tavern won't be open for another hour yet. So I give Ruth a call hoping to catch her at home.

"Hey, Chris," she says. "What's up?"

"Did you know Dave Braggart's in town?"

The line goes silent, and I hear hushed whispers, but can't make out the words. Finally, she comes back with, "No. When did he arrive?"

"I'm not sure, but he showed up at the diner this morning."

"Oh, my God. Did he speak to Jennie?"

"I'd say he did a lot more than speak to her. They got into it in her office."

"Damn it. Is she all right?"

"She's okay. Shaken, but she's managing. I walked her home. That's where she is now."

Again, the line goes quiet, and I hear muffled talking. I imagine she's filling Jack in. Jack hasn't lived here that long, so he'd have no idea who Braggart is.

A moment later, she returns to the line. "She had a restraining order against David, but that expired years ago. She'll probably have to get a new one. If he's back, it's because he wants something from her. He's not going to stop harassing her until he gets it."

"I'm trying to fill in the details. Can I stop by so we can talk?"

"I'm sorry, Chris," she says. "I'll have to say no. If Jennie wants you to know, she'll tell you herself. It's not my place."

"I appreciate you trying to respect Jennie's confidence, Ruth, but I'm worried about her. I saw Dave accost her this morning in her office. If I hadn't been there—hadn't stopped him—who knows what might have happened. Jennie was terrified."

"She has good reason to be afraid. Talk to her, Chris. I can't tell you what went on between them, but I will say it wasn't good. And that's the understatement of the year. Jennie is one of my nearest and dearest friends, and I won't betray her trust. So you need to get her to tell you. Do whatever it takes."

"I understand. Thanks."

"For what it's worth, Jack and I will keep an eye on her. So will Maggie. And if we have to, we'll call in the others to fill in. We're not leaving her unprotected. She dealt with him on her own the first time around. That was before we'd become friends. But we won't let it happen again."

After I get off the phone with Ruth, I go into the archives and pull the case files on Braggart from a decade ago. I pour myself a cup of black coffee and sit at my desk, ready for the long haul of wading through dozens of reports.

I am not prepared for what I read.

Domestic violence. Bruises. Lacerations. A concussion. Multiple visits to the hospital in Estes Park. Accusations of physical abuse. Accusations of sexual abuse. Finally, a restraining order forbidding Mr. Brag-

gart from coming near Mrs. Braggart.

I can barely bring myself to look at the photos included in the reports. Vivid bruises on her face and wrists. Red, angry cuts. A swollen lip. A black eye. *What in the fucking hell!*

It's sickening to think she endured this on her own. Physically, she's no match for Braggart. He's easily twice her size. Plus, he's a bully. Emotionally and mentally, she's no match for him.

This time, it will be different. She's not alone. She has friends who will protect her.

Starting with *me*.

* * *

After leaving the station, I head out to the Braggart ranch outside of town. I'm going to have a chat with Dave. Maybe I'll get lucky and find another reason to arrest him.

I'm guessing he's staying at his parents' ranch, even though they're out of town right now. The Braggarts own a thousand-acre cattle ranch east of Bryce. They're outside the township limits, but they're in our county, so they fall under my jurisdiction.

When I pull through the main gate of the Triple B Ranch, I follow the long, winding drive up to the main single-story house. To the right of the house are several massive barns and a number of chicken coops. To the left of the house is forest. It's an impressive spread.

The Braggarts are undoubtedly the wealthiest people in these parts. That meant their son, Dave, was by association the wealthiest kid in our school district. He was also the biggest jerk.

I park in front of the sprawling ranch-style home and walk up to the door. I guess I should say *doors*, as there are two of them, at least eight feet tall, hand-carved wooden monstrosities. I guess if you've got the money, go ahead and flaunt it.

I ring the bell, and a moment later the door opens. I doff my sheriff's hat at the middle-aged Hispanic woman wearing a gray uniform dress and a white apron. I'm guessing she's the housekeeper. "Ma'am. Is Dave here?"

The woman nods. "*Si.*"

"Would you tell him Sheriff Nelson is here to see him?"

She frowns, looking like she'd rather not do any such thing.

"*Por favor, senora?*" I give her a friendly smile. "I'm not looking for trouble. I just need to speak to your boss's son."

She reluctantly nods and steps back so I can enter. "Just a minute, please," she says as she walks away, leaving me alone in a spacious foyer with high ceilings and what I guess is expensive artwork hanging on the walls. Overhead hangs a fancy chandelier dripping with crystals that shed refracted light on the walls and polished parquet floor.

From where I'm standing, I can see into what looks like a home office to the left, a dining room to the right, and straight ahead I can see part of a gourmet kitchen and a living room.

It's not long before I see Dave walking toward me down the center hallway. He's wearing a pair of cut-off denim jean shorts and nothing else. No shoes, no shirt. He's holding a sandwich in one hand and a beer bottle in the other.

"My parents are out of the country," he tells me as he talks around a mouthful of food. "You'll have to come back in a month."

"I'm not here to see your folks, Dave. I'm here to see you."

"What for? I don't think my business is any of yours."

"That's where you're wrong. Why are you here? From what I've heard, you left Bryce years ago and haven't been back. Why now? Especially if your folks are out of the country. You obviously didn't come back for a family reunion."

His smile fades. "That's where *you're* wrong, Sheriff. That's exactly why I came back—for a family reunion. I came to reunite with my *wife*."

Hearing him call Jennie his wife makes my gut knot. "She's not your wife. She hasn't been for a long time. And the last time you were here, she had to get a restraining order against you."

Dave scoffs. "That expired years ago. We're gettin' a fresh start, Jennie-bean and me."

I'm not in the mood to play games with this clown. "Why are you really here?"

"I told you. I came back to reunite with my wife."

"She has no interest in seeing you, so I suggest you take yourself back to wherever it was you came from. Vegas, if the rumors are correct."

The man's eyes narrow on me. "You shouldn't believe rumors."

It looks like I hit a sore spot. "Everything that happens in Vegas stays in Vegas, right?" I ask.

"Get out of my house, *Sheriff*." He sneers that last word. "You have no business here." He nods to the door. "Marguerite! Show the sheriff out."

The housekeeper materializes out of nowhere as if she'd been lurking around the corner just waiting to be summoned.

"I'll go," I say. "But the minute you give me an excuse to return, I will."

He points to the doors. "Get out!"

"Steer clear of Jennie—unless you actually want me to arrest you."

"*You* arrest *me*? Ha! I'll believe that when I see it. The son of the town whore isn't fit to step foot in my home, let alone think he can tell me what to do."

He loves throwing the memory of my mother in my face. She was a sad case, that's true. But at least she always made sure I ate three square meals a day. The real irony is, Dave's father—David Braggart, Sr.—was a regular visitor at our trailer. "Tell your dad I said hi. I haven't seen him in a while."

"Get the fuck out, you crack-addict bastard!" Dave storms off in the direction of the kitchen. Halfway there, he throws his beer bottle on the ceramic tile floor, and the bottle shatters. "Clean that up, Marguerite!"

The housekeeper opens the door for me, and I walk outside. After my chat with Dave, I head back to Jennie's place. I want to make sure she's okay, but I also need to talk to her about going back to court to get a restraining order. I don't want Dave anywhere near her.

* * *

When I arrive at Jennie's house, I park in the driveway and walk up to her side door. I knock quietly and wait.

A few moments later, someone pulls back the curtain hanging over the window and peers outside.

I wave to Jennie, and immediately she unlocks the door and opens it.

"Sorry to come over unannounced," I say. I keep my voice low because the lights are out and the house is quiet. I suspect that means Granny's napping again. Jennie says she's been sleeping a lot more lately.

"It's okay," Jennie says as she closes and locks the door behind me.

"Granny's sleeping?"

She nods. "Can I get you something to drink? Or food? Are you hungry?"

"I am thirsty. I'd love some water."

While she pours me a glass of water from the pitcher in her fridge, I study the kitchen. It hasn't changed much since we were kids. There's still the same floral striped gold wallpaper dating back to the seventies or earlier. The same oak cabinets. The same faded linoleum flooring. The same table and chairs. It's vintage, but it's clean. It feels homey rather than outdated.

She hands me the glass of water. "Let's sit here in the kitchen. Granny is in her chair in the living room."

She seems nervous.

"Hey. This isn't an interrogation, Jennie. Relax. I just want to talk to you."

She takes a seat. I take the chair opposite her and set my glass on the table.

"So, what do you want to talk about?" she asks. She crosses her arms over her chest in a classic defensive posture.

She's not just nervous. She's scared. But of what? Or of whom? Surely not me. "Let's start with last night at the tavern when you rushed off the dance floor."

She shakes her head, brushing off my concern. "I was just tired. That's all. Don't read anything into it."

"Jennie."

Her dark eyes flash defensively. "I'd had a long day at the diner."

I'm used to interrogating suspects. Victims and witnesses, too. I know avoidance when I see it, and she's avoiding the truth about last night.

"Last night, when we were dancing, I reached out to fix your hair, and you flinched."

Her eyes widen. It's barely perceptible, but I'm used to watching for small tells. She shrugs. "I told you, Chris. It was nothing."

"Sweetheart, it wasn't nothing. It was an automatic response. *You flinched* when you saw my hand coming at you." I pause a moment to give her time to process what I'm getting at. She has to know where this is going. "I know he was physically abusive."

She just stares into my eyes, but says nothing.

"I need to understand why you married him, Jennie. Please. And why you never told me."

She looks away a moment, as if collecting her thoughts. When she looks back at me, her dark eyes are flashing with emotion. "I never told you because I was ashamed and embarrassed, all right?" She's trying to keep her voice down. "I didn't want you to know what a horrible mistake I'd made."

I reach across the table, my hand open, palm up. I'm hoping she'll give me her hand, but she doesn't.

"I left for school in August, and you married him in November, right? Tell me how you married a complete stranger in three months."

"It seems so stupid now, but back then, it made sense."

"How so?"

She shakes her head. "After you and Micah left Bryce, he started coming into the diner, nearly every day. He always asked for me to wait on him. He was so funny and charming back then. Believe it or not, he can be very charming when he wants to."

"He was courting you."

She nods. "He was always around the diner. He offered to help out at the house. In the beginning, Granny loved him, and he was good to her. Grandpa was still alive then. They hit it off well, watching football games together. David helped Grandpa in the yard. He took over the mowing and raked the leaves. He shoveled the snow that winter. He gave me rides to the diner when the streets were covered in snow and ice. It was... nice. It was what I needed at the time."

She says *it* was what she needed, and not *he* was what she needed.

"You were lonely?" I ask gently.

Frowning, she nods. “With you and Micah gone, I had no one. And that’s when Grandpa started getting ill. It was a stressful time. I was alone and vulnerable, and David realized he easily control me. Back then I had no idea what a narcissist was.”

My chest tightens. *She’d been lonely.* For the first time since we’d met in third grade, she’d had no one. “God, Jennie, I’m so sorry.”

“You have nothing to be sorry about, Chris. You guys were living your lives. That’s how it should be. I don’t blame you for that.”

I went away to school in an effort to forget about her. I didn’t want to spend the rest of my life pining for her, so I left, hoping I’d meet someone who could take my mind off Jennie. I didn’t. I dated in college, yes, but it never amounted to anything serious. When I returned home after four years of schooling, I was as much in love with her as I’d always been.

I can see the pain filling her eyes. “I was so wrong about him. He was just pretending in the beginning. He pushed and pushed for us to make it official. Once we tied the knot, I started seeing glimpses of the real David. Our marriage quickly became abusive.” She sighs deeply. “It wasn’t long before I realized he didn’t want me. He wanted access to my money—my grandparents’ money.”

“But why? The Braggarts are loaded. Why did he need money?”

“They’d cut David off, financially. I didn’t find out until after we were married. I guess I should have wondered what was up when he insisted we get married at the courthouse. His parents weren’t even involved. I guess they knew him better than I did.”

“And you think he’s back for your money?”

“Why else would he come back? His parents disowned him years ago. I'm his only connection here in town."

"I want you to request another restraining order to keep him away from you. In the meanwhile, I'll keep an eye on you—and him. I won't let him bully or pressure you."

Tears pool in her eyes. "This isn't your problem, Chris. You shouldn't have to—"

"Any problem of yours is a problem of mine. You're not alone this time, Jennie. You've got me—and Micah. We've got your back. The three *amigos*, right?"

She finally lays her hand on mine. "I've made so many mistakes in my life, Chris."

"It's okay. Mistakes were made to be fixed."

"Some mistakes can't be fixed."

"Why do you say that?"

She links our fingers. "Because it's too late."

10

Jennie

I press my palm to Chris's and link our fingers together. As usual, he's being wonderful when I don't deserve it. The mess I'm in is of my own making.

The biggest mistake I made wasn't marrying David. It was saying no to Chris all those years ago when we were in school. I thought I was protecting him. I was bullied so badly for being an outsider—a brown girl in a school full of white kids. I was the half-breed Mexican-American, and I wanted to spare him that pain—the jokes, the slurs, the hateful looks. The name-calling. He was already being bullied because of his mother, and I didn't want to add to his misery.

So, instead, I drove him away—literally, he left town because of me. I know he did because his mother told me so not long before she died of an overdose. I can still hear Kitty Nelson's voice in my head. *"You drove my son away, you fucking slut! What, you think you're too damn good for my boy? Well, to hell with you."*

It was ironic that she called me a slut when I was still a virgin, and she was the notorious town prostitute.

I want so badly to tell him how I feel—how I've *always* felt about him. But it's far too little, too late.

"I should never have gone away," he says, his voice low and tight, laced with self-recrimination. "I should never have left you." He squeezes my hand. "God, I wish I could go back and do things differently." His eyes tear up. "I just couldn't handle it at the time. Now that I'm older, I—"

"Handle what?" I ask. My heart starts pounding.

"Pining for you like a lovesick teenager. Being around you all the time, knowing you didn't feel the same way I did—it *killed* me."

I didn't feel the same way? My throat seizes up on me. My pulse is galloping, and I can't catch my breath. "Chris, of course I—"

"JENNIE!"

Granny's hoarse cry rattles the windows. I jump up and run to the living room, where she's napping on her recliner. She's flailing her hands, clearly frantic.

"Granny, what's wrong?" I ask. I notice Chris hovering just outside the room.

"Where's George? Where's my husband?"

My heart sinks. I can't tell her the truth. It's been years since he passed, and she still asks for him. "He's out in the garage," I tell her, feeling sick to my stomach for lying to her. But a white lie to spare her feelings is better than the cold hard truth.

She glances toward the big window. It's starting to get dark out. "But it's late."

"You know how he gets when he's working on his car. He'll be along soon." I guide her to lie back down and straighten her blanket. "Go back to sleep, Granny."

"He's been gone a long time." She sighs. "I miss him so much."

I freeze when I hear that moment of clarity coming from her. "So do I, Granny."

She notices Chris in the doorway and points at him. "It's your husband."

This time I don't want to fudge the truth. "No, Granny. I divorced David, remember? He wasn't very nice."

"Oh, I don't mean *him*. I mean this one. Chris. The sheriff." She yawns. "I always liked him better. He's a good man." As she rolls onto her side and closes her eyes, Pumpkin lies against her, purring loudly.

"Sorry about that," I whisper to Chris, who follows me back to the kitchen.

I pick up my empty tea cup and rinse it out in the sink. My nerves are frayed. After seeing David again, I feel like my emotions are all over the place. As I stand at the sink, busying myself with unnecessary tasks, Chris takes the hint.

He walks up beside me and rests his hand on my shoulder. "I guess I should go. I'm sure you're tired after all the drama today."

My throat tightens as I nod. "Yeah. I guess so." I came so close tonight to confessing how I feel about him. I want to tell him, but I'm worried about how he'll take it. Will he hold me accountable for all the time we've wasted? I wouldn't blame him if he did.

"Okay, then. Make sure you lock up." He pats my back and lets himself out the door without another word.

I'm such a coward.

* * *

After spending a quiet and relaxing Sunday with Granny folding towels, watching *Little House on the Prairie* reruns, and working on a puzzle, I return to work as usual on Monday.

That afternoon, I'm standing beside a booth at the front of the restaurant, taking an order, when an unfamiliar car goes speeding up Main Street so fast, it catches nearly everyone's attention. A moment later, Chris speeds by in his sheriff's SUV, sirens blaring and lights flashing.

The wide panel windows actually shake.

And right on Chris's heels come two deputy patrol cars running their lights and sirens as they follow in hot pursuit.

A male customer walks out onto the sidewalk and gazes down the road in the direction the vehicles were driving. When he returns, he shrugs. "I couldn't see anything. They all kept on going out of sight."

I say a silent prayer for Chris and the deputies, hoping they'll be safe. It must be serious if they're willing to pursue a car at high speed. I know Chris frowns on those high-speed chases. "Only when someone's life or liberty is at stake," he always says.

I resume taking my customers' orders, but before long, we're interrupted by the sound of yet more approaching sirens. This time, we all glance out the window to see a paramedic squad speed by, followed by a firetruck.

My stomach drops.

Someone's hurt.

Please let Chris be all right.

After I turn in my customers' orders, I sneak back to my office and call the police station.

Darlene answers. "Sheriff's office. How may I direct your call?"

"Darlene, hi. It's Jennie. We just saw Chris and some deputies speeding up Main Street, followed by paramedics. Is everyone on the force okay?" *Please say yes.*

She hesitates a moment before answering, which makes my anxiety skyrocket. "Jennie, I really can't—"

"Darlene, please! I'm worried about Chris and the deputies. At least tell me they're all right."

Darlene sighs. "Normally I wouldn't share information like this over the phone, but I know you and Chris are close. I think he'd want you to know. There was an accident. Chris and the guys tried to box the suspect in, but the suspect managed to ram Chris's vehicle and drive him off the road. The suspect then lost control of his car and crashed into a tree."

I drop into my chair as I try not to hyperventilate. "Is Chris okay?"

"Honestly, I don't know. All I know is Ricky called for the paramedics. Oh, wait—" She's silent a moment. When she comes back to the phone, she says, "The suspect died at the scene, but the little girl is okay. Chris is being taken to Estes Park Health."

That's the main hospital in Estes Park, known for their critical care services and emergency room. "Oh, my God. Is it—is he—is it serious?"

"I'm sorry, but I don't have any more info than that. I wish I did."

My mind is racing, and all I can think of is that I need to get to the hospital. I need to be with Chris. "Wait—you mentioned a little girl?"

"Yeah. It was a carjacking at a gas station south of town. The suspect dragged the father out of his car and took off with the man's three-year-old daughter still in the car. Thank God she was still strapped into her car seat. It probably saved her life."

After I hang up the phone, I inform my staff I'm heading to the hospital. I also text Micah to let him know where Chris is and what's happened.

I jog home to get my car.

When I fill Dawn in, she tells me not to worry about Granny. She'll stay with her until I can return home.

I hop in my car and head south to Estes Park, fudging a bit on the speed limit. I hardly remember the drive. I've made it so many times, I can do it by rote. When I arrive at the hospital, I park in the ER lot and walk in.

* * *

When I reach the information desk in the ER department, I blurt out, “Where’s Sheriff Nelson? He was just brought in.”

A middle-aged woman glances up at me. “Are you family?”

Chris doesn’t really have any next of kin, at least no one I know of. “Yes!” I say without hesitation. “I’m his fiancée.”

The woman checks her computer screen. “He’s in room eight.” She points to a set of double doors. “Go through those doors, then turn right and follow the signs. The door numbers are marked.”

I follow her instructions, and after wandering around a bit, I find Chris’s room. He’s lying on a bed. His forehead is bandaged, as is his right shoulder. The sheets are bloody, and so are the bandages.

I step into the room and try to be quiet so I don’t disturb the nurse who is gently wiping blood off his face. My heart is in my throat, threatening to choke me.

When she spots me standing here, she smiles and waves me closer. “It’s okay. You can come talk to him. I’m just getting him cleaned up.”

His eyes are closed, but based on his ragged breathing, I sense he’s awake.

I lean close. “Chris? It’s me. I’m here.”

He cracks open his eyes and squints at me as he winces in pain.

“It’s okay. You don’t have to talk.” I reach down and squeeze his left hand, the only part of him not covered in blood. “I came as soon as I heard.” I glance up at the nurse, who’s just about done cleaning him up. “Is he okay?”

“His vitals are stable,” she says. “He has a superficial cut on his forehead—hence all the blood. Scalps bleed a lot. And his right shoulder is dislocated. Once we get someone in here to address that, he should be good as new."

"Oh, thank God." Relief washes through me, leaving my knees weak. I pull a chair up to the side of the bed so I can sit near him.

He's clinging to my hand, and apparently neither one of us wants to let go.

"Are you okay?" I ask when we're finally alone. "I saw you drive past the diner when you were chasing that suspect. I heard the little girl is fine."

When he shifts position, he cries out. "Damn it, that hurts!" He blows out a breath. "Yeah, Ricky told me she was okay. I saw the suspect crash, and I was afraid for the kid. I'm just glad she's all right."

There are fine lines bracketing his mouth, and his breathing is ragged. I can tell he's in a lot of pain. "Hopefully they'll fix your shoulder soon. At least it's your right shoulder. That's a good thing, right?" Because he's a lefty.

Chris nods, but even that seems to hurt him. He sucks in a sharp breath. "Sorry."

"Don't you dare apologize for being human, Chris. I know you're in pain. It's okay."

I sit with him, holding his hand and gently stroking his hair. He seems to have dozed off a bit, lying quiet and so still.

I notice movement at the door to Chris's room. Deputy Ricky Stephens is standing just outside.

"You can come in," I say, motioning for him to enter.

He walks into the room, dressed in his uniform, but looking a bit disheveled. "How's he doing?"

"His shoulder is dislocated, and he's in a lot of pain. But otherwise, he's okay."

Ricky nods. "Good. I'm glad to hear that. His SUV took quite a beating, so I wasn't sure how serious his injuries are."

"Everyone else is okay?" I ask. "Except for the carjacker. I heard he didn't make it. But the little girl is okay?"

Ricky nods. "She was taken to the Children's Hospital to be checked out, but they said she's fine. Her parents are with her now. Looks like Chris saved the day." He comes closer to the bed to glance down at Chris, who's sleeping. "When he wakes up, please tell him his duty belt, badge, and gun are at the station."

"I'll tell him."

Ricky leaves, and I maintain my vigil, leaving only once for a few minutes to visit the restroom and get a bottle of water at a vending machine. When I return, he's still asleep.

I'm reading on my phone when I hear him groan. When I glance up, he's awake, watching me. "Hey," I say.

"Hey," he replies, his voice subdued.

I reach for his hand. "Just hang in there. I'm sure someone will come in before long to take care of your shoulder."

* * *

Half an hour later, the nurse returns with a syringe and an alcohol pad. She wipes a spot on his arm and prepares the syringe. She looks at me. "This is a mild sedative to help him relax." After she has administered the medication and applied a band aid to the injection site, she says, "One of the physicians will be in soon to take care of his shoulder. Just hang tight."

The nurse leaves once more, and we're alone again.

I resume stroking his hair, and he moans softly. "I was so scared when I saw the paramedics go by."

His eyelids flutter open, and he stares at the ceiling. "You don't—have to—worry," he says. The words come out between shuddering breaths.

"Of course, I worry. If something happened to you—"

He squeezes my hand. "Nothing's going to happen to me. I'm tough as an old goat." His eyelids drift shut as the sedation starts to kick in. He keeps talking, but his words are mumbled. He's practically slurring them like he's drunk. I guess this is a good thing. It'll help him get through the upcoming procedure. I'm sure it's going to hurt something awful.

Right on time, the nurse and a physician enter the room. While the nurse is checking Chris's vitals, the physician addresses me. Chris is pretty much out of it now.

"I'm Dr. Talbott," he says. "This won't take long at all. He'll feel some discomfort during the procedure, but he won't remember it afterward. Once his shoulder is back where it should be, we'll let him sleep off the effects of the sedative, and when he's alert, and assuming the shoulder is functioning correctly, he'll be able to go home."

The nurse confirms Chris's vitals, giving Dr. Talbott the okay to proceed. She pulls down the top half of Chris's hospital gown, and Dr. Talbott steps right up to him, takes hold of his arm and shoulder, and makes a quick snapping movement.

It happens so quickly. There's a muffled popping sound, and Chris cries out sharply, but then he's quiet again.

Dr. Talbott rotates Chris's shoulder a few times, I guess to make sure the bone is where it's supposed to be and he can use his arm. "I'll come back in a little while to see how he's doing. He should be able to leave in an hour or two, depending on how quickly he wakes up. I assume you'll be driving him home. He shouldn't operate any machinery or heavy equipment for the rest of today. I'll send care instructions home with you."

"Yes, I'll be driving him home. He'll stay with me until he's fully recovered from the sedative."

"Perfect," the doctor says. "I'll check back in a little while to see how he's doing."

"How long before he's himself again? How long until the sedation has fully worn off?"

"Anywhere from four to six hours, but I'd give him until morning to be back one hundred percent. Don't let him make any big decisions tonight, okay?" The man chuckles. "Don't let him buy a new car or take out a loan."

"Got it. Thanks."

We're alone once more. Chris is sleeping now, his bed at a slight incline, and he seems more comfortable. His breathing is more even. I remain in my chair so I can keep a close eye on him.

I text Micah with an update, and he tells me he's already on his way to the hospital with a clean change of clothes for Chris. Thank goodness, because Chris's uniform is ruined.

I call the station and let Darlene know how he's doing, and I ask her to pass the information along to the rest of the department. I reply to texts from Maggie and Ruth and Hannah, who are all checking on not just Chris, but me as well. Word got around quickly, but that's no surprise.

While I wait for Chris to sleep off his sedative, I sit beside his bed reading on my phone.

A quiet male voice says, "Hey there."

I look up just as Micah walks in carrying a canvas bag. "Clean clothes and sneakers. I brought sweats because I figured those would be easier for him to get on." He sets the bag down on a vacant chair and walks over to the far side of the bed to gaze down at our sleeping friend. "How's he doing?"

"So far, so good. His shoulder was put back into place. They gave him a light sedative, which is why he's out."

Micah looks at me. "How are you holding up?"

"I've had better days. When I heard he'd been in an accident and they were taking him to the hospital, I feared the worst. I was terrified, Micah." I reach over and squeeze Chris's good hand.

"What are we going to do with him tonight?" Micah asks. "He won't be fit to drive."

"I'm taking him home with me." The words just pop right out of me without thought. He's mine to take care of.

"You sure? I can stay until he's released and take him home with me. We've got room."

I shake my head. "That's okay. I've got him for tonight. He can stay with me as long as he needs to."

"He'll need more clothes, then," Micah says. "I'll drop some things off for him at your house in the morning."

"Thanks."

Micah gazes down at Chris and frowns. "He could have been killed today, Jen. I worry about him. I swear, he's got a hero complex. He's always the first one to put his life on the line to rescue someone."

My throat tightens because I share Micah's concerns. "He is who he is. I don't think either one of us would want to change him."

Micah hangs around for a little while hoping Chris will wake up. But after a while, it seems that's not going to happen anytime soon.

"I guess I'll take off." Micah walks over to me, leans down, and kisses the top of my head. "Let me know if either of you needs anything tonight. I'm just a phone call away."

"I will. Thanks. Give Robyn my love."

Micah hasn't been gone long when the patient finally begins to stir. He moans groggily, which tells me he's still pretty much out of it.

"Hey, Sheriff," I say as I reach for his good hand. "How do you feel?"

He slowly turns his head toward me, and his eyes widen in surprise. "Jennie Lopez! What are you doing here?"

Yep, he's still out of it. "I came to check on you."

He looks around, clearly confused. "Check on me? Why? Where am I?"

"You're in the hospital in Estes Park. Do you remember what happened?"

He frowns. "No."

"You were in an accident."

"Seriously? How bad was it? Was anyone hurt?"

I don't want to go into all the gory details, so I just tell him he was chasing a carjacking suspect who had kidnapped a little girl.

"Did we catch him?"

"Yes."

"Is the kid okay?"

"Yes, the little girl is fine. There's nothing to worry about, so just relax."

"What about my vehicle?"

I frown. "Honestly, I'm not sure. You crashed in a ditch."

He frowns. "I hope it's not totaled." He looks disappointed. "Well, at least the kid is okay." He sighs as he gazes at me for the longest time. "You're so pretty, Jennie."

I smile. Sedation has such an interesting effect on people. "Thank you. So are you."

He shakes his head. "Be serious. I'm not pretty, but you sure are." Then he giggles. "I always thought you were the prettiest girl in school. You're an angel, Jennie, you know that? And I don't just mean because of looks. I mean you're an angel on the inside, where it really counts. You're the nicest, kindest, sweetest girl in the world. You're *beautiful,* inside and out."

He may be awake, but that sedative is really messing with his head.

I squeeze his hand gently. "Thanks. I think you're pretty awesome yourself."

Suddenly, his smile turns into a frown, and he shakes his head. "You don't get it. But how could you? I never told you." He looks devastated.

My pulse starts tripping. "You never told me what?" I'm almost afraid to hear his answer. Whatever he's about to tell me, it's clearly under the influence of a sedative. There's no telling what he's going to say, or even if it's true.

I'm about to change the subject to something much safer when he blurts out, "I never told you how much I love you."

11

Jennie

My heart jumps into my throat, and my ears are ringing. *Chris loves me?* I know it's the sedative talking. It has to be! He doesn't know what he's saying. "Chris—"

"I've loved you for so long I can't remember a time when I didn't love you. But you always turned me down, so I stopped asking. I didn't want to be one of those jerks who pester girls, ya know? And I understood why you didn't want me back. I mean, what girl would?"

It shocks me to hear Chris speak of himself like this. No, it breaks my heart, and I'm ashamed I played a part in how he saw himself.

"I was a nobody back then," he continues, his mind wandering.

"Still am, to be honest. I'm still just the bastard son of the town whore. A drug addict's kid." He turns to face me, his eyes bleak. "I don't even know who my dad is. My mom didn't know either. It could be anyone—the butcher, the baker, the candlestick maker." He laughs at his own lame joke.

But then, just as suddenly, his mood changes again, and he frowns. "God, I hope it's not David Braggart, Sr. That would fucking suck if Dave turned out to be my half-brother. When I was young, David Braggart, Sr. came by our place *a lot*, so I know he was doin' my mom. He probably had been for *years*. That's why you could never love me back, Jennie. I am literally a bastard, and you deserve better."

I try to decide how best to respond. I'm so tempted to tell him how I feel about him, but now is definitely not the time. He probably won't even remember this conversation tomorrow. "Chris—"

But his eyes are closed now, and he's softly snoring.

My mind is reeling after the things he said, and I need time to process it all.

He loves me? He always has?

But how do I know he's telling the truth? He's under the influence of a drug. He's loopy right now.

* * *

Sometime later, Dr. Talbott returns to assess Chris's shoulder. He applies a sling to help immobilize the arm while the shoulder joint is recovering. "You'll be sore for a few days, but there shouldn't be any lasting damage. I advise you to take a few days off work and rest." Then to me, the doctor says, "Just keep an eye on him tonight. Would you like me to prescribe something for the pain?"

Chris shakes his head adamantly. "No!" he replies, way too quickly. "Thanks, but I'll be fine."

"Well, if you get too uncomfortable, you can take something over the counter."

Chris nods, but doesn't say anything. I'm not surprised. He has an aversion to taking *any* medication because of his mother's drug addiction. He's afraid it could happen to him.

When the doctor leaves, I begin the arduous process of helping Chris change into the clothes Micah brought. I help him sit up, being as gentle as I can, and still he grimaces throughout the process.

He chooses to forgo the underwear. "It'll be easier if I go commando."

Blushing, I avert my gaze as I help him slip his bare legs into a pair of gray sweatpants. He stands on shaky legs, gripping my shoulder with his good hand as I work the sweats up to his waist. Once he's seated again, I help put on his socks and sneakers. Getting his T-shirt on is just as difficult because of his sling and his immobilized right arm. Fortunately, the nurse comes in at that moment—bringing a wheelchair—and she helps me. He grits his teeth and closes his eyes, so I know he's in pain, and yet he never says a word. He never complains.

After the doctor officially releases Chris, I wheel him out to my car and help him get settled into the front passenger seat of my Honda Civic. "Sorry," I mutter as I lean across him to buckle his seat belt.

"S'okay," he mumbles.

I catch him observing me a couple of times, but each time he quickly looks away. Obviously, something is bothering him. On the drive back to Bryce, he stares out the passenger window at the passing scenery, saying nothing.

I feel the need to break the silence. "In case you're wondering, I'm taking you back to my house to stay the night."

He winces as he rotates his right shoulder. "That's all right." He can barely meet my gaze. "You can drop me off at my house. I don't want to inconvenience you."

"Humor me, please. Stay with me for at least one night. Your doctor said the sedative won't wear off fully until the morning." I can't help wondering if he remembers any of what he said to me earlier. Does he remember spilling his guts, and now he regrets it? "Chris, please. It's just one night."

"All right," he says reluctantly.

"Thank you."

* * *

It's evening when we arrive back at my house. I unlock and open the door for him so he can step through.

Dawn, who's putting dirty dinner dishes into the dishwasher, scans him from head to toe. "How're you doing, Sheriff? I'm glad to see you're all in one piece. I heard what happened."

"I'm still standing," he says.

Right now, he's acting a bit hung over. I assume it's because of the sedative.

"Granny and I had pot roast for dinner this evening," she says. "There's plenty of leftovers in the fridge. Enough for the both of you. There are some dinner rolls, too. Help yourselves."

As I watch Chris drop down heavily onto one of the kitchen chairs, I suspect he's hurting more than he's letting on. I pat his good shoulder. "How about something cold to drink?"

Wordlessly, he nods.

"Is Granny in bed?" I ask Dawn as I hand Chris a glass of fresh-squeezed lemonade. It's eight now. Granny's usually in bed by seven.

She nods. "Sound asleep. She asked for you at dinner. I told her you were working late tonight."

"I can't thank you enough, Dawn." I give her a hug as I walk her to the door.

"Oh, I forgot! There's blueberry cobbler on the counter."

I lock the door after Dawn leaves, and then I turn back to face the patient. "I'll get you some dinner."

Chris sits at the table nursing his lemonade while I heat up the leftover pot roast in the microwave. As that's warming, I set a basket of dinner rolls and the butter dish on the table. I keep myself busy until the microwave beeps, indicating our food is ready. I dish it out and set the plates on the table, along with silverware and a glass of lemonade for myself.

"Dig in," I say. "You must be hungry. You probably haven't eaten since breakfast."

He scoops a forkful of food in his mouth and grunts as he chews. "It's good," he says after he swallows.

"Would you like something for the pain?"

"I'm fine. Just sore."

"Let me know if you change your mind." I hate pestering him, but it bothers me that he's hurting and I can't do anything about it.

He manages a few more bites and half a roll, but he mostly pokes at his food. Usually, he's a good eater, but I'm afraid he's preoccupied with something.

Of course I can't help thinking he must remember what he said to me at the hospital. He's probably embarrassed, or maybe he regrets saying anything at all.

My phone chimes with an incoming message. I glance at the screen. "It's Micah."

Micah: Checking to see you two got home okay

Micah: Send proof of life

"He's checking to make sure you made it here all right." I take a picture of a sullen-looking Chris spooning some of the pot roast into his mouth and send it to Micah. "A picture is worth a thousand words."

Micah: He looks like shit. Tell him I'll bring more clothes in the morning

I bite back a chuckle as I pass along the message.

"You guys don't need to fuss over me," Chris says, frowning.

"No, but you're our friend, and we care about you."

Chris reaches for his glass and downs the rest of his lemonade. "Thanks for dinner. It's been a long day, and I think I'll turn in."

"Dawn made a blueberry cobbler. Would you like some?" This guy *loves* cobbler.

He shakes his head. "Nah. I'm good."

I've never known Chris to turn down cobbler, so something is definitely wrong. But I don't want to push him because I'm pretty sure I already know what it is. He remembers what he said, or at least some of it, and he regrets it. And that makes me sad.

Chris carries his plate and silverware to the sink, rinses them off, and puts them in the dishwasher. Then he turns to face me. "Thanks for having me over tonight, Jennie. I'm pretty wiped out, so I'll say goodnight. I think I remember where the guest room is."

He takes a couple of steps toward the arched doorway, stops, and turns back to me. "Did I say anything earlier to you, at the hospital? I mean, anything inappropriate? I was kind of out of it."

My chest tightens. I'm right. He does remember at least bits and pieces. I honestly don't know how to respond to that. It's getting late, and he's exhausted and in pain. Now is not the time for me to pile more worries on his conscience. "No," I say easily, lying through my teeth. "You didn't."

He doesn't look convinced. "If I said anything I shouldn't have, I'm sorry."

"No worries." I do my best to give him a reassuring smile, when deep down inside, I'm hurting. He might have said those things, but I doubt he meant them.

He nods. “If you’re sure. Goodnight then. I’ll see you in the morning.”

The house is eerily quiet after Chris goes to bed. I’m tired, and it’s been a long day, and I should be sleepy, but I’m not. I keep replaying our conversation at the hospital over and over again.

How can I take him at his word when he was under the influence of a sedative? He couldn’t have been serious, could he? I’m thinking no, especially not when he clearly acts like he regrets it.

12

Chris

I am such a fucking idiot! I stare at my reflection in the bathroom mirror, watching rivulets of water stream down my face. It's damn hard to wash your face when one of your arms is completely immobilized. It's even harder to lower my sweats one-handed so I can take a piss. It's even harder to pull them up when I'm done.

Jennie always keeps a stash of new toothbrushes in the bathroom cupboard for guests. I snag one and brush my teeth. Then I head for the guest bedroom and wrangle my clothes off one-handed, which isn't easy. It looks like I'm sleeping in my sweats tonight since I passed on the underwear at the hospital. I hope Micah thinks to bring me some in the morning.

After yanking the covers down, I crawl onto the bed and lie staring at the ceiling.

I am such a fucking idiot!

Jennie denied I said anything inappropriate to her at the hospital, but I know better. I know what I said, or at least most of it. I told her I fucking loved her. That's true, of course, I do. But I wasn't supposed to say that out loud. And now I've put her in an awkward position, and God knows what kind of damage I've done to our friendship.

I'm afraid I just ruined the most important relationship I have. If I lose her as a friend, I don't know how I'll ever recover from that.

I lie here for the longest time, rehashing what I *might* have told her, overthinking everything, and generally driving myself crazy. The house is silent, and I'm wondering what Jennie is doing. Has she gone to bed? Or is she sitting up wondering what she's going to do about me and my unrequited love for her?

Fuck!

It feels weird even being here tonight. It's been years since I stayed over at Jennie's. When we were kids, Rosie let me and Micah spend the night sometimes. We'd stay up all night watching scary movies and eating popcorn and M&Ms until Rosie made us go to bed.

Micah and I would crash in sleeping bags on the living room floor. In the morning, Rosie would make us pancakes before she had to head off to the diner. George would give me and Micah rides home after breakfast.

The nights I slept over here meant the world to me. It was such a luxury to sleep in a clean, secure home where I didn't have to watch my back constantly. I lost count of how many of Mom's tricks tried to make a move on me when she was out cold in her bed, usually after a drug binge.

In the trailer, I slept on the sofa in the living room, so the tricks would have to pass by me on their way out in the middle of the night. Some of them propositioned me, offering me cash for a blow job. Some of them offered me money if I'd let them fuck me. I was probably twelve then. It got so bad, I started sleeping over at Micah's house a lot.

Jennie never knew about any of that kind of shit. I wanted to protect her from it. I was also ashamed of where I came from. I didn't want her to know how bad it was.

It's why I went into law enforcement in the first place—to protect those who can't protect themselves.

My shoulder is aching like a bitch, but that's just too bad. I won't take so much as an aspirin. I'm terrified of ending up an addict like my mom. Her addiction to drugs and alcohol is the reason she ended up like she did. I always wondered what kind of mom she would have been if she hadn't gotten hooked on the stuff. I like to think she'd have been a good mom if she could have stayed sober.

I never blamed Jennie for saying no to me when we were kids and I stupidly asked her to school dances. What girl would have wanted to go to a dance with a kid like me? I didn't even own a decent pair of pants. All I had to my name was ripped jeans, and not the fancy kind, but jeans that were so old and threadbare the fabric tore.

I never blamed her.

But I never stopped loving her either... I just did it quietly, from afar.

* * *

I must have eventually fallen asleep because the next thing I know, the sun is peeking through the blue gingham curtains, and birds are singing outside my window.

After making the bed as well as I can with only one hand, I grab my phone and head to the hall bathroom to pee, wash my hand, and attempt to tidy my bedhead. It looks like that's not going to be possible, so I figure a shower is in order. But I can't very well take a shower with my arm in a sling, so I slip it off and set it on the counter. When I straighten my right arm, pain radiates up into my shoulder and neck, and I bite back a curse.

My phone chimes then with a message from Micah.

Micah: Hey, you doing okay?

Me: I'm alive.

Micah: I just dropped supplies outside Jennie's kitchen door. Jeans, T-shirt, underwear and socks. You need anything else?

Me: Thx. I owe you. Maybe a ride later this morning to the station?

Micah: Sure. Just txt when you're ready.

I go ahead with my shower, moving very slowly because every time I use my right arm, pain streaks along my spine. I manage to bathe one-handed. I even wash my hair one-handed.

I dry my feet on the bath mat, and with nothing but a towel wrapped around my waist, I slip out of the bathroom and head to the kitchen door to open it. Sitting on the top step is a paper grocery sack. I grab it and take it back to the bathroom so I can get dressed.

Besides more clothing, Micah also packed my deodorant. Good man! At least one of us is thinking clearly this morning. Maybe my brain is still a bit addled by the sedative.

The house is quiet, so I don't think Jennie and Rosie are out of bed yet. I head for the kitchen, flip on the lights, and start the coffeemaker. While I'm waiting, I pace nervously. I'm not sure how Jennie will respond to me this morning.

I'm just about to pour myself a cup when I hear someone walk into the room. Bracing myself, I turn to see who it is, and I'm majorly relieved to see it's Rosie in her floral bathrobe and pink bunny slippers. "Good morning, Granny."

"Hello, Sheriff." Fortunately, she doesn't question my presence in her home. "Is there a cup of coffee with my name on it?"

"There sure is, ma'am. Have a seat, and I'll bring it to you."

I pour her a cup, add the French vanilla creamer she likes, and set the cup in front of her on the table.

She takes a sip and says, "It's perfect. Thank you, dear."

"How about some breakfast? I was planning to make scrambled eggs. Would you like some?"

"I believe I would, honey."

So, I get out a skillet and some oil and the carton of eggs from the fridge. It takes me a couple of tries to master cracking eggs one-handed, but I manage. Just as the eggs start cooking, Jennie walks into the kitchen. Her hair is damp, so she must have just showered. She's wearing blue jeans and a white T-shirt that beautifully hugs her breasts. I force myself to look away.

"Morning," she says.

"Morning."

"Where's your sling?"

"In the hall bathroom."

"You should be wearing it."

I shrug. *Ouch.* "I'll put it on after breakfast."

"Speaking of breakfast," she says, eyeing my efforts at the stove. "You're cooking."

"Yeah. It's the least I can do."

She goes to pour herself a cup of coffee and takes a seat at the table. "How's your shoulder?"

I flex a bit, wincing because it's sore as hell. "A lot better today, which is a good thing. I don't want to miss any work."

"Chris." She levels her *let's be reasonable* gaze on me. "Dr. Talbott said you need to take it easy for a few days. Maybe even a week. You should take some time off."

"I can still work. I'll catch up on my paperwork in the office and leave the patrolling and chasing to the deputies. Micah offered to drive me to the station later this morning."

I can tell she's not happy with my reply.

The eggs are done now, and so is the toast. I fix up three plates and plan to carry them to the table—one at a time—but Jennie jumps up.

"I've got this," she says. "You sit down and rest your shoulder."

"George must have gone to the grocery store to buy cat food," Granny says as she takes a bite of her toast. She reaches down and scratches Pumpkin's chin. "I swear, that man dotes on this cat."

"Yes, he does," Jennie says, a bittersweet smile on her face.

Pumpkin saunters over to me and throws himself against my shin. "Well, who can blame him?" I ask as I pat the cat.

I love how Jennie keeps her grandpa's memory alive for Rosie. There's no point in reminding her on a daily basis that her husband has passed, not when a little white lie will make Granny happy.

Jennie's gaze meets mine as she gives me a grateful smile. And for a moment, she lets the pain shine through. Her grandfather's passing left a big hole in her heart, too.

My chest hollows out, leaving an aching hole. I'd take that pain for her if I could.

Did I tell you I love you, Jens?

I can't help dwelling on the fact she remembers exactly what I said yesterday, and like me, she's pretending she doesn't.

I guess we're both going to pretend it never happened.

13

Jennie

Granny is the first one done with breakfast. She excuses herself from the table and goes to her room to get dressed. Pumpkin follows right behind her.

As we sit at the table eating, I can't help noticing how Chris's chest fills out his T-shirt. It hugs his torso like a glove, outlining his muscles. His shirt is short sleeved, baring his muscles and the thick veins running down his forearms. There's not an ounce of flab on him. I wish I could say the same about myself. His feet are bare. His hair is damp, so I'm thinking he managed to sneak in a shower this morning.

"I see Micah made good on his promise to drop off more clothes."

Chris nods as he sips his coffee. "So, what's on your agenda for today?"

He knows it's my day off. "Granny and I will hang out here and keep ourselves busy."

Chris sets his mug on the table. "Jennie." His voice is heavy, laced with intention. He's staring at the table top, tracing the pattern of a flower on the tablecloth. He's nervous. He's fidgeting.

My pulse picks up. "Yes?" My stomach is in knots because I know what's coming. *Questions.*

"Yesterday, at the hospital," he begins. "I'm pretty sure I said some things to you."

There's no point in playing dumb. If he wants to talk about it, the least I can do is meet him halfway. "You did." I'm a nervous wreck because I don't know where this is going. Does he want to take it back? Ask me to pretend it never happened?

I decide the best course of action is to give him a graceful out. "Chris, you were under the influence of a sedative, so I won't hold you responsible for the things you said."

He's so unsure as he forces himself to look at me. "That's just it, Jennie. I meant what I said—every word of it. I just never meant to tell you."

My heart stops, and I swallow hard. "Why wouldn't you tell me, if that's how you feel?"

"I didn't want to put you on the spot or make things awkward between us. You made it plenty clear in the past that you aren't interested in me, not like that." He runs his fingers through his hair and grimaces, but it's emotional pain on his face this time, not physical pain. "God, I'm sorry," he says. "I wish I'd kept my damn mouth shut." His brown eyes radiate pain and regret. "I would never want to do anything to jeopardize our—"

"Chris, stop." I reach for his good hand.

He pulls it back, as if touching me is simply too much right now. "Jennie, I—"

"No, please, let me speak."

He nods and goes back to tracing the pattern on the tablecloth.

Now it's my turn to bare my soul. I should have done this a long time ago. "One of my biggest regrets in life is saying no to you all those years ago."

His head snaps up, and he stares at me in disbelief. "What?"

"I thought I was protecting you back then, from all the bullying and slurs that were leveled at me. I knew you had it rough already, because of your mom, and I didn't want to add to that."

He looks at me like I'm speaking a foreign language, and he doesn't understand a word of it.

"The truth is," I say, forcing myself to continue before I lose my nerve, "I feel the same way about you. I always have." Tears blur my vision. "But I was stupid and afraid, and ended up ruining everything. I'm so sorry."

Now he's the one reaching for my hand. He squeezes it so tightly, I wince. "Sorry," he says as he gentles his grasp. "Jennie, sweetheart, you could never ruin anything." He looks me in the eye. "Say it again."

I laugh shakily. "Say what?"

"What you just said."

Suddenly, I'm feeling as bashful as a middle-school girl again talking to the boy she's crushing on. "That I feel the same way about you?"

When he smiles at me, a terrible weight is lifted from my shoulders. I don't see blame or accusation in his eyes. I see something that looks an awful lot like relief mixed with joy.

"Jennie—"

Our heartfelt moment is interrupted by the sound of multiple sirens in the distance. Every second, they get louder and louder, as if they're coming our way.

A chill skates down my spine. "Are those—"

He nods. "Police sirens, yes."

They sound so close!

Too close!

We stare at each other. "What—" My cell phone, which is on the nightstand in my bedroom, starts ringing. "I'd better grab that in case it's the diner."

Before I'm even out of my chair, Chris's cellphone starts ringing.

Then my landline starts ringing.

Three phones ringing at the same time? That can't be a coincidence.

Chris answers his. "Nelson here. Darlene, what's up?" His expression changes instantly as he puts his phone on speaker. "Repeat that, Darlene. I've got Jennie right here with me."

Darlene's voice comes over the speakerphone. "There's a fire at the diner. The fire department is on their way."

"Oh, my God!" As I jump up and race to my bedroom, I can hear my phone ringing *again*. I grab it off my nightstand and check the screen to see I have two missed calls from Robert. He's in the process of leaving me a voice message when I call him back.

"Robert!" I say when he picks up. "I heard about the fire. I'm on my way. Are you okay?"

"I'm fine."

"Is anyone else—"

"No. I was the only one here when the smoke alarms went off." He pauses to cough before he adds, "Jennie, the fire is in your office."

"What!" It wouldn't surprise me to hear there was a fire in the *kitchen*, but in my *office*? There's nothing flammable in there. "Stay outside and let the fire department handle it. They're on their way. So am I." And then I end the call.

I return to the kitchen as Chris is attempting to tuck his T-shirt into his jeans.

"I talked to Robert," I say. "He's safe. He said the fire started in my office."

The look on Chris's face surely mirrors mine. *That's impossible.*

I call Dawn to tell her about the fire and ask if she can come stay with Granny.

"Of course!" she says. "I'll be right there." Hardly two minutes later, there's a knock at the door. When I open it, Dawn rushes in, breathless.

I pull her into my arms for a hug. "I can't thank you enough!"

She gestures at the door. "You two, go. I've got everything covered here."

"Your sling!" I remind Chris.

He waves me forward. "There's no time for that. We need to go."

I drive us the two blocks to the diner. Two cruisers with lights flashing are parked behind the building.

"Park over there on the side street," Chris says. "The firetrucks will need to get close."

As we approach the rear of the building, a firetruck pulls in and comes to a stop. Firefighters jump out and begin donning the rest of their protective gear.

From where we're standing, flames are visible through my office window, and the back door is blocked by a deputy. "Go around to the front," he yells at us over the commotion. "This way isn't safe."

Chris and I round the block to the front of the shopping center, where a small crowd of onlookers has gathered in front of the diner. They're peering through the front windows as they try to see what's going on. Robert is standing out front. When I spot him, I rush to him and wrap my arms around his waist.

Robert hugs me back. "I'm so sorry, Jennie." He coughs again, probably because his throat is irritated by the smoke. "I didn't see or hear a thing until the smoke alarms went off. As soon as I heard them, I searched for the source of the smoke, and when I opened your office door, I saw the flames. There was no way I could put it out with a fire extinguisher. Not on my own. It was already too involved. It's arson, honey. It has to be. Your desk was on fire, nothing else."

The diner door opens, and Deputy Stephens comes out. "Hey, boss," he says to Chris. "They're putting the fire out now. It's nearly extinguished."

"How extensive is the damage?" Chris asks the deputy.

"Jennie's desk and computer are destroyed. The whole thing was engulfed in flames when I arrived."

"Was there anything flammable on your desk?" Chris asks me.

I shake my head. "No. Nothing that would spark a fire. Just my computer, some notepads, pens, a stapler, and a landline. Some picture frames. That's it."

"We need to look at security camera footage," Chris says to Officer Stephens. Then he turns to me. "Obviously, your computer's no use now. Can you access the footage from your phone?"

"Yes!" I can't believe I hadn't already thought of that. I pull up the security app on my phone and look at this morning's recordings.

We see video of Robert arriving at six, as he always does. Then, at six-fifteen, someone dressed in black, their face obscured by a black ski mask, walks up to the camera at the rear entrance and smashes it with a hammer. The same thing happens to the camera positioned in the hallway right outside my office door.

"Someone did this on purpose?" I ask. It's a rhetorical question, obviously, because the proof is staring me in the face. I just can't believe it.

A few minutes later, the white-haired fire chief walks through the dining room and joins us out front. "Fire's out," he says in a gruff voice. "The desk and chair are destroyed, and the floor underneath is scorched. There's soot on the ceiling and plenty of smoke damage. My best guess, from what I can see, is the fire started in the trashcan beside the desk. We found an empty gas can on the floor nearby." The man frowns. "I'm sorry, ma'am. The fire inspector is on his way."

A wave of dizziness hits me, and my knees practically buckle. Chris catches me with his good arm and eases me down on the sidewalk. "Sit right here, sweetheart. I'm going inside to take a look at your office."

Just as Chris and the fire chief head inside, Maggie, Ruth, and Jack appear on the sidewalk.

"Jack and I checked the police scanner as soon as we heard the sirens," Ruth says.

Maggie crouches down beside me. "Ruth called me, and I came as soon as I could. Was there anyone inside?"

"Robert was the only one in the building at the time, and he's fine," I say. My head is still reeling from the fire chief's initial assessment. "The fire started in my office. It looks like arson."

Jack's customary dark expression darkens even more, if that's possible. "Where's Chris?"

"Inside with the fire chief. He wanted to see my office."

Jack walks into the diner. Maggie takes a seat beside me on the curb, and Ruth sits on my other side.

Maggie grabs my hand. "Are *you* all right?"

"Yes. I think I'm mostly in shock. Chris and I were at my house eating breakfast—"

Ruth looks at me curiously. "Chris?"

Oh, that's right. They don't know. "Chris slept over at my house last night."

"Really?" Ruth asks, seeming quite interested.

"They gave him a sedative at the hospital when they fixed his dislocated shoulder. When he was released, he was still a bit loopy and wasn't permitted to drive, so I thought it would be best if he came home with me so I could watch over him."

I skip telling them about the confessions he made at the hospital as well as our follow-up discussion at the breakfast table.

"Do they know how the fire started?" Maggie asks.

"The chief said it started in the trashcan beside my desk. He found an empty gas can nearby."

"Did any of your cameras pick up anything?"

"No. Whoever it was destroyed the cameras."

While we're waiting, Cara and Michelle arrive for work. They both look shellshocked at the sight of the firetrucks and police cruisers.

The crowd of pedestrians has grown outside the diner, all of them staring through the front windows.

"If the fire hadn't been contained so quickly," I say, "it would have spread to the kitchen, and we'd be out of commission for a good long while." I shudder at the thought. "I can't imagine who would do a thing like this."

"Can't you?" Ruth asks, giving me a telling look.

"What are you—who—?"

"Who do you think?" Maggie asks.

My face grows cold. "Do you mean David?"

"Who else?" Ruth asks. "He's done nothing but cause you trouble since he returned."

At that moment, Chris and Jack return.

Chris walks up behind me, lays his good hand on my left shoulder, and leans down to kiss the top of my head. "You doing okay?"

I nod. "As good as can be expected."

And then it dawns on me—he kissed me in front of our friends, who are all staring at me like I just grew a second head. Granted, it was just a friendly kiss on my head, but still. He's never done *that* before.

"Jack and I are going to look around out back and see if we can find any evidence," Chris says. "We'll also check the Tavern's rear cameras. Hopefully they're still intact and caught something." He squeezes my shoulder once more. "I won't be gone long."

Once Chris and Jack are out of sight, Maggie and Ruth both turn curious eyes on me.

"What did I just see?" Ruth asks.

Maggie grins at me. "Is there something you should be telling us?"

Now my face is overheating. "It's complicated."

They both start laughing.

"Of course it is," Ruth says. "Isn't it always? Now, please enlighten us."

I'm not ready to tell them Chris confessed his feelings for me when he was under the influence of a sedative. "We've been talking."

Ruth raises an eyebrow. "*Talking?* And?"

"Well," I begin, unsure how much to share this soon. Chris and I have hardly had a chance to discuss it. "It's complicated."

Before anyone can say another word, Chris and Jack return. Maggie, Ruth, and I all stand for the update.

"The building is safe now," Jack says. "The fire is out. Jennie, your office is off limits until the fire inspector can investigate. But the room is pretty much destroyed. The wood floors around the desk are badly singed and will need to be repaired. Your desk, chair, and computer are ruined. And there's smoke damage in the kitchen and dining room."

"Don't worry," Chris says. "Your insurance should cover everything. Once the fire inspector gets here and makes his report, we can start on repairs."

"Did anyone say how long the diner will be closed?" I ask as this is starting to sink in.

"I'm guessing a few days at least," Chris says. "You won't be able to reopen until the health department gives you the okay." He pulls me close, wrapping his good arm around me. "It's going to be okay. No one was hurt. That's what's important. The rest can be fixed."

* * *

Officer Stephens offers Chris a ride to the station so he can requisition a temporary replacement vehicle until there's a determination on his SUV as to whether it's repairable or not.

"We'll give you a ride home," Chris says. "There's nothing you can do here right now. Besides, it's not safe. No civilians are allowed in the diner until further notice."

"Ruth thinks David might have done it," I whisper to Chris.

Chris nods. "Believe me, he's my number one suspect. I'm going to pay him a visit this morning to see if he has an alibi." Then he surprises me when he reaches for my hand and gives it a gentle squeeze.

As I nod, I get a whiff of his scent—a combination of clean laundry, soap, and something distinctly male. Something that makes my insides quiver in anticipation.

And then, to everyone's surprise—including mine—he kisses my cheek.

Our avid audience—Ruth, Jack, Maggie, and the servers—are watching our interaction.

Chris's deputy gives me a ride home. When we pull into my driveway, I thank him for the ride and tell Chris I'll see him later.

Chris gets out of the vehicle to walk me to my door. He leans close and whispers in my ear. "We need to continue our discussion from earlier." Then he slips his good arm around my waist and kisses me. "Go inside, and lock the doors. I'll come back after I question Braggart."

It's not until Chris and his deputy drive away that I realize he forgot to put on his sling.

14

Chris

"Let's head straight to the Braggart ranch," I tell Ricky. My gut tells me he started the fire in Jennie's office. On the way there, I realize I forgot to grab the sling, but that's too bad. There's no time to go back for it. My shoulder will just have to keep aching like a bitch.

When we arrive at the Braggarts' place, Ricky pulls up to the circular drive in front of the house. We get out of the cruiser and approach the front door. He knocks while I peer through the front windows trying to get a bead on Dave's location, assuming he's even here. But I don't see anyone.

The housekeeper, Marguerite, comes to the door. When she sees us standing here, her eyes widen. "Yes? Can I help you?"

"Is Dave here?" I ask.

"No, sir. He left early this morning, and he hasn't been back. I don't know where he is."

I need to search this house to be sure he's not here. I can't take the housekeeper's word for it. I also need to look for evidence of arson, both in this house and in his vehicle.

"Looks like I need a search warrant," I tell Ricky. "Let's head back to the station. We need to put out an APB on Braggart. He's got to be around here somewhere. I want all eyes looking for him."

On my way back to the car, I call Jennie to let her know Braggart's not at home. That means I have no idea where he is, and I want to give her a heads-up.

When she answers my call, I say, "He's not at home, Jennie. We'll keep looking. In the meanwhile—"

"Chris, he's—!" Whatever she was going to say is cut off, and all I can hear is her muffled voice.

"Jennie!" I cry as I run to the cruiser.

"Hello, Sheriff." It's a familiar male voice, arrogant and lazy. "I imagine you're looking for me right about now."

My chest tightens as panic floods me. That *son of a bitch!* "Braggart, I swear to God, if you hurt—"

But the line goes dead.

Ricky's already seated in the driver's seat. I slide into the front passenger seat, and we tear off back to Jennie's. On the way, I get on the radio and call for back-up to meet us there.

15

Jennie

I wave to Chris and the deputy as they pull out of my driveway and head for David's parents' house. When they're out of sight, I unlock the door and step inside.

And here he is.

David is seated at my kitchen table with Granny, drinking a cup of coffee like he doesn't have a care in the world. Like he didn't just attempt to burn down my diner. Dawn is standing across the kitchen from them, leaning against the counter.

My lungs seize up, and suddenly I can't breathe. I meet Dawn's eyes—hers are wide with fear. We stare at each other for a long moment, and I can only hope we're on the same wavelength. "Thanks for staying with Granny this morning," I say, my voice impressively calm. Totally nonchalant. "You should head on home now."

She nods. "Sure. Anytime." And then to Granny, she says, "I'll see you Monday, Rosie."

She says that like it's any other day. Like it's no big deal. We're all just going to ignore the narcissistic monster seated at the kitchen table.

Dawn gathers her purse and crochet bag and calmly heads out the door. *Without locking it.*

Thank you, Dawn!

Dawn will call for help the moment she gets into her house, and Chris and his officers will come. In the meanwhile, I just need to keep David occupied.

"What are you doing here, David?" Miraculously, I manage to keep my voice even.

"Is it a crime for me to want to spend time with my favorite girls? With my *family*?" He reaches across the table for Granny's hand and gives it an affectionate pat.

She pulls her hand back, lays it in her lap, and gives me a beseeching look. *She's scared.* She never liked David, and she's aware enough at the moment to know he shouldn't be here.

She knows we're in trouble.

"You shouldn't be here," I say, still managing to sound calm when I'm anything but inside. My pulse is racing. I'm literally shaking. "I'd like for you to leave."

Mentally, I'm calculating how long it will take Chris to get here.

Three minutes? Five? Ten?

David leans back in his chair and crosses his arms over his chest. "I'm not going anywhere, Jennie-bean."

God, just hearing him use that nickname brings back a wave of painful memories. How many times did he whisper that in my ear when he was hurting me? "I told you not to call me that!"

"Why not?" He sounds truly perplexed. "I'm just being affectionate, sugar."

"Trust me, there's nothing affectionate about you."

David's face reddens as he shoots to his feet and stalks toward me. I back up hastily until I hit the counter and can't go any farther. He crowds me, getting right in my face, his hands caging me in. His hot breath hits me in the face when he grates out, "I'll call you whatever the fuck I want to call you, *Jennie-bean.* Won't I? And you'll *like* it."

I wince. This close, I can smell the alcohol on his breath. I think it's whiskey. Now a dangerous man is even more dangerous. David becomes a real monster when he's intoxicated.

He leans in closer and skims his nose along my cheek. "You'll like it, won't you, Jennie?"

He wraps his fingers round my throat, not enough to cut off my air, but enough to make his point. My voice shakes when I say, "Yes."

He runs his nose up the side of my face and into my hair. "God, you always smelled so good. That's what I missed the most after you divorced me. I missed smelling you." One of his hands slides between my thighs, and he cups my crotch firmly. "Every damn inch of you." He growls. "God, I've missed you, beanie."

I feel nauseated—by his touch, by his nearness, and by his threats. And I'm not the only one who's concerned. Granny's afraid, too. I need to get him away from her.

My phone rings then, and we all flinch.

"Who's that calling you?" David asks. He grabs my phone out of my back pocket and stares at the screen. "That fucking sheriff again!"

He accepts the call and puts the phone on speaker.

"He's not at home, Jennie," Chris says. "We'll keep looking. In the meanwhile—"

"Chris, he's—!" David grabs me in a choke hold and covers my mouth.

I hear Chris cry my name.

"Hello, Sheriff," David says, sounding perfectly at ease. "I imagine you're looking for me right about now."

"Braggart, I swear to God, if you hurt—"

David ends the call. "That moron thinks he's God's gift to the world. Well, let me tell you, he's not." He leans in to kiss me, and when I try to push him back, he tightens his grasp on my throat, squeezing nearly hard enough to cut off my air. "We don't have much time, J-bean. It looks like the cavalry's on its way."

I don't want Granny to see this, so I manage to rasp out, "Let's go in the other room."

Apparently, he likes this suggestion because he releases my throat. "Good idea."

As he pushes me out of the kitchen, into the hallway, I frantically try to decide what I should do. I need to keep him away from Granny. I also need to stall him until the police get here.

I'm not surprised when he herds me into my bedroom and shuts the door. He glances around. "This hasn't changed much since the last time we fucked in here. I figure we have just enough time for a quickie before all hell breaks loose. Won't your sheriff just love that? You, full of my cum?"

As I stare at the gleam in his eyes, a frisson of fear streaks down my spine. He's not a narcissist. He's *insane*.

I back away from him, toward the window, hoping I might catch a glimpse of police cars arriving. I just need to stall. "We're not having sex, David, so you can put that thought right out of your head."

He laughs. "Remember how I had to gag you when we fucked in here, so your grandparents didn't hear us?" Smirking, he shakes his head. "It wasn't easy keeping you quiet, sugar, because you are a screamer."

Something sour shoots up into my throat. I swear to God, if he lays one finger on me, I'll throw up. If I screamed before, it wasn't from pleasure. It was from pain, because he liked hurting me. "David, I'm begging you, please go. There's nothing left for us. We're through, and I'm never taking you back."

His smile disintegrates. "We never should have divorced in the first place. I've come back to rectify things. We're going to get married again, you're going to liquidate everything, and we're leaving this God-forsaken town once and for all. I've got a place in Vegas—"

"You just want my money. That's what this is about."

"It should be *my* money, sugar. The inheritance you got from the old man, the diner, this house—this should be mine."

"The house and the diner don't even belong to me. They're Granny's."

"They'll be yours one day, and based on Granny's condition, that won't be long from now. Besides, if you ask her nicely, I'm sure she'll be happy to sign everything over to you."

"If it's money you want, I'll pay you to leave and never come back. How much will it take? I've got my inheritance from Grandpa—"

When I hear the muffled sound of a car door shutting, my heart stutters. *Are they here?*

David must have heard it, too, because he rushes to the window and looks out at the street. We don't see any cars, but then we hear another car door, and another.

"Looks like your boyfriend's here." He growls at me. "This isn't over, Jennie."

He has to realize what's about to happen. Out of spite, he pushes me up against the wall, grabs my wrists, and holds them captive above my head. His free hand slides up beneath my top, and he grabs one of my breasts.

When I try to pull free, he squeezes my breast hard, making me cry out in pain. He crushes his mouth to mine, muffling my cries, nearly gagging me with his tongue.

My bedroom door bursts open, and men flood inside, shouting demands. Two pairs of hands yank David off of me and throw him face down on the floor. A separate pair of hands catches me when my knees give out.

"I've got you, sweetheart," Chris says. He helps me to my feet and walks me out of the room and down the hall to the living room, where he sits me down on the sofa. I'm shaking violently as my mind tries to catch up.

The sound of utter chaos comes from my bedroom—shouts and grunts and scuffles—as the officers fight to subdue and cuff David.

"Where's Granny?" I cry, panicking. "Is she—"

"She's in her room with an officer. She's safe. Are *you* all right?" Chris sits beside me and takes my hands in both of his, squeezing them reassuringly. "Jennie, did he hurt you?"

Overwhelmed, I can't formulate an answer. Instead, I burst into tears.

Chris pulls me against him, wrapping both of his arms around me. "It's okay. I've got you, and he's going to jail."

I feel Chris's arms around me, so solid and strong. I feel his lips press against my temple, so very welcome, as he murmurs something unintelligible.

It takes me a full minute to realize it's *his* arms that are shaking, not mine.

"You're still not wearing your sling," I remind him.

His chest vibrates as he chuckles. "I know. It just doesn't seem important right now."

16

Chris

I've never been so scared in my life as I am when we enter Jennie's house through the unlocked side door. Dawn Keller had called the station, and Darlene forwarded her message to me. Dawn had left the side door unlocked.

When we arrive, it's still unlocked, and that buys us several precious seconds. I, along with five other officers, sweep into the kitchen. We find Granny seated at the table, alone, looking terrified. The moment she sees us, she points toward the hallway. "That bad man is in Jennie's room."

We waste no time getting to her door and find it unlocked—

thank God because every second counts. Jace turns the handle and kicks the door in so hard it bounces off the wall. Immediately, we spot Braggart pressing Jennie up against a wall.

The thoughts going through my head at that moment are chaotic and crazy. I want to kill him. I want to get my hands around his throat and choke the bloody life out of him.

But before I can act on this impulse, Jace and Randy grab Braggart and haul him off Jennie. She immediately sinks to the floor. I help her up and walk her to the living room so I can assess her condition. She and Braggart were both still fully dressed, so that allays one of my worst fears. But that doesn't mean he didn't hurt her.

She's too distraught right now to answer any more of my questions, so I just hold her in my arms and let her cry.

"He's going to jail for a very long time," I tell her. "It's over. No more fires. No more threats."

Randy and Jace strong-arm Braggart, who's cuffed, out of the bedroom. They drag him, kicking and cursing, toward the kitchen.

I start to set Jennie aside, so I can assist in getting Braggart out of the house and into a patrol car, but she clings to me, refusing to let me leave. And I don't have the heart to release her just yet.

I can hear him scuffling with the officers as they drag him toward the door.

"You bitch!" Braggart yells. "You're making a huge mistake! I'm the best thing that ever happened to you!"

Jennie flinches in my arms.

"Get him out of here!" I tell my deputies. Then, to Jennie, I say, "I'm sorry, but I'm going to have to go to the station. I need to oversee his booking and shove him into a holding cell myself. I'll call someone to come sit with you."

"Call Maggie," she says. "Her brother usually takes over for her in the afternoons. She should be free."

I make the call. Maggie promises to be here in fifteen minutes.

"I don't want to leave you, but I have to," I tell Jennie.

She nods. "I know." As she turns to face me, she takes my good hand in both of hers. "Chris." She can barely meet my gaze. "I'm so sorry. I've been so stupid."

"Hey, no. Don't say that."

"But it's true. When we were in school, I made some bad choices. I thought I was protecting you, but in reality, I hurt us both. And then later, with David, I made a monumental mistake that's haunting me still to this day."

I link our fingers, our palms pressing together, and bring her hand to my lips to kiss.

Her hand comes up to touch my face, her fingers gentle as they trace the edge of my cheek. Unshed tears glimmer in her dark eyes like stars in a night sky. "I don't deserve you," she says as she presses her forehead to mine.

"Well, if we're going down that route, I don't deserve you either. I'm the damn fool idiot who sent you into this house where that motherfucker was waiting. I practically handed you right over."

She shakes her head. "It's not your fault. You couldn't have known he was here."

And then there's a knock on the kitchen door.

"Jennie? It's me, Maggie. I'm here."

Jennie pulls back from me, her eyes glistening. "We're in the living room!"

Maggie walks into the living room.

Jennie practically jumps off the sofa and nervously tidies her hair and clothes.

"Is that awful man gone?" Granny asks as she walks out of her bedroom.

"Yes, Granny, he's gone," Jennie says as she goes to put her arm around Rosie's thin shoulders.

"You need to put him in jail, young man," Rosie says to me. "He's a vile monster. He hurt my granddaughter."

I stand. "Yes, ma'am. I'm on my way to do that right now." To Maggie, I say, "Thanks for coming. I've got to get to the station so I can oversee Braggart's booking. We can't afford to screw this up and give him any leverage when he goes before a judge tomorrow."

"It's no trouble," Maggie says. "Owen is at home with Claire, so I can stay as long as I'm needed."

Maggie opens her arms, and Jennie walks right into them, undoubtedly needing a hug after what she's been through today. First the fire, and then Braggart attacking her in her own home.

When I reach Jennie, I pause long enough to hold her a moment. "Everything will be okay," I murmur to her. "I promise you." And then, after giving her a quick kiss, I head for the kitchen.

"Are you all right?" Maggie asks Jennie. "Did he hurt you?"

"I'm okay," Jennie says, but her voice is quiet and subdued.

I pause. "He did hurt her," I tell Maggie. "And I'm going to make sure he pays."

* * *

I head to the Larimer county jail to be present when Braggart is booked and placed into a holding cell. As soon as I walk into the jail, I hear him yelling his damn fool head off.

"Do you know who I am!" he shouts. "Who my parents are? They won't stand for this. You can't treat me like this!"

When Braggart sees me walking toward him, he grows even more livid. "Arrest him!" he yells, nodding in my direction. He would point at me if he could, but his hands are cuffed behind him. "Arrest the fucking sheriff!"

Rolling my eyes, I ask the booking staff if they've performed a breathalyzer test on him yet. I could easily smell the alcohol on his breath back at Jennie's.

"We sure did," Officer Cindy Carver says with a grin. "We could smell it on him the minute he walked in. It read zero-point-one-six." That's twice the legal limit.

"Good. Add three more charges: public intoxication, disorderly conduct, and DUI. And that's on top of the kidnapping, assault, and battery charges." I'm going to throw the book at him. See how he likes cooling his jets in jail.

Braggart is still screeching his head off, demanding that someone call his parents and his attorney.

"Hold your horses," I tell him. "You'll get your phone calls."

After he's processed, he's permitted to make a call to his attorney. Then he's put in a holding cell, where he'll stay until his arraignment. He might get to see a judge tomorrow, if he's lucky.

I can't help stopping by his cell to see him behind bars. "Just making sure you're in for the night."

Braggart is sitting on a bench seat in his cell, arms crossed over his chest. He sneers at me. "You're gonna regret this, Nelson. When my parents find out about this, they'll have you removed from office. You can't do this to a Braggart."

I smile smugly. "You sound like you're twelve years old and still need your mommy and daddy to bail you out of trouble. I'm sorry to break it to you, pal, but you're a grown up now. You have to face the consequences of your actions."

He surges to his feet and rushes the bars, reaching out in an attempt to grab me. "You're a fucking idiot, you know that?" he sneers.

I step back easily, beyond his reach. "Actually, I'm feeling pretty good right now. You're behind bars and off the streets, and Jennie can rest easy tonight. I hope the judge denies you bail and you rot in jail until your trial."

He scoffs. "I'll be a free man tomorrow, I guarantee it."

God, I hope not.

I leave the jail then and head home so I can pack a few days' worth of clothes and necessities. There's no way I'm leaving Jennie home alone right now. At least not until Braggart is incarcerated. I'll sleep in the guest room, of course. I have no expectations.

I'm going to talk to Jennie about requesting a restraining order. If the judge does give Braggart a bond, he'll likely pay it and be out on the street by the afternoon.

As I drive the four blocks to Jennie's house, my shoulder is on fire. Fortunately, my sling is still at Jennie's house. I think it's time to put it back on.

17

Jennie

Maggie and I are cleaning up after dinner when there's a knock on the kitchen door. When I jump out of my skin, Maggie lays her hand on my back. "I'll get it. It's probably Chris."

I'm holding my breath as Maggie peeks out the window.

"It's Chris," she says as she unlocks the door and opens it. "Hello, Sheriff."

"Hi, Maggie." He walks in, and his gaze goes right to me. "You doing okay?"

I nod. "As good as can be expected."

Then he glances at Granny, who's seated at the table. She's petting Pumpkin, who's rubbing against her skins. "Hi, Granny. How are you?"

Hearing her name, Granny lifts her face and smiles at Chris. "I'm fine, young man. Thanks for asking." And then to me, she says, "It's your nice husband, honey. I don't like the nasty one."

I smile apologetically at Chris, and he just shrugs. He's used to her saying things like this. "I'm just glad I'm the one she likes," he murmurs.

Maggie says her goodbyes then, and after we hug, she heads home to her family.

Granny stands. "That's my cue. Goodnight, everyone. Come along, Pumpkin." And she heads out of the kitchen, the cat racing along after her.

"I should go help Granny get ready for bed," I tell Chris. "Have a seat and relax. I'll join you in a few minutes."

After Granny finishes in the bathroom, she finds me waiting for her in her bedroom, ready to help her change into her nightgown. She doesn't really need my help, but after all the stress she experienced today, I just want to provide some extra support.

"Are you doing okay?" I ask her.

"Of course. Why wouldn't I be?"

I'm not sure if she's forgotten the episode with David, or if she's just suppressing it. "Well, we had a rough day today, didn't we?"

She looks confused, like she's searching for a memory and can't find it.

Once I have her safely tucked in bed, I kiss her forehead. "Goodnight, Granny. I'll see you in the morning."

She grabs my arm. "He's staying, isn't he? The good one."

Sometimes I'm surprised by how insightful she can be. "We'll have to see, Granny. Chris is a busy man. He's got a lot of responsibilities."

"Yes, but none of his responsibilities are as important as *you*. That boy has waited all his life for you." She reaches up to boop my nose. "You remember that, young lady. A man who puts your needs first, over his own, is a keeper. Just like my George."

"I won't forget, I promise." I kiss her again. "Sweet dreams."

I walk out of her room, leaving the door open just enough so Pumpkin can come and go as he pleases.

When I return to the kitchen, Chris isn't there. I double-check to make sure the door is locked before I go in search of him. It doesn't take me long to find him in the guest bedroom, struggling to put his sling back on.

"Here, let me help you," I say as I take it from him and untwist the straps.

"Thanks. It's harder than it looks."

I hold the sling for him so he can slip his right arm into it. "I imagine your shoulder hurts."

"Yeah, it does."

The fact he's admitting it so readily makes me think it probably hurts a lot more than he's letting on. "And you won't take anything for the pain."

"I'd rather not."

I think it's unnecessary for him to pass on over-the-counter painkillers, but I understand why he does it, and I won't argue with him about it.

He winces when I cinch the sling in place.

"Then how about a glass of wine and a cold pack for your shoulder?" I ask. "That might help."

He nods. "Sure, I think I can handle that."

He follows me to the kitchen, where I pour us each a glass of red wine. Then I grab a bag of peas from the freezer and a linen hand towel.

We end up on the sofa in the living room. I wrap the bag of frozen peas in the linen towel and gently place it on his right shoulder. Then I hand him his glass of wine. He takes a sip and makes a face.

"You don't like it?" I ask.

"I'm more of a beer guy." Still, he takes a good swig, nearly emptying his glass before he sets it on the coffee table. "I'd like to spend the night again, if you don't mind. I know Braggart's behind bars tonight, but I don't feel right leaving you two alone. I'll sleep in the guest bedroom, of course. I just wanted to make that clear."

If I'm disappointed about him choosing the guest room—which admittedly I am—I try not to show it. Just because we exchanged some words, as well as some kisses, doesn't mean he's ready for more.

"Granny asked if you'd be staying tonight. She'll be pleased to see you're still here at breakfast."

"What about you, though? Are *you* okay with me staying again?"

I nod. "Yes, I want you to." Actually, I want a whole lot more than that, but I don't think we're there yet. I take a sip of wine and set my glass down next to his.

"About this afternoon—" I say.

"About earlier—" he says.

We both grow quiet, both of us smiling. At least we're both thinking about it.

"Why is this so awkward?" I ask. "We're both adults."

"It's because we waited so long. We let this go on far longer than we should." He reaches for my hand. "Jennie, in case I haven't been clear enough, I want you to know—I've loved you for as long as I can remember. I never stopped. Not even when I went away to school."

It's clearly time for honesty, for sharing long-held secrets and allowing ourselves to be vulnerable. "When you left for Phoenix, I was sure you weren't coming back. I'd convinced myself you'd meet someone in Arizona and decide to stay."

"I dated in college," he admits. "I was hoping to meet someone who could take my mind off you."

"Did it work?" I guess it didn't, or he wouldn't be sitting here beside me now.

"No, it didn't." He absently rubs the back of my hand. Without warning, he lifts my hand and kisses the back of it. Then he presses my hand to his face. "Not one bit. What about you? Did you date anyone besides Dave while I was away?"

"No. David was the first and only. When he finally left town after our divorce was final, I realized I'd dodged a bullet. I was afraid to date again after that. I no longer trusted my own judgment."

"Do you trust me?"

I smile. "Absolutely."

At that moment, Pumpkin races into the room and jumps up on the back of the sofa. He starts rubbing against the back of Chris's head.

"Cats are good judges of people," I point out. "If Pumpkin trusts you, I certainly do."

Chris smiles at my comment, but only for a moment. Suddenly, he's back to being serious. "We need to talk about Dave."

"I'd rather not, if you don't mind."

He smiles ruefully. "I know. But we have to be realistic. He's going to get out on bail sooner rather than later. I doubt the judge will deny him bond, even though I think that's what should happen. Assuming he's going to be released, as soon as tomorrow I'm afraid, you're going to need to get a restraining order."

I sigh. "I'll go to the courthouse tomorrow to fill out the paperwork. Hopefully the judge will approve it quickly."

He reaches for my hand and links our fingers together. "Are you sure Braggart didn't hurt you earlier? I saw he had you pinned against the wall."

"He had his hand around my throat, and he grabbed one of my breasts really hard, but that's it."

"*That's it?*" Chris is furious. "Hell, he never should have touched you at all!"

"This isn't personal for him, Chris. It's not about sex. It's not even about *me*. It's about control and money. He just wants my money."

"But his folks are loaded. Why does he need money?"

"His parents disowned him after our divorce. They disapproved of how he was treating me. And they only knew half of it, trust me. I don't know for sure, but I suspect he's broke, or close to it. I can't think of any other reason why he'd come back here. He assumed the house and diner were in my name, but they're not. Not yet, anyway. Granny had a trust drawn up after Grandpa died, even before her mind started deteriorating. Everything goes to me after she passes."

"Well, I'm not after your money," he says with a chuckle. "I make decent money as a sheriff, and my house and truck are paid off."

I start tracing a vein that runs from the back of his wrist all the way up to his elbow. When I skim my finger back down his arm, following the path of that thick ropey vein, he shivers.

"I'm about three seconds away from kissing you," he warns. "If you don't want me to, or if you're not ready for that, just say so. I'll understand."

I see hunger in his eyes, but also caution. Maybe he thinks I'm not ready for intimacy after what happened with David today. But I am ready, because what happens between *us* has absolutely nothing to do with David.

It's time for another confession. "I've been waiting years for you to kiss me."

He goes still, except for his breathing. His chest rises and falls heavily as he stares into my eyes, searching for something. I guess he finds what he's looking for because he leans closer.

And then it's just like it is in the movies. We gravitate toward each other in slow motion, in perfect sync, our gazes locked. And when his lips settle on mine, warm and sure, everything falls into place.

I breathe in his scent—warm male skin, clean laundry, a hint of cologne—and my body comes alive. My nerve endings go off like fireworks, shooting delicious tingles throughout my body.

When the kiss deepens, he groans, the sound rough and needy. His free hand is suddenly in my hair as he clasps the back of my head and holds me to him. I slip my arm around his waist, careful to avoid his injured arm.

Our first real kiss.

When Pumpkin lies down on the back of the sofa and starts purring, I chuckle. "We have an audience," I murmur against his lips

Chris pulls back with a smile as he looks into my eyes. "Tell me what you want, Jennie." His voice is rougher than usual. "Where do we go from here?"

"What do I want?" My pulse is racing as it tries to catch up with reality. The one thing I've wanted for so long is right here, practically in my lap. I'm afraid to move forward, but I'm terrified of staying frozen in place. Finally, I take a leap of faith and blurt out what I want. "I don't want you to sleep in the guest room. I want you to sleep with me."

His eyes widen as if he's surprised by my answer. "Just to sleep? Or, *to sleep?*"

I smile. "Not just to sleep."

As my words sink in, it takes him a moment to respond. "You're sure?"

"Yes."

"Okay." He nods, but a second later, he frowns. "Shit! Do you have condoms?"

"No. Do you?"

He shakes his head. "Sorry, no." He rests his forehead on my shoulder and groans. "I can't believe this."

I run my fingers through his hair, which elicits a moan from him. "Actually, I'm kind of glad you don't carry condoms with you."

"I guess you're not on the pill," he says.

"Nope. No need for it."

I can tell he's wracking his brain for a solution. "I could run to the store," he offers.

"Since it's a Sunday night, all of the local stores are closed by now," I point out. "I suppose you could try the gas station. They're open late."

He shakes his head. "I'm not leaving you and Granny here alone."

I muster all the courage I have. "There are *other things* we could do, you know—activities that don't involve the risk of pregnancy."

The look on his face is priceless. "You'd be okay with that?"

I brush the hair back from his forehead. "Yes, I'd be okay with that."

He stands. "I'd sweep you up in my arms and carry you to bed, but unfortunately" —he glances at his sling— "that's not in the cards tonight."

"Don't worry about your shoulder. I promise to take good care of you tonight." And then I stand, take his good hand, and lead him from the living room, down the hallway, and into my bedroom.

Pumpkin follows us, but I gently guide him out of my room.

"Not tonight, Punky. Mommy's got company."

And I quietly shut the door.

18

Chris

I might actually be dreaming right now. I'm thinking this has to be a dream because I'm in Jennie Lopez's bedroom, and the door is closed. We're alone, just the two of us, and she's gazing up at me with these gorgeous dark eyes filled with desire. I've had this dream so many times before, and each time I woke up alone in my bed, wishing it were real.

Right now, she's reaching for the hem of my T-shirt. Hell, I never got this far in a dream before.

"We'll have to pick up some condoms tomorrow," she says casually, as if she's making a grocery list. She attempts to work my shirt over my head and off of me without disturbing my sling, which is impossible.

"I don't think this is going to work, honey," I say. "I'll have to take the sling off."

"But your shoulder!"

My shoulder is the *last* thing on my mind right now. "It'll be fine."

She unclips the strap on the sling and gently slips it off me, biting her lip the entire time like she's defusing a bomb. Finally, she helps me out of my shirt.

"Please tell me this isn't a dream," I say as she folds my T-shirt and lays it on her dresser.

Dimples appear in her soft round cheeks as she grins. "I'm pretty sure we're both awake. I know I am."

I'm growing harder by the second, and pretty soon she's going to notice. It's impossible to hide a hard-on when it's at full staff and tenting pants.

She stares at my chest and arms long enough I start to feel self-conscious. I'm no gym rat, but I'm also not a couch potato. I have a decent amount of muscle on me, not from lifting weights but from chopping wood, shoveling snow, and chasing down suspects. Is she disappointed?

She lays her palms against my chest, fanning them out over my pecs. She skims her delicate fingertips across the little bit of chest hair I have. For a moment, I'm distracted by her pretty fingers topped with peach nail polish. She has a few dark tatts on the fingers of her left hand, symbols that I'm sure carry important meaning for her. There are three thin black lines tattooed around her arm just below her left elbow.

"What do these three lines represent?" I ask as I trace the ink.

She smiles at me. "What do you think they mean?"

She's looking at me like I should know the answer. "The three of us? You, me, and Micah? The three *amigos*?"

Her entire face lights up. "Yes. I got them right after you guys left Bryce. The tattoo made me feel less alone, like we were still together even if we'd gone our separate ways."

My heart cracks open. "God, I was such a selfish asshole back then. I didn't stop to think about what our leaving would do to you."

"Don't you dare blame yourself," she says. Her eyes start to glisten as she's on the verge of tears. "You weren't being selfish. You were just living your life. I would never want to be the friend who held you back."

I cup her face with my left hand. "I don't deserve you, but as I already admitted, I'm a selfish asshole." I lean down to kiss her, my mouth settling on hers. She opens for me, and I slide my tongue inside, licking and tasting and stroking her. She tastes like red wine.

Jennie's fingers skim down my chest, following the trail of dark hair that bisects my abdomen and disappears beneath the waistband of my jeans. Her fingertips pause a moment to ring my belly button before continuing down to my waistband. I suck in a breath in anticipation of what she's going to do next.

When she reaches for my belt buckle, I take a step back. "Maybe we should hold off on that a bit." When she looks confused, I add, "It's been a while for me, Jennie."

She still looks confused. "It's been a while for me, too."

"Yeah, well, I'm a guy. It's not going to take much for me to go off like a rocket after a long dry spell, if you know what I mean."

"Oh." She smiles.

"So, let's just focus on you tonight, all right?"

She grabs the hem of her top and whips it over her head like it's nothing. Her confidence is a total turn-on. Even after all she's been through, she's not afraid.

The sight of her in a plain white bra is enough to make my brain explode. I've imagined this sight a million times, but it was never this good. I stare at the round tops of her breasts peeking out above the cups, the soft brown of her skin contrasting against the stark white material of her bra. I can make out the dusky shadows of her nipples beneath the fabric.

Before I can even fire off a coherent thought, she reaches back and unclips her bra, letting it fall to the floor. Her breasts—*my God.* I swallow hard. "You're trying to kill me, aren't you?"

She smiles again, which eases some of the concern I have that this is too much, too soon, after what she's been through. But she doesn't seem timid or unsure. Quite the contrary, she seems confident, which I find hot as hell.

I can't help staring at the most beautiful pair of breasts I've ever seen. They're simply gorgeous. Her lush brown nipples are a darker shade than her skin. I lift my good hand and cup her right breast, which fills my hand perfectly. When I brush her nipple lightly with my thumb, it tightens into a sweet little point.

When she leans into my touch, pressing her breast into my palm, it's like she lit a fire in me. I drop my hand to her lower back and draw her in closer. My mouth returns to hers, my lips gliding over hers, coaxing them, nudging them open.

Our kiss heats quickly, our lips and our tongues striving to get closer. We're both breathing hard, panting, trying to catch our breath. I cup the back of her head, threading my fingers through the silky strands of her hair. God, I've always wanted to touch her like this. To kiss her, breathe her in, immerse myself in her. But I sure as hell never dreamed this day would come.

She grasps the waistband of my pants and pulls me closer, sucking in a breath when she feels my erection pressing against her body. But she doesn't shy away from the contact. If anything, she urges me closer. It's like neither one of us can get close enough.

I know how to fix that.

I walk her to the foot of her bed and start unfastening her jeans. It's difficult for me to do one-handed, and she quickly realizes what I'm trying to do and jumps in to help me. She kicks off her sneakers, and soon her jeans and pink cotton panties are lying on the floor at our feet.

"Lie back," I murmur.

She sits on the edge of the bed, and when I push her gently, she falls onto her back. She scoots up until her head rests on a pillow.

For a moment, I'm rooted to the spot, unable to look away. She's shamelessly and gloriously naked, right in front of me, and my brain is short-circuiting. I run my hands up her legs, from her ankles to the tops of her thighs. Her body is gorgeous, with all its dips and curves and lush flesh. I run my hands over her hip bones and over her soft, rounded belly.

I'm trying not to be greedy, but I want to eat her up. I want to breathe her in, taste her, lick and suck every single inch of her.

I move up onto the bed to lie beside her. I kiss her forehead, her cheeks, the tip of her nose. My mouth settles on hers once more, and we share the same air, our ragged breaths mingling just as our tongues do. I trail kisses down the side of her face to her neck, her throat, down to her clavicles.

Her hands are on my back, gripping and stroking me. She drags her nails down my spine. And the sweet sounds she's making are driving me crazy.

When I finally reach her breasts, I draw a nipple into my mouth and suckle it. With a soft cry, she arches her back and pulls me closer. "Chris!"

My name has never sounded so good coming from anyone's lips.

I switch to her other breast and place a soft kiss on that lush, pouty tip. I lick my way down her torso and nuzzle her belly. Slowly, I keep moving down, giving her time to get used to my touch, wanting to be sure she's okay with this.

When my tongue reaches the junction between her legs, she stiffens, her muscles going taut.

I lift my face and catch her gaze.

Are we okay? Do you want me to stop?

Her only response is to grip my hair tightly and raise her hips. She wants this as much as I do.

With a loud groan, I lose myself in her. I wallow in a fantasy come true. I use the fingers of my good hand to open her up, and then my tongue shows no mercy, licking and teasing and tormenting.

As my tongue worships her clit, my index finger slides lower, through her silky arousal, to tease her wet opening. Her thighs stiffen when I slip just the tip of my middle finger inside her, giving me a reason to pause. But the way she moans my name and how she claws at my hair are all the green lights I need. After waiting and praying for this moment for so long, I won't risk fucking it up over mixed signals.

Her thigh muscles finally relax, and she lets her legs fall wide open. I coat my finger in her slick arousal to ease the way, and then I slowly slide my finger into her, searching for her sweet spot. When I find it, I stroke her there, gently, relentlessly.

She gasps my name. "Chris!" She sounds so surprised, as if she's never come this way before. Her fingers dig into my scalp.

My finger keeps on mission, stroking that ridged spot inside her, and my tongue never lets up. Soon, her thighs are shaking. She's breathing like she just ran a marathon.

"Oh, my God, Chris!" she keens softly. She pulls a pillow over her face to muffle her voice.

I imagine she's keeping her voice down to avoid drawing attention. Granny's bedroom is right next door to ours.

I know the moment her orgasm hits her. Her thighs quiver. Her pussy flutters around my finger. She bows her back, lifting her torso off the mattress as a garbled cry escapes her. "Chris!" Her body gradually gentles, and now she's petting my hair instead of trying to pull it out.

Suddenly, she reaches for me, inviting me to lie beside her. I move carefully, trying not to jostle my right arm, which is on fire now, and settle down beside her. I'm half on her, half off, as I settle my mouth over hers.

We kiss for a long while, slowly, languidly. My good hand travels over her body, finally coming to rest on her breast. I gently roll her nipple between my index finger and thumb, and it tightens into a peak. As I take it into my mouth and suckle it, she moans beneath me.

My cock is a throbbing, aching bystander that wishes he could get in on the action, but we don't have a condom, so he'll have to stay in timeout. If we're lucky, and we get a second try at this on another day, he can have his way.

When Jennie reaches between us and presses her hand to the length of my erection, I choke out a garbled cry. Before I can get out a coherent word, she's stroking me through my jeans, her fingers curling around me.

My dick is throbbing, and it wouldn't take much to set me off.

I lay my hand over hers, stilling her movements. "Honey, I'm about two seconds away from coming in my underwear."

"That would be a shame, wouldn't it?" she asks as she presses her hand to my chest and pushes me onto my back.

"What are you—" But there's no use finishing that sentence, because she's unbuckling my belt. "Jennie—" I gaze up at her determined expression to see a woman who looks like she's on a mission to save mankind. My heart explodes. "Jen—"

She pulls my belt free of its loops, unfastens my pants, and kneels on the bed so she can tug my jeans and underwear down... all the way down to my ankles, which is when she realizes I still have my shoes and socks on.

With a huff, she unlaces my shoes, pulls them off, along with my socks, and drops it all to the floor. My jeans and boxer-briefs follow.

I reach out and touch her cheek. "Jennie."

Her dark brown eyes flash at me with fire and determination. "Yes?"

"What are you doing?"

Her brow furrows quizzically. "Isn't that sort of obvious?"

"Yes, but honey." I catch one of her hands in mine. "You don't have to. Next time, I'll have a condom, I promise."

"We don't need a condom for this."

"Yeah, but—" And then I am rendered speechless because my cock is in her beautiful, generous, mind-blowing mouth. She's leaning over me, bobbing her mouth on my erection, stroking my length with the flat of her tongue. One of her hands circles the base of my cock, squeezing and stroking so damn perfectly I could cry.

Fuck! I'm not going to last a minute. I'm going to embarrass myself.

My dick is throbbing and aching, and my ballsac feels heavy and tight. Fire races along my spine, and my heart is pounding.

Twenty-eight is too young to have a heart attack, right?

My mind might be tripping, but my body knows what it's doing. I raise my head so I can watch—seeing it is half the pleasure. When she runs the tip of her tongue around the broad head of my cock, catching a trickle of precum, I completely lose it.

I'm done for. I'm—

"Jennie—" I try to warn her so she can pull back, but she takes me in deep again.

Before I can utter another word, my orgasm slams into me. I cry out hoarsely as my cum shoots down her throat. My erection kicks and bucks in her mouth, and dear God, she doesn't miss a beat. She doesn't pull back. She's still bobbing on my cock, her hand gripping the base and squeezing and stroking me through my climax. I come and come and come.

Finally, once the ejaculations slow to a stop, she releases me. Ribbons of cum cling to her lips before she licks them away.

She smiles so shyly at me, as if to say, *How was that? Did I do it right?*

I close my eyes and groan. "I'm dead."

19

Jennie

When I wake Monday morning, Chris is lying on his back, and I'm pressed up against his left side with my arm over his waist. We're both still naked, lying skin to skin.

Last night was absolutely amazing. Even without a condom, and without intercourse, it was perfect. I knew he'd be a kind and generous lover. I never once doubted that.

I check the clock on my nightstand. It's nearly eight, and the house is silent. I guess we all slept in this morning.

Chris mumbles something in his sleep and turns toward me,

pressing his lips against my hair. "Good morning." His voice is gruff from sleep.

His arm doesn't seem to be bothering him too much because his right hand starts roaming over my naked body, first cupping a breast and thumbing my nipple until it shrinks into a little pebble. Then his hand moves lower, stopping to stroke my belly. He doesn't seem to mind the soft, pudgy parts of me. Finally, he groans as his hand slips down between my legs, where I'm still wet from last night, and he starts rubbing circles on my clit.

Neither one of us says a word, but my breathing picks up. So does his. I part my legs to give him easier access. As he rubs and rubs and rubs my tender nerve bundle, he trails kisses across my shoulder and the back of my neck. When he hits a particularly sensitive spot behind my ear, I shiver.

I gasp when an orgasm sneaks up on me, making my belly quiver and my thighs shake. I press my face into my pillow to muffle the sounds coming out of me—high-pitched, girly sounds.

All of a sudden, my bedroom opens and Granny peers inside the room. I bite back a squeal. Chris casually pulls the blankets up to cover our bodies.

"Is it time for breakfast?" Granny asks. "I'm hungry. So is Pumpkin." She pauses a moment to study the man in my bed. "Oh, good. He stayed." She turns and walks away, muttering, "Him, I like. Not that other one."

I roll to face Chris and press my face into the crook of his neck. "I guess Granny approves."

"Thank God," he says as he pushes the covers back and sits up. "I guess we'd better go make her something to eat."

This morning, it's French toast and bacon for breakfast. And coffee, of course, with French vanilla creamer.

"So, what's on the agenda for today?" Chris asks as we're eating.

It looks like neither one of us has to go to work today. Chris is on a brief medical leave because of his shoulder, and the diner will be closed for the next day or two for repairs. I'm hoping we'll be allowed to reopen on Wednesday.

"I've got to call the insurance company, and the contractor who's doing the repairs. And I need to go to the grocery store."

Chris's phone rings and he checks the screen. "This is one of my contacts in the DA's office." He takes the call. "Sheriff Nelson."

He listens for quite a while, his expression turning darker by the minute. "All right," he finally says. "Thanks for the update." He ends the call and looks at me. "Braggart's hearing is scheduled for this afternoon at three. His attorney is going to request a personal bond."

I frown. "What does that mean?"

"It means he can walk right out of jail without having to pay any bail. He'd be out on his own recognizance. The DA is going to ask that a personal bond be denied due to the nature of the offenses and the number of charges he's facing."

My chest tightens. "What do you think will happen?"

"I hate to say it, but I think he'll get what he's asking for."

"After what he did yesterday?"

Chris nods. "Afraid so. His parents have a lot of clout. I'm sure they know about Braggart's arrest by now, and they've been busy making phone calls. We need to plan for the worst, and that means going to the courthouse today to request a restraining order. If he violates it, I can arrest him again. And if he gets arrested again, it'll be harder for him to get bail."

I call Dawn and ask her if she can stay with Granny while we go to the courthouse in Estes Park. She says yes.

After I help Granny get cleaned up and dressed for the day, I sit her on her favorite recliner in the living room and give her a skein of yellow yarn to wind into a ball. This is one of her favorite activities, and it keeps her happily occupied for a good while. I also put more episodes of *Little House on the Prairie* on the TV.

"I really need a shower," Chris tells me when I return to the kitchen. He has already cleared off the kitchen table and is now rinsing the dishes and putting them in the dishwasher. He makes a show of lifting his good arm and sniffing his armpit. He makes a face, which makes me laugh.

"You smell perfectly fine," I assure him. "I should know."

He grins, probably blushing beneath his trim beard. "Seriously, though, I do need a shower." He raises an eyebrow. "Wanna help me?" He nods to his sling. "Cause I'm injured?"

"Yes, I'll help you. We can shower together."

That certainly piques his interest. He whispers, as if he's afraid Granny will overhear us from the other room. "That reminds me—we need to stop at Maggie's today to get condoms."

"We can stop on our way home from the courthouse."

* * *

Dawn comes over at noon, and Chris and I leave shortly after for the courthouse in Estes Park. I drive since Chris is partly out of commission. We arrive half an hour later.

Once we're in the courthouse, Chris directs me to where I need to go and shows me what papers I need to fill out. I admit my mind is doing its best to dissociate from the process. I did this once. I never dreamed I'd have to go through it again.

"She'd like to request a temporary restraining order," Chris tells the staffer. "Her ex-husband is likely to be released from jail today, and she needs protection now. I think she's in immediate danger."

I submit the paperwork to the courthouse staff who will send it on to a judge for a prompt review.

We sit and wait over two hours before we get a reply.

"Judge Connelly has issued a temporary restraining order in effect until your court hearing," the staffer says. "The hearing is scheduled for two weeks from today." She hands Chris a reminder of the hearing date. "Do you have someone who can serve this temporary order to the object of the RO?"

"I'll do it," Chris says. He flashes her his badge.

"Well, I guess you can." She hands him a copy of the order. "Serve this to the recipient and then file proof of service with the court."

Once we're back in my car heading home, Chris watches me as I watch the road.

"Are you doing okay?" he asks.

I nod.

He lays his left hand on my thigh. "You're awfully quiet."

"I don't think a piece of paper is going to stop David from harassing me."

"Maybe not, but *I* will stop him. As soon as I get word he's been released, I'll track him down and serve him with this temporary protection order."

We make a quick stop at Emerson's Grocery Store to pick up a few things I need, plus the condoms. Maggie's working. When she spots us walking in, she stops what she's doing and comes to greet us.

"How are you holding up?" she asks as she hugs me.

"As well as can be expected, I guess. We just left the courthouse in Estes Park. I was granted an emergency temporary order, and my hearing for a permanent one is in two weeks."

While Maggie and I are chatting, Chris wanders away, pushing a grocery cart. On the drive here, I gave him a list of what I needed. Basics mostly—bread, butter, milk, chicken breasts, carrots, and a few other things. He seems to be making his way through the store, so I imagine he's getting everything. I notice he stops in the personal care section.

Maggie eyes him a moment before redirecting her attention to me. "How is everything going?"

"Good," I say.

"Any word on when the diner can reopen?"

"Not yet. I was told it would be a day or two at the very least. I'm hoping to get the report from the fire inspector today, and from the health inspector tomorrow. If everything looks good, we should be able to open on Wednesday."

Chris parks the cart beside me. "I think I got everything."

I glance in the cart, noting that everything's there, including a jumbo box of extra-large condoms, ribbed for her pleasure, no less. I can feel my cheeks heating up.

Maggie notices them, too, and gives me a look that speaks volumes. "Hey, Chris. Owen's in the back room doing inventory. Why don't you go say hi?"

Chris rolls his eyes. "That was subtle, Maggie. You could have just told me to go wait in the car so you can grill Jennie."

Maggie smiles sweetly at Chris. "Either go talk to Owen, or go wait in the car, Sheriff. Your choice."

"Fine. I'll go talk to Owen." He squeezes my hand. "I won't be far."

As soon as Chris is out of earshot, Maggie rounds on me. "Okay, time to spill the beans. Why did Chris put a huge box of condoms in your shopping cart?"

I try not to grin. "Because he's optimistic?"

"I'm serious, Jennie!" She's trying not to laugh. "Tell me."

I sigh. "Well, in a nutshell, we're in love, and we slept together last night. Well, I guess, technically, we made out because neither one of us had a condom. We had to improvise."

She's trying so hard not to laugh. "I'm so happy for you, honey." That earns me another hug. When she pulls back, she grins as she looks me in the face. "Everyone's going to be thrilled when they hear the news. It's about time, girl! We told you he was crazy about you. Is this a big secret, or can I tell people?"

"I don't think it's a secret. Granny knows. She walked in on us this morning."

Maggie bursts into laughter. "I would have paid good money to see that."

"It was fine, really. She likes Chris. She told me last night she wanted him to stay over."

Maggie rings up my groceries, and when we're done, she uses the intercom to call back to Owen in the storage room. "Honey, please tell Chris the coast is clear. He can come back out here."

When Chris rejoins us, Maggie gives him a hug. "You'd better do right by her, mister, or you'll have half the town to answer to."

"Not a problem." Chris smiles, and I imagine it's because he's relieved the cat is out of the bag. He puts his arm across my shoulders and pulls me close so he can kiss my temple.

"This is going to take some getting used to," Maggie says.

We head back to my house, and as we're unpacking the groceries, Chris's phone rings. It's his contact at the courthouse.

I can tell by the look on his face it's not the news we wanted. He ends the call. "He got out on a personal bond." He mutters a curse under his breath. "What a joke!"

"How could they do that?" I don't know whether to be disappointed or downright angry. "He forced his way into my house, and then he assaulted me!"

"His attorney argued before the judge that Granny invited him in."

"She wouldn't do that. She hates him."

"I know, but it's his word against hers, and we can't very well have her testify."

"No, we can't. But what about the assault? He attacked me in my own bedroom."

"He claimed you asked him to come into your bedroom. He said you were giving him mixed signals."

That shuts me up quick, because it's true. I did suggest we take it in the other room. "I was just trying to get him away from Granny. I didn't want her to witness him manhandling me."

Chris pulls me close and wraps his arm around me. "I'm sorry, Jennie. His parents are pretty influential in this area. That's why he got the benefit of the doubt. It's a good thing we applied for the restraining order. I'll serve him the papers today."

I blink back tears. Not only am I not safe, but I'm worried about Granny, too, and Dawn.

"Do you mind if I move in for the time being?" he asks. "Just until this is resolved one way or another."

Right now, I have trouble seeing any of this ever getting resolved. And I hate feeling like a coward, but the idea of Chris living here with us fills me with immense relief. I cup his handsome face. "I would love for you to stay with us. Thank you."

"Consider it done," he says, and then he kisses me.

Granny walks into the kitchen. "More kissing, I see. Well, good for you. Is it time for dinner yet? I'm hungry."

20

Chris

I'm furious that Braggart got out on a personal bond. I can't believe he just walked right out of that courthouse a free man.

"That's my cue," I tell Jennie as I grab my keys and phone. "Time to serve Braggart with the restraining order."

"Wait, can you drive? What about your arm?"

She's right. I won't be able to shift gears with my right arm in a sling. "Help me take this off. I'll put it on when I get back."

After she helps me out of the sling, she says, "Be careful," as she walks me to the door. She cups my face and leans up to kiss me. "Come home as soon as you can. I'll be waiting for you."

Home. I really like the sound of that. "You can count on it."

I head home first to pack a suitcase. While I'm there, I change into my uniform. I'm going to pay a visit to Braggart in my official capacity as sheriff. Then I stop at the station to collect my badge, duty belt, and firearm.

Jace stops by my office as I'm gearing up and says, "I thought you were taking some time off because of your shoulder."

"No time for that. I'm off to serve Braggart with an RO."

"Then let me grab my hat. I'm coming with you, boss. I'll drive."

Jace drives me to the Braggart ranch and parks in the circular drive. Marguerite answers when I knock on the front door.

"Is he here?" I ask her.

"I'm sorry, but no, sénior. He's in jail."

"He was released half an hour ago. He's a free man."

Her neutral expression changes instantly into a frown. "I see."

"I'll be waiting for him right here. I have words to say to him."

She nods as she closes the door.

Jace and I wait in the cruiser until an unfamiliar black Mercedes pulls into the drive about twenty minutes later. I spot two men in the front seat. One is likely Braggart. The other one is probably his lawyer.

The car comes to a stop near the front walk. The doors open, and two men step out. One is Braggart, with a shit-eating grin on his face. The other is a pretentious dude in an expensive suit. I guess I was right on both accounts.

Braggart heads right for me on unsteady legs, his arms open wide. "Look who it is, Jeff!" Dave must have stopped at a bar on his way home. Clearly, he's drunk. "It's my good buddy Sheriff Nelson, here to welcome me home." He gives me a smarmy smile—one I'm tempted to knock off his face. "Are you here to congratulate me on my release? I told you they wouldn't hold me long."

"I hate to disappoint you, Dave, but no. I'm here to give you this." I hold out the notice.

He takes it from me. "What's this?"

"You've been served, Braggart, very conveniently in front of a witness, no less." I eye his attorney for emphasis. "This afternoon, a judge approved a temporary restraining order against you. You're not to step foot within five hundred feet of Jennie, her home, or her place of business. And there's a no-contact provision. If you violate this order, I'll gladly arrest your ass. The official hearing is scheduled for two weeks from today. Don't miss it."

Braggart laughs. "You think a piece of paper is going to keep me away from my wife?"

My blood burns like acid. "She's not your wife, Dave."

"She *was*. That's a helluva lot more than *you* can say." God, he loves throwing that in my face. "Hell, you couldn't even get her to go out with you."

"Stay away from her, Braggart. This is your last warning."

His expression goes ice cold. "I'd like to see you stop me."

"All right, that's enough," the attorney says as he steps between the two of us. The man looks me in the eye. "You've served the notice, Sheriff. I think it's best that you leave now. Please stop antagonizing my client. He's had a rough twenty-four hours."

"*He* has?" God, I want to wring both their necks. Instead, I smile, doff my hat, and say, "Have a nice evening, gentlemen."

I have no desire to be around Braggart a second longer than I have to, so I walk away, Jace following. When we get back into the cruiser, I text Jennie to let her know Braggart has been served. I tell her I'm on my way back to the courthouse to hand in my sworn statement that I served the notice to Braggart.

It'll be official this afternoon. Jennie has a restraining order.

* * *

When I finally get home—to Jennie's house, I mean—she's waiting for me at the door. She lets me in and wraps me in her arms.

I could definitely get used to being greeted like this.

She pulls a key out of her pocket and drops it in my hand.

"What's this?" I ask.

"A key to my house. Since you'll be staying here a while, you'll need a key."

I pull out my keychain and add hers. "Thank you. Does this mean we're going steady?" It was supposed to be a joke, but as soon as the words are out of my mouth, I realize I mean it.

She seems to realize it, too. Her eyes widen as the weight of my words sink in.

"Sorry," I say, chuckling, hoping to let her off the hook. "I didn't mean that literally. It's way too soon, right?"

But she's not laughing. "Chris, we've been dancing around each other for *years*."

"Yeah, but—" God, I don't want her to think I'm rushing her for a commitment or anything. We've hardly started dating. "It was—"

"Please don't say it was just a joke."

I grow serious. "No, it's not a joke. It's just probably too soon for you, right?"

She glances away a moment, as if to collect herself, then she turns her gaze back to me. "I don't think it's too soon. I've waited years for you."

I cup one side of her face with my good hand. "I don't want to rush you. You need time to think about it."

She laughs nervously. "I think we're well past the thinking stage, don't you?"

"Yeah, I guess so." *I love you.* I want to say it so badly, but I don't want to put her on the spot.

I'm shocked when she beats me to it. "I love you, Chris Nelson. I don't need time to think it over. If you want me, I'm yours."

"If I want—are you crazy, woman! Of course, I want you!"

Granny waves from the kitchen table, where she's eating spaghetti with marinara sauce and garlic bread. "If you two are done canoodling, come eat dinner before it gets cold."

"Yes, ma'am," I say as I take off my hat. I start to unbuckle my duty belt. "Is there somewhere safe I can hang this?"

Jennie nods. "My bedroom closet." And while I'm off to do that, I hear her say, "We're coming, Granny."

* * *

After we eat, the three of us hang out in the living room on the sofa watching an episode of *Little House on the Prairie*. The funny thing is, I remember watching this show here at Jennie's house when we were kids. The *déjà vu* I'm feeling right now is pretty intense.

A little after seven, Jennie helps Rosie with a bath and gets her dressed for bed. Once Rosie's tucked in, Jennie returns to the living room and snuggles beside me on the sofa.

"It's funny how the tables have turned," she says. "When I came to live here, she and Grandpa took care of me like I was their own child. Now, it's my turn to take care of Granny. Life comes around full circle, doesn't it?"

She pauses a moment, deep in thought, before she adds, "You know, if you want a life with me, that includes Granny. I plan to take care of her for the rest of her life, whether that's one year or a decade."

I bring her hand to my lips and kiss it. "I'm all in, Jen. Rosie was more of a mother to me when I was growing up than Kitty ever was. Rosie was the one who patched my boo-boos. She was the one who helped me with my homework. She's the one who baked me a birthday cake every single year, without fail. She did more for me than my own mother ever did."

Jennie has tears in her eyes at this point. My chest tightens, and there's a knot in my throat. I love this woman, and I want to be part of her life. "I love you, Jennie. I always have. All I've ever wanted is to be part of your family."

She stands, takes my hand, and pulls me to my feet. "The condoms are in my top nightstand drawer just waiting to be used."

I smile, feeling like a kid whose dream has come true. "You don't need to tell me twice."

* * *

This time, it's going to be different. There's nothing to stop us, nothing to come between us. We love each other, and we both know it.

I feel like I'm getting the biggest do-over in my life.

We step into her bedroom and close the door quietly behind us.

"Help me take the sling off." I want both of my arms functioning for this, both of my hands available to touch her and hold her. To make love to her with all my heart and soul and body.

She makes a face that says, *Are you sure this is a good idea?* "Dr. Talbott said—"

"Hey." I press a finger to her lips. "Trust me, Dr. Talbott would be okay with me ditching the sling to have sex with you."

She laughs. "Really? Is this some kind of guy code thing?"

"Yes, it is. Now help me, please."

"I'm going on record saying I think it's a bad idea." But still, she helps me release the buckle and allow the sling to fall away.

I gingerly flex my right arm, slowly moving it, rotating it, wincing a bit. I extend my arm slowly and then retract it. It's stiff and more than a bit sore, but not enough to change my mind. "See? It's all good."

"Do you want to know what my fantasy is?" she asks.

My mind goes blank as my dick grows hard as a pike and starts throbbing. All my blood is rushing south, and I feel lightheaded. "Tell me. Please."

She grins. "How about I show you instead?"

21

Jennie

This is my fantasy come to life—*Chris*, all mine. As I undress him, he undresses me. It's almost a race to see who can finish first. When he's naked, I push him, gently because of his arm, onto the bed.

He falls on his back, grinning, and scoots up the bed so his head is on a pillow. "Go easy on me, honey. I'm *injured*."

"Trust me, I am going to go easy on you. In fact, I'm going to do all the work this time, so you can just lie back and relax. Remember I told you I'd show you what my fantasy is?"

He swallows hard, his Adam's apple bobbing sharply. I think I have his attention.

I open the top drawer of my nightstand and retrieve a condom packet. I tear it open and toss it on the bed beside him. "We'll get to that in a bit. Just relax for now."

I crawl over to him on the bed and start kissing him. Not surprisingly, he wraps his arms around me and pulls me to his chest, so my breasts are pressed against him.

Also not surprising, he winces and groans—and not in a sexy way. His shoulder is hurting him.

"I told you to leave the sling on. Now you're going to overuse your arm."

"Don't care. I want my arms around you—both of them." He pulls me close and kisses me. His mouth is hot and hungry, like he can't get enough. I guess, like me, he's waited a long time for this.

I rise up on my hands and knees so I can maneuver better. I crawl over him and lean down to kiss his throat. He arches his neck to give me better access. I trail kisses along his good shoulder and down his arm. His biceps are rock hard. Everything about him is lean and firm, quite a contrast to my body, which is pretty much the opposite. I never have time to exercise, and I taste way too many of my pies and donuts.

He moans when I kiss my way across his chest. When I flick one of his flat nipples with the tip of my tongue, he cries out, arching his back off the mattress. He fists the sheet beneath him, straining to lie still.

"Careful," I remind him. "Your shoulder."

He gasps. "Fuck my shoulder. Honestly, I couldn't care less about it right now."

I chuckle. "You will tomorrow morning."

He chokes back a laugh. "You're assuming I'm going to survive tonight."

My tongue follows the path of his happy trail, that thin line of dark hair that leads to his groin. That's where I'm headed.

When I finally wet my lips and take him in my mouth, he swears a blue streak. He pets my head, his fingers alternately burrowing into my hair, gripping, flexing, and gripping again. "Oh, God, baby."

I glance up at him. His teeth are gritted, his eyes tightly closed.

I taste his precum on my tongue, savoring the warm, salty tang. I feel so safe with him, so free, like I can do anything I want, and it'll be okay. I won't be judged or criticized. That was all David ever did—criticize me.

I shake all thoughts of my ex from my head. He's out of the picture now. I have a restraining order against him. Surely that will be enough to keep him away from me. He'll have to go find his pot of money at the base of some other rainbow.

I reach for the condom packet and open it the rest of the way. As I roll it onto his erection, I realize it's a good thing he bought extra large.

"I promise to be gentle with you," I say as I throw my leg over his hips.

When he realizes what I'm about to do, his eyes widen. "God, you really are trying to kill me."

I position myself over his hips and reach between my legs to wrap my fingers around him and put him where I need him. When

I sneak a peek at his face, I see that his gaze is locked on my hand. I don't think I've ever seen him so intense.

"It's been a while for me, so don't expect much," I say. It's true. I haven't been with anyone since David. "It's like starting all over again, right?"

He grips my thighs with both hands. "Honey, you couldn't do it wrong if you tried."

Bolstered by his encouragement, I start to lower myself, stopping abruptly when I feel the broad head of his cock right at my entrance. I know I'm wet. I'm so aroused, I'm aching. My body is so *ready* for this. But he's on the big side, and my body has been in hibernation for a long time.

Slowly, I sink down, driving the head of his erection into me. I feel a delicious stretch and a slight burn that makes me gasp. His hands clamp down on my thighs, squeezing so strongly, a pained whimper escapes me. He releases me immediately and pets the area in apology.

I rise up and lower myself, over and over, each time sinking a little farther down on him, taking more of his length into me. His chest rises and falls hard, as if he's struggling to catch his breath.

I'm only halfway there when he says, "It's okay if you can't—"

"Shh! I've got this." And sure enough, with a few more tries, he's all the way in. I pause for a moment and just breathe as my body accommodates the intrusion. When I raise myself, he sucks in a breath, flexing his fingers on my thighs.

"Oh, God, sweetheart." He groans, low and long. "You feel—it's so—holy shit."

My body continues to soften, like it knows how this is supposed to go. I raise and lower myself on him again, several more times, until it becomes easier. I'm so wet, he's sliding in and out of me perfectly. The stimulation and the friction are sublime, and I angle myself so that the head of his cock brushes me in just the right spot.

He reaches up and cups my breasts, gently squeezing and molding them. He plays with my nipples, tweaking them, gently pinching and rolling them, with just the right amount of pressure. I feel a connection between my breasts and my pussy. When he tweaks the one, I feel tingles in the other.

Pretty soon, I'm moving easily on him, rocking myself. He's touching me, all of me, my breasts, stroking my thighs, threading his fingers into my hair which hangs down around my face like a dark curtain. At one point, he leans up to kiss me, and our lips cling together as we both try to catch our breath.

When he lies back down, he grits his teeth as he watches me move on him. I think he's trying to hold off his climax, waiting for me.

"This is my fantasy," I confess. "Riding you like this."

Instantly, he explodes. His cock bucks and throbs inside me. His expression tightens, his whole body does as he shoves himself into me, gritting his teeth.

And suddenly, watching him come triggers my orgasm. My vagina clamps down on his erection, squeezing him so tightly. He groans harshly and grips my thighs hard as he keeps bucking his hips up into me.

Even though he's wearing a condom, I can *feel* him ejaculating. I can feel the throbbing and the pulsations deep inside me.

He pulls me forward so that our chests are touching. He kisses me like he's starving for it, his chest heaving as he tries to catch his breath.

Eventually, I collapse on him. He catches me and rolls us so that we're lying on our sides facing each other.

He brushes my hair back from my hot face. "You are so incredibly beautiful. I always knew you were the prettiest, nicest, and smartest girl in school. Now I know you're also the sexiest."

I close my eyes and drink in his kisses, his words, his gentle touches. I waited a long time for this. I guess that's because we save the best for last. When I finally get around to opening my eyes, he's watching me, smiling.

"I love you, Jennifer Lopez," he says. "And if you let me, I'll love you for the rest of our lives."

And that's when I burst into tears. Ugly, soul-sucking sobs.

"What's wrong?" He sounds truly alarmed. "Are you hurt? Did I do something?"

I'm crying so hard I can't even form a coherent statement. All I can do is shake my head.

"Jennie, please. Talk to me."

"I'm—sorry!"

"Sorry for what?" He props himself up on his good elbow and leans over me. "Jennie—"

"It's all my fault!" I struggle to talk as tears clog my throat and nose. I can hardly see past the tears. "All those wasted years! Saying no to you when my heart was crying out *yes*." I press my face against his chest and let years of longing and pain pour out.

He wraps his arms around me and starts rocking me gently. "Shh, no, it's okay, sweetheart. It's not your fault. None of it's your fault."

"Yes, it is." I know he's just trying to be kind, but it's true, and we both know it.

"It's really not, sweetheart."

I realize he's shaking. When I pull back and gaze up at him, I see the glimmer of tears in his eyes. Knowing he's hurting, too, breaks something wide open inside me. "I was afraid," I say through my own tears. "All the hateful things the kids said to me. The bullying—I didn't want that to rub off on you, too. You were already the object of so much bullying because of your mom. I couldn't add to it." I blow out a shaky breath. "I was afraid you'd grow to resent me, and I'd rather have stayed your friend forever than risk losing you altogether. I was a coward, Chris. All these years, I wanted you, but never believed I deserved you. Not after what I put you through."

Chris leans over me and opens my nightstand drawer. I wonder what he's doing when I hear him tear open another condom packet. I watch as he removes the first one, sets it aside, and then sheathes himself all over again.

When he comes over me, I automatically open my legs for him, and he settles between my thighs. He guides himself into me, so carefully, even though there's no need because my body is so wet and slick after my orgasm.

He begins to move then, so gently, every action tender. He gazes down into my face and brushes my hair back. "No more tears. No guilt, and no blame. We're starting over right now. We're starting fresh." He kisses me sweetly. "I love you more right now than I ever have in my life. And I'll love you even more tomorrow."

He thrusts slowly, in and out, over and over, in no hurry. Time stops for both of us, and we just exist in this moment. Slow strokes, soft kisses, gentle flutterings in my belly and between my legs. This is so achingly delicious.

This is making love in a transcendent way I've never experienced.

When an orgasm gently sweeps through me, I gasp in surprise. He comes right after me, bowing his head as he rests his forehead against mine.

I'm exhausted, both physically and emotionally. Chris disappears into my bathroom to dispose of both condoms. He returns with a warm, wet washcloth, which he wipes tenderly between my legs.

A moment later, he's back in bed with me, and he wraps himself around me, spooning behind me, holding me safe and secure.

I exhale a long, shaky breath and let sleep overtake me.

* * *

Tuesday is a quiet day. Chris and I stay home in the morning with Granny, helping her fold towels and wind another skein of yarn into a ball. Granny and I sit on the sofa watching an old rerun of the original game show *The Price Is Right*, while Chris sits on the floor at my feet, with his sling back in place, playing fetch with Pumpkin. Yes, Pumpkin is a cat who likes to play fetch. Go figure.

That afternoon, I get a call from the health inspector, who asks me to come to the diner to discuss his final assessment.

I call Dawn and ask if she can come over for a little bit to stay with Granny while Chris accompanies me to the diner. Once she's here, Chris and I head over to the diner.

He's dead serious about me not walking anywhere alone while David's in town.

We walk through the rear entrance and find the health inspector in the kitchen.

The machines that draw out the smoke are still running. The rehab crews are still at work cleaning the kitchen equipment and appliances, as well as the tables and chairs in the dining area. Everything looks—and smells—clean to me. That awful smoke smell is gone.

Chris introduces me to Denny Haskins, the health department inspector.

"So, what's the verdict?" Chris asks.

"It's looking good," the inspector says. "Fortunately, there was limited damage outside of Jennie's office. The restoration crew has done a thorough job. Everything looks as it should. You can re-open for business as usual tomorrow."

"Wonderful!" I say. "My customers will be thrilled."

After we return home, I call all of my employees to let them know they can resume their regular schedules tomorrow.

"I guess I'll be back bright and early tomorrow morning," Dawn says.

I hug her tightly. "I can't thank you enough, Dawn. I couldn't work if I didn't have you to watch Granny."

We invite Dawn to stay for dinner. After we're done eating, and Dawn has left for the evening, Chris and I clean up the kitchen together and then go hang out with Granny in the living room until her bedtime.

Once she's tucked safely into bed, I return to the living room to spend a relaxing evening with Chris.

"I'll be so glad to be back in the diner tomorrow," I say. "I've missed making the pies and donuts. I've missed my early morning chats with Maggie and seeing you and Micah come in for lunch."

"I'd say it's time for me to get back to work, too." He peers down at his sling. "Well, I can do paperwork at least, and other administrative tasks. Maybe some light patrolling." He lays his good arm across my shoulders. "From now on, until this situation with Braggart is resolved, I'll drive you to and from work. Promise me you won't walk home alone."

"What about the times I come home between the meal rushes to spell Dawn a bit? I can't expect her to watch Granny for twelve hours straight."

"Not a problem," he says. "I'll time my patrolling around your break schedule so I can drive you. And if for some reason I am delayed, I'll have Jace or Ricky drive you. Okay? No walking home alone."

"Okay." I sit on his lap, straddling him, and lean in to kiss him. "I never realized you were so protective."

He kisses me. "I never had something so precious to protect before."

"Oooh, that's a good one, Sheriff. You just earned yourself a blow job."

He grins. "Damn. I should have used that line on you a long time ago."

22

Jennie

Wednesday morning, it's business as usual. Chris and I get up before Granny this time. We both get ready for the day, and breakfast is almost on the table when Granny walks into the kitchen, Pumpkin right on her heels as always.

"Good morning, everyone," Granny says as she takes her seat at the table. "It's a beautiful day, isn't it?"

Actually, it's kind of dreary, and it's been drizzling all morning, but we're not going to argue with her.

Chris pours her a cup of coffee and adds creamer. "You're right.

It is a beautiful day," he says as he winks at me.

I plate some French toast and bacon and set it in front of her. She enjoyed the French toast so much the other day, I thought she'd like it again.

"What's this?" Granny asks as she stares at her plate.

"It's breakfast, Granny," I say as I set the butter dish and the pitcher of warm maple syrup on the table. "French toast and bacon."

She makes a face. "Do I like this?"

"You do. You had it the other day, and you said it was delicious."

She frowns. "I did?"

Smiling, I nod at her. "You did."

Then her frown transforms into a bright smile. "Well, if you said I liked it, then I'm sure I do."

Some days her mind is sharper than others. It looks like today isn't going to be one of those days. I feel a pang of sadness that she's slowly slipping away from me. But no matter what, I'll hang on to her as long as possible.

"Why don't you take a bite and try it?" I suggest. "If you don't like it, I'll make you something else, okay?"

"Oh, no, dear. I don't want to be any trouble." She takes a cautious bite. Then another. "This *is* delicious." And then she proceeds to devour the rest of her meal.

Chris and I join her at the table to eat our meals. He keeps looking at me with a slight grin on his face, as if he's thinking about last night. Remembering what we did and how we slept entwined in each other's arms all night long. He's making me blush.

There's a knock at the door.

"That'll be Dawn," I say as I start to get up from my chair.

"I'll get it," Chris says as he stands. "I need to go get dressed. You finish your breakfast."

After he lets Dawn in, Chris returns to my bedroom to grab his hat and duty belt. He's in the process of buckling it around his waist when he walks into the kitchen.

"What about your sling?" I ask.

"I can't wear it and drive, so I'll have to do without. I'll put it on in the evening to rest my arm."

I've seen him in his uniform a million times, but for some reason, it's hitting me differently this morning. I get up and run my hands over his shirt, smoothing the tan fabric. "You look so handsome in your uniform. I've wanted to tell you that for years."

He cups my face and leans in to give me a kiss. "I wish you had. I've always been so desperate for your attention. The smallest little crumb from you—every smile, every wave—made my day."

And I withheld that from him for so long because of my own insecurities. My eyes prickle as tears form.

"Hey," he says with a smile. "No tears. No guilt. Remember?"

I nod. "Yeah. I remember." But that's easier said than done.

We say our goodbyes to Granny and head out the door.

Chris drives me to the diner in his loaner car. "Have a good day," he says as he pulls up to the back entrance. He leans over to kiss me. "I'll see you later, honey." He smiles. "This is all very domestic, isn't it? Me, dropping you off at work." He looks so happy.

"It is. What do you think about that?"

"What? Us, doing partner things? I love it." He pats my thigh.

"Give me a heads up when you're ready to take a break. I'll pick you up."

"Are you sure? It's a terrible inconvenience. You can't plan your whole day around me."

He grins. "Watch me." Another kiss. And then he says, "Now go, before I have second thoughts about us working at all today."

Laughing, I get out of the car. "See you later, Sheriff." After closing the door, I turn and walk in through the back door.

My office looks pretty empty now, with no desk or chair, but I'll order new ones today. I can hear easy jazz music coming from the kitchen as Robert goes about prepping for breakfast.

I poke my head through the kitchen doorway. "Good morning, Robert."

He's in the middle of rolling out the dough for biscuits when he gives me a big smile. "Welcome back, boss!"

"Thanks. It's good to be back."

I've got a ton of work to do this morning after an unexpected three-day break. My routine for making the pies and donuts is all messed up, and I'll be pressed for time this morning to catch up. Fortunately, I've got some fresh dough I can use for the pies. I prep two and get them in the oven as soon as possible so I can start on making some cake donuts. Today I'm feeling like chocolate icing and strawberry. I'll have just enough time to make a few dozen before the diner opens for business.

Cara and Michelle wander in shortly and go about their assigned tasks in preparing for our morning customers. Chad saunters in and gets to work.

When I turn on the OPEN sign and unlock the front door, I find the line of customers waiting outside is longer than usual. I think the fire on Sunday is the reason for that. Folks haven't been able to eat here for a few days, and suddenly they miss the place. And, I'm sure a lot of them are simply curious and are here for the gossip.

I feel like I'm running non-stop all morning, just trying to play catch-up. As soon as the donuts are ready, I take a box next door to Maggie.

The rest of the day progresses normally, with no drama, no fires, no sightings of David, and no obnoxious customers. On the David front, now that he's been served the restraining order, I hope I've seen the last of him. Part of me realizes that's wishful thinking. As I told Chris, I don't think a piece of paper is going to stop him from doing what he wants to do.

Chris manages to make himself available each time I need to run home to spell Dawn for a bit.

* * *

When it's nearing time for me to head home at the end of my work day, I text Chris to let him know. He replies right away.

Chris: I'll be there in five mins

Sure enough, he pulls up to the back of the building, where I'm waiting at the back door. I climb into the front passenger seat of his borrowed cruiser.

He leans over to kiss me. "How was your day?"

"Good. And busy! We were slammed all day. I guess having a fire is good for business."

"Most of them are a bunch of busybodies," he says. "Hoping to get the juicy details."

We're halfway to the house when my phone rings. I check the screen. It's Dawn. "Hi, Dawn. What's up?"

"Jennie!" The quaver in her voice puts me instantly on alert. "Oh, Jennie, I'm so sorry!" She's crying.

A chill crawls down my spine. "Dawn, slow down and tell me what's wrong?"

Chris turns to me, instantly on high alert. "What is it?"

"Pumpkin got out," she says. Her voice is shaky as she talks through her tears. "I went to look for him, but I must have forgotten to lock the door because when I returned home—with the cat—the door was ajar, and Rosie was gone. I've searched every inch of the house twice, and the garage, but she's not here."

I mute the call for a second to tell Chris, "Granny got out. She's missing."

Immediately, Chris hits the accelerator.

"Dawn, we're on our way. We'll be home in two minutes."

As soon as we're home, Chris jumps out of the car and runs inside.

When I walk into the kitchen, Dawn is sitting at the table and Chris is crouching in front of her. He's holding her hands as she sobs, trying to coax her into telling him everything that happened.

"Pumpkin slipped outside when I went out to get the mail," she says to Chris. "I went to find him, but I guess I left the kitchen door unlocked. When I returned, Rosie was gone. I've searched everywhere."

At that moment, Pumpkin saunters into the kitchen, purring loudly as he rubs against Chris.

"I'll check again," I say as I begin a thorough search of the house, checking every room, every walk-in closet and bathroom, the laundry room, the furnace room. I even run out to search the detached garage, but it's empty. I check the yard. I call her name. And as every second passes, my heart contracts painfully into a tighter and tighter ball.

When I race back inside, Chris looks my way for an update. Sadly, I shake my head. *Nothing.*

Chris rises. "Stay with Dawn," he tells me. "Try to calm her down. I'll canvass the neighbor to see if anyone has spotted Rosie." He cups my face and pulls me close to kiss my forehead. "Don't worry. We'll find her."

My heart is in my throat. I can't even imagine what Granny is thinking right now. She must be so confused, and so scared. "I want to look with you," I say.

Chris eyes Dawn, who is crying hysterically. "I really think you should stay here. I'll call the station and get everyone out looking for her. Can you send me a recent photo of her that I can pass around? I'll call Micah, too. He'll help."

"Do you remember what she was wearing?" Chris asks Dawn.

"Her floral robe and pink slippers," she answers.

"She hasn't been gone long, sweetheart," Chris says to me, "so she couldn't have gotten far. She's probably just a couple of blocks away at most." He squeezes my hands. "I promise you, we'll find her."

My stomach drops as I watch Chris walk out the door.

The first thing I do is scroll through my camera roll to find a good, clear image of Granny. I text that to Chris.

At the sound of Dawn's heart-wrenching cries, I say, "Let's go sit in the living room." I take her hand and coax her to her feet. "We'll be more comfortable in there."

Even though she's still crying, she complies. Once I have her sitting on the sofa, I put my arm around her and hold her close. "It's okay, Dawn. It was an accident. It's not your fault."

She stops crying long enough to say, "But it is! I left the door unlocked."

I don't try to argue with her, because—well, there's no point. I know she didn't do it on purpose, and that's what really matters.

Chris texts me.

Chris: Micah, Jack, and Ruth are on their way

Me: Thx. Pls keep me posted.

Chris: Will do. And three deputies are out looking. I gave them her pic.

"It shouldn't be too hard to spot an eighty-year-old woman wandering around the neighborhood in a floral bath robe and pink slippers."

Emotionally exhausted, Dawn lays her head on my shoulder. I reach for her hand in hopes of comforting not just her, but myself, too.

Granny, where are you? Please come home. Please let them find you.

* * *

I'm mentally and physically numb. Time crawls by, minute by minute, and then an hour passes as we continue to wait for news.

When I hear the kitchen door open, I jump to my feet and race into the kitchen.

Ruth walks in, her demeanor stoic as usual. She wraps her arms around me. "I wanted to check on you, sweetie, to see how you're doing."

Now it's my turn to fall apart. I've been trying to be strong for poor Dawn, but now with Ruth here, her strong arms around me, I crumple. She's the closest thing I have to a mom these days. "I'm so scared."

"I know, honey." She runs her hand up and down my back.

"Have they heard anything at all? Has anyone seen her?"

"No, surprisingly, no one has seen her. But given the time of day, most folks are busy with supper, so it's unlikely they would have seen her walking through the neighborhood. Owen has joined the search. Robyn's out there, too. Hannah and Killian are mobilizing the rest of the search and rescue team. They're on their way. And Hannah's bringing Scout. This is what Scout is trained to do—find people."

Hannah's been training her Belgian Malinois for a year and a half now to find missing people. Already, the dog has been credited with locating several missing hikers up in the mountains. The dog even located a kidnapped woman once.

As frightening as this situation is, I know these people—these friends of mine. They're capable of extraordinary things, including finding my grandma.

The side door opens once more, and Chris and Micah walk in. With a cry, I run into Chris's arms, and he holds me close, wrapping both arms around me.

"Your shoulder," I say, my voice muffled against his shirt.

"It's fine, honey," he says. "You don't need to worry about me." Then he kisses my forehead.

Ruth crosses her arms over her chest. "Is there something you two need to share with the rest of us?"

Chris and I break apart.

"Oh, right," I say. "We haven't had a chance to tell you guys."

"Tell us what?" Micah asks, raising a curious brow.

"Jennie finally took pity on me," Chris says with a pleased grin. "We're, um, dating."

We hear a lot of commotion outside as multiple vehicles arrive. A moment later, Hannah McIntyre and her husband, Killian Devereaux, walk into the house. Hannah unfolds a county map and spreads it out on the kitchen table. "We'll use your house as our command center, if that's okay."

"Of course," I say. "Anything you want."

Hannah notices Chris's arm around me, but doesn't say anything. I guess now is not the time.

Killian pulls out a pen and starts drawing a search grid on the map.

"We searched the town in all directions," Chris says, "but we didn't see her. We're going to have to expand the search grid."

"But she couldn't have gotten that far," I say. "She doesn't have enough stamina. Unless someone gave her a ride." That thought terrifies me. I pull Chris aside. "Do you think David could have anything to do with this? Could he have picked her up and driven her somewhere?"

Chris isn't surprised at my question. "That has occurred to me," he says, his voice low. "I've put out an APB on him as well. We're looking for him, if only to rule him out as a suspect."

My stomach plummets at the thought of him having my grandmother. She already doesn't like him, or trust him. I find it hard to believe she'd get in his car.

Chris's phone rings. "It's Jack," he says. "Go ahead, Jack." He listens a moment, and then he says, "I'm putting you on speaker, Jack. Repeat what you just said."

"We found a pink slipper at the mouth of a trail leading into the woods two blocks east of Jennie's house. I'll send you a picture."

Her slipper? That means she's heading into the woods with at least one bare foot.

Chris's phone chimes, and he shows me the image Jack sent him. It's a very familiar fuzzy pink bunny slipper. "Yes, that's hers," I say.

While Killian redirects his focus to the start of the trail, he draws new search patterns on the map. Hannah starts assigning teams.

Maya McKendrick and Travis Hicks walk into the house then,

followed by Maggie.

Maggie hugs me. "I'll stay here with Dawn so you can join the search," she says.

"Thank you," I whisper as I hug her back. "You're a mind reader."

"I figured you'd want to be there." She presses her hand to her abdomen. "Owen doesn't want me out looking. Actually, it was his idea. Paul is watching the store." Paul is her brother and a co-owner of Emerson's Grocery.

"Thank you," I say. "I need to be out there looking, but Dawn shouldn't be here alone. She's distraught."

"Where is she?" Maggie asks, glancing around the crowded kitchen.

"She's in the living room."

"Jennie, I need a piece of clothing Granny wore recently," Hannah says. "Maybe her pajamas from last night? Something that would have her scent on it."

I run to Granny's room and grab the nightgown she wore to bed last night and hand it over to Hannah.

"Do you mind if I take this with me?" she asks.

"Go right ahead."

"All right, everybody, listen up." Hannah announces the team assignments. "We need to find Mrs. Johnson soon. The temperature tonight is going to drop, and we're expecting rain." As Killian hands out radios, she adds, "Keep in touch. Report anything you see that might be relevant."

While I grab my jacket and put on my hiking boots, Chris grabs a backpack from the coat closet and stuffs it with Granny's sneakers and a jacket.

Soon, we're all out the door. I'm shocked to find nearly two dozen people loitering in my driveway—the search and rescue team members, deputies from Chris's department, and quite a number of neighborhood volunteers.

Hannah hands out grid assignments to the leader of each group. The teams will spread out and search as much of that section of the woods as possible.

Chris takes our instructions. We're teamed up with Micah and Robyn. "Let's go," he says.

Hannah, Killian, and Scout are already heading toward the path where the slipper was discovered.

"Let's go find her," Chris says to me, taking my hand.

For the first time since I heard Granny was missing, I finally have hope we're going to find her safe and sound. We have to. The alternative is something I can't even bear to contemplate.

23

Chris

The members of the search and rescue team converge at the spot where Jack found Granny's slipper. Hannah presents the nightgown to Scout, who sniffs it thoroughly. "Go find!" she tells the dog. "Go find!"

Scout takes off down the path, stopping every few feet to smell the ground and sniff the shrubs lining the path. The dog moves at a good clip, Hannah and Killian easily keeping pace with him. Soon, they're so far ahead on the meandering path we lose sight of them.

Jennie and I, along with Micah and Robyn, follow the same path as the dog. The others have branched out from the path and are cutting through the trees in different directions.

I really wish Jennie had stayed at home. It's getting close to dark now, and the temperature has dropped quite a bit. Even though she's wearing a jacket, I still catch her shivering.

But I understand Jennie's need to be here. Rosie is the only family she has. Rosie is family to me, too, as far as I'm concerned. She took care of all of us when we were kids, not just Jennie but her two wayward friends as well—me and Micah. If it weren't for Rosie, I never would've had a birthday cake when I was a kid.

High-powered flashlights are shining in all directions. Here in the woods, with the thick canopy overhead, it's pretty dark.

Micah and Robyn are behind us on the trail, about ten feet back. Like us, they shine their flashlights into the trees and the undergrowth on both sides of the path. It's not exactly a trail we're following—it's nothing official, nothing marked. It's just a well-worn dirt path made from years of kids and adults traipsing through these woods.

"Granny!" Jennie calls loudly. "Granny, can you hear me? It's Jennie."

"Ms. Rosie!" Robyn calls.

As we move deeper into the trees, we can hear voices echoing throughout the woods as they call her name. *Granny! Rosie! Mrs. Johnson!*

The entire SAR team is in these woods. The deputies and neighborhood volunteers continue to canvass the houses in this area in hopes of meeting someone who has seen her.

"Granny!" Jennie trips on a root sticking out of the packed dirt and nearly falls forward.

I manage to catch her and steady her. Her hands are like ice. "The temperature is dropping fast, Jennie. Let me take you home. I'll come back to rejoin the search."

"Thanks, but no. I'm staying until we find her."

I can respect her need to be part of the search, but I don't have the heart to tell her it's possible we won't find Rosie tonight. The fact we haven't found her yet is concerning. But there's no point in saying that now. Not until we know more.

I'm still hopeful we'll find her safe and sound, but in my line of work, it pays to be realistic. I've seen a lot of similar situations—a missing vulnerable adult—that didn't turn out well. God, I hope that's not the case here. It would devastate Jennie if she lost her grandmother this way.

Lights flicker throughout the woods as the other groups shine their lights into the trees.

I think we should stick to the worn trail because at her age, Granny's not likely to stray off the path. The woods on either side are just too dense with shrubs and other ground cover for her to easily manage.

Sometime later, we hear an excited dog barking somewhere ahead of us.

Jennie looks to me, her eyes wide and hopeful. "That's a good sign, right?"

"It could be," I say. I don't want to get her hopes up to then have them crash.

I'm about to call Hannah on the radio to ask for an update when she beats me to it.

"Hannah to Chris," Hannah calls over the radio. "Tell Jennie we found her grandmother. Rosie's in good health. Over."

"Copy that, Hannah. Is she on the path? Over."

"Affirmative. Just keep walking and you'll run right into us."

Once she hears this, Jennie picks up the pace, and the rest of us keep up with her. As we get closer, and can hear voices up ahead, Jennie breaks into a run.

We come across our group standing in a huddle. Scout is sitting quietly behind Hannah, and Killian and Jack stand on either side of her. And right there in front of them is Rosie Johnson, seated on a fallen log that had been placed conveniently at the side of the path to give hikers a place to rest.

Her hair is wild. Her cheeks are flushed, and her eyes are bright as she chats happily with her rescuers.

"Granny!" Jennie cries as she runs up to her grandmother. She drops down beside her on the log and wraps her arms around Rosie. "Are you okay?" She pulls back and scans Rosie from head to toe. "Are you hurt?"

"I'm not hurt," Rosie says. "But I'm tired and cold. Can we go home now? I'm sure it's past my bedtime."

Jennie lays her arm across her grandmother's shoulders and leans in to kiss the older woman's cheek. "Yes, ma'am," she says with a tearful laugh. "We can do anything you want."

"My foot's cold." Rosie lifts her bare left foot. "Has anyone seen my slipper?"

"How about we put some proper shoes on your feet?" Jennie

retrieves the sneakers and jacket from the backpack I'm carrying. She puts the shoes and jacket on her grandmother. "Let's go home now.".

As soon as we reach an area where I can get a decent cell signal, I call Maggie to let her know we've found Rosie. As I deliver the good news, I can hear Dawn crying again, undoubtedly this time in sheer relief.

I also radio the deputies and the volunteers to let them know Jennie's grandmother has been found, and that they are all welcome to call it a night.

* * *

When we arrive back at Jennie's house, Jennie takes Rosie inside, where Dawn is waiting eagerly to see her old friend. Dawn nearly smothers Rosie in a bear hug, alternately laughing and crying.

"What's wrong, Dawn?" Rosie asks her, clearly perplexed. "Why are you crying?"

"I'm crying because I'm so glad to see you, that's why."

"You see me all the time, dear. There's no reason to get excited."

Jennie takes Rosie off for a hot bath and then bed.

Poor Dawn, who is clearly exhausted, says goodnight and heads home, promising to be back bright and early the next morning.

After everyone has had a chance to warm up, they all head home. Hannah, Killian, and Scout. Ruth and Jack, Owen and Maggie, Maya, Travis.

After they've all gone, the house is quiet. I sit in the living room waiting for Jennie to reappear.

A short while later, looking ragged after a traumatic evening, Jennie walks into the living room. "She's already asleep. She was exhausted."

Jennie drops down onto the sofa beside me and bursts into tears.

"It's okay, honey," I say as I put my arm around her. "I think you're exhausted, too. Let's get ready for bed. Tomorrow morning will be here too soon."

That night, after we're settled in Jennie's bed, she turns to me, cups my face, and kisses me. It's a soft kiss, a gentle one, and I'm not sure if it's a gesture of gratitude for helping in the search or an invitation for something more. After what she's been through today, I wouldn't want to assume anything.

When her hand travels down my chest, past my abdomen, to my groin, I realize it's an invitation. "Are you sure?" I ask. I don't want to take advantage of her emotional state.

Instead of answering me verbally, she wraps her soft fingers around what is now a full-blown erection.

I suck in a breath. "I'll take that as a yes."

She laughs softly and then presses a kiss to my throat. I wonder if she can feel my pulse pounding.

We make love then, slow and easy. And if it weren't for having to get up and dispose of the condom, I would have fallen asleep inside her.

24

Jennie

The morning after her harrowing escapade, Granny is starving when she comes to the kitchen for breakfast. The three of us eat together, and as we're cleaning up, Dawn arrives.

Dawn seems a bit subdued after the events of yesterday, but Granny is absolutely fine. She doesn't mention anything about wandering away from the house. I suspect she doesn't even remember doing it.

Chris drops me off at the diner at six-thirty, and I get started on pies and donuts. I'm still trying to catch up after the fire.

Thursday and Friday are very routine, and it looks like we're getting back to normal. Chris is still on limited duty because of his shoulder injury. He has a doctor's appointment in Estes Park coming up soon, and he's hoping to be cleared to return to full duty.

On Friday evening, Chris comes to the diner at seven, just as we're closing up, so we can join our friends next door at the Tavern for our weekly meet-up. Mrs. Robinson is on Granny duty this evening.

As we walk into the tavern, I realize it's the first time we're socializing with our friends since Chris and I became a couple. I mean, they already know because they saw us together during the search for Granny. They saw us holding hands and hugging, but we really didn't have a chance to talk about it. It wasn't the priority at that moment.

But now... as we walk into the tavern, all eyes are on us. They've pushed two large tables together so we can all sit together for a change—the guys with us women. Everyone else is already here, and they saved two seats for us, side by side. We take our seats, and Chris puts his arm along the back of my chair. His thumb brushes my shoulder.

"All right, spill the beans!" Maya says. "I saw you two holding hands the other night. So?" She gives us a coaxing grin. "Come on! Spill the tea."

I can feel my face heating up, like I'm in middle school again, and the other girls just found out I have a crush on one of the boys. I shrug because there's no point in drawing this out. "We're together."

To emphasize the point, Chris leans in and kisses my cheek.

Everyone at the table cheers. Jack wads up a napkin and lobs it at Chris's face. Chris tosses it right back.

Micah, who's on Chris's other side, smacks him on the back. "It's about time, Sheriff! I told you to go for it."

I look to see Chris's reaction to all the teasing, and he's sitting there with a big grin on his face, clearly unfazed by the attention.

Jack jumps up and runs to the bar to grab a tray of pitchers.

Ruth follows carrying glasses for everyone. "Drink up!" she says. "We have a lot to celebrate tonight—Rosie is safe and sound, and these two lovebirds finally got their act together. Food is on the way."

Owen goes to the bar to get a Coke for Maggie. Ruth, Gabrielle, and Maya fetch platters of hot *hors d'oeuvres* for everyone to share.

Chris and I field so many questions.

Who admitted their attraction first?

When was our first kiss?

And then the questions get far more personal, leaving me in tears of laughter.

The evening is absolutely perfect, and I can't imagine anything better. That is, until Chris holds out his hand to me and says, "May I have this dance?"

Ah, yes. This is the better part. "I would love to."

We receive lots of hoots and hollers from our friends as we walk onto the dance floor.

"I've been looking forward to this," Chris says. "All the times we've been here, I wanted you to be mine. I wanted the right to hold you, touch you, kiss you. Dance with you, not as your *friend*, but as your *boyfriend*."

I blink back tears. "You're going to make me cry."

He cups my face. "I hope they're tears of joy."

Sniffling, I nod. "They are."

We dance several dances before we return to the table for a cold drink and more teasing.

* * *

On Saturday, when I work a half-day, Chris stays home with Granny.

On Sunday, we spend the day together, the three of us. Early afternoon, Chris runs back to his house to get his mail and check on things. When he returns, he brings more clothes and his laptop.

After dinner, Chris makes popcorn for us, and we watch *Mary Poppins*—the original Disney classic. It's another one of Granny's favorites.

Granny's in her recliner, covered with her favorite crocheted throw, Pumpkin napping on her lap, happily munching on her bowl of popcorn. Remarkably, she's no worse for wear after her walkabout adventure.

Chris and I are stretched out on the sofa, his arms are around me, his nose is buried in my hair.

This is heaven.

Originally, Chris said he wanted to stay here with me because of David, but now that David seems to be behaving himself—I haven't seen or heard from him since Chris served the notice of the restraining order—does this mean Chris will go back to his own house? I'm afraid to ask him. I'm afraid of his answer. Because I don't want him to leave. But I also don't want him to feel obligated to stay.

I'm amazed at how easily we've fallen into a comfortable routine living together. His shoulder is doing much better. It still bothers him, but not nearly as much. We'll find out more at his doctor's appointment coming up.

Everything's perfect.

* * *

Chris invites me to go with him to his orthopedic appointment in Estes Park on Monday. We leave around noon. I'm driving so he can give his shoulder a rest.

His doctor checks his range of motion during the appointment and asks what his pain level is. Chris says he's healing well, and the doctor seems to agree.

"I'd say you're fit to return to work, but please take it easy for a couple of weeks. Let the other officers do the chasing and the heavy lifting, all right?"

As we're leaving the doctor's office, Chris says, "We have some time before we have to be home. How about a dinner date?"

"A date?" I smile. I realize we've never gone on an actual date. I mean, we do things together all the time now, and we eat meals together. We even sleep together. But we haven't gone on a *date*. "I would love that."

"What sounds good?" He rattles off a list of popular local restaurants, everything from American cuisine to Italian to barbeque to a steakhouse.

"How about the Italian restaurant?" I suggest.

"Mama Rose's, it is," he says. He pulls up directions on his phone.

We arrive at the restaurant at an odd hour, 3 PM, so there's no wait. We're seated by a window overlooking the riverside patio.

I order fettuccine Alfredo. He goes for the lasagna. Our server brings us breadsticks and salads to keep us busy while we wait for our entrees to arrive.

"How's your food?" Chris asks right as I'm taking a bite.

I chuckle as I chew, holding up a finger. *Just a minute.* "It's delicious," I finally say. "How's yours?"

Our meal is relaxing. I keep catching Chris watching me, to the point I start to feel self-conscious. "Why are you staring at me?"

He laughs it off. "I'm not."

"Yes, you are."

"Maybe it's because I like looking at you." He holds his hand out, and I give him mine. "And maybe it's because I still can't believe this is real."

"I know what you mean. It does seem unreal sometimes."

"When you want something so badly, for so long, and all of a sudden you have it, well, sometimes it feels too good to be true. I keep expecting to wake up and find it's all just a dream."

I squeeze his hand. "It's not a dream, Chris."

He reaches into his jacket pocket and pulls out a small square box. "Now, this isn't what you think it is," he says, clearly cautioning me.

I grin. "And what would that be?"

He offers me the box. "This is something practical. Open it and see."

I take the small box from him and pry the lid open. Inside is a gold chain with a silver pendant attached. "What is it?"

He takes the chain out of the box and opens the silver pendant, revealing a small button. It's clearly not a jewel or any type of decorative ornament. It's something else. Something practical.

"This is a panic button," he says. "If you push this button, it sends an alert to my phone, letting me know you're in trouble. It's got GPS, so it will give me your exact location. I'd be able to track you."

I'm a bit stunned. I mean, I wasn't expecting jewelry or anything like that. It's way too soon. But this—this means he's worried about my safety.

"Look," he says. "Braggart is still out there, a free man. And a restraining order can do only so much. If he refuses to honor it—well, I'd feel a lot better if you wore this. Please, Jennie, for my peace of mind, will you wear it?"

I nod, suddenly all choked up. I'm touched that he took the effort to get me something like this. It's even more meaningful than a ring. He wants to keep me safe.

Chris leans close, holding out the chain. I meet him halfway so he can slip the chain around my neck. "If you don't want anyone to see it, you can slip it beneath your top. Just please, promise me you won't go anywhere without it."

A knot forms in my throat. "I promise."

He wipes an errant tear from my cheek. "I didn't mean to make you cry."

"It's okay," I say as I glance down at the pendant, which rests between my breasts. The truth is, this feels a lot more personal than something as simple as a ring. This is about my *safety*.

This also tells me he doesn't have much faith in the restraining order, and that scares me.

25

Chris

"Mornin', boss!" Ricky says when I walk into the station the following Monday morning.

"Morning, Ricky." I pick up the mail in my inbox. It's my first full day back to work after dislocating my shoulder.

"There are donuts in the break room," Darlene says, pointing across the room. "Jace brought them in fresh from Estes Park this morning."

"What was Jace doing in Estes Park?" He lives in Bryce.

Darlene grins. "He's got a new girlfriend. Looks like they had a sleepover last night."

"Speaking of sleepovers," Ricky says, "I happened to drive by Jennie's house early this morning on my way to work, and I spotted your loaner parked in her driveway. Is there something you want to tell us?"

I bite back a grin. "Nope."

I join Ricky in the break room, and we each polish off a glazed donut while we're waiting for the coffeemaker to work its magic.

Darlene pops her head through the open doorway. "Better get those ropes out, boss. The goats are in Mrs. McPherson's flower garden again."

Yeah, it's good to be back.

After wrangling half a dozen goats and returning them to their rightful owner, Ricky, Jace, and I head back to the station. I'm hoping to get good news today on my SUV. It's taken this long for the insurance adjuster to get out to Micah's Auto Repair to get a look at it.

* * *

As it turns out, my SUV is totaled. I was afraid of that, but I'd been holding on to the hope it could be repaired. It looks like I'll have to put in a requisition for a replacement vehicle. In the meanwhile, I have my loaner cruiser to drive.

I resume my normal patrol schedule. I've got eyes and ears out on Braggart, but so far, he's been quiet. No one has spotted him in town, which is fine with me. I'm hoping his fancy attorney put the fear of God in him and explained that if he violated that restraining order, his ass would end up back in jail. And this time, he wouldn't find it so easy to get bail.

Life at home with Jennie is wonderful. Maybe we're still in the so-called honeymoon stage, but it's been going really well. I get to go to bed with her each night and wake up with her every morning. We take turns cooking breakfast and doing the dishes.

I manage to drive her to and from the diner most of the time. When I can't, one of our friends stands in for me.

I notice she's been wearing the pendant consistently, which makes me happy. I'm debating whether or not to suggest to Jennie that we put one of these pendants on Granny. Then, if she goes on another walkabout, we'll be able to track her easily.

* * *

I'm sitting at my desk when my phone chimes with a notification. When I check the screen, my heart stops. It's an automated alert from Jennie's panic button.

"Fuck!"

Immediately, I check her location, and according to the app, she's at the diner. I grab my duty belt and race out of my office.

"Where are you off to in such a hurry?" Jace asks as I rush past him to the exit.

"Jennie's panic alarm just went off!" I tell him. "I'm going over to the diner to check on her. Be on stand-by in case I need you."

"Will do," Jace says as he follows me out the door. "It probably got pushed on accident!" he hollers as I run to my cruiser. "I'm sure she's fine!"

On my way to the diner, I call Jennie's phone. It rings several times before I hear, *"Hi, this is Jennie. Please leave me a message."*

Damn it! My anxiety is climbing with every second that passes.

I text her.

Me: Jennie? Everything ok?

But there's no answer.

So I call her phone again. Same thing. It rings a few times and then I hear her voicemail greeting.

My pulse is racing now, and I'm trying to shove back the panic. Panicking won't help the situation. Usually I'm pretty calm when I'm stressed, but this is *Jennie!*

When I arrive at the diner, I pull up at the back door and run inside. I check her newly furnished office, which is empty. I check the storage room, then the kitchen. "Have you seen Jennie?" I ask the kitchen staff. Both cooks and the dishwasher are here, up to their elbows in work.

"Yeah," Chad says as he pulls a tray of plates and silverware out of the dishwasher. "She was taking out the trash."

The trash dumpster is right outside the back door. I would have seen her. "When was this?"

Chad shrugs. "I dunno. Just a few minutes ago, I think. I'm not sure. I haven't seen her come back in, so she should still be out back."

"She's not," I say. Then I head for the dining room. It's packed with customers, and I see Cara and Michelle waiting on customers, but no Jennie.

I snag Michelle's arm. "Have you seen Jennie?"

"She said she was going to take out the trash. Why?"

Fuck!

I race back outside and search the area between the back door and the dumpster. There, on the ground, is Jennie's pendant. My hand shakes as I pick it up. The chain is *broken*, as if someone ripped it from her neck. *Damn it!* I can't track her location.

I call her again, and I'm not really surprised when I hear her phone ringing in the dumpster.

My blood turns to ice as I force myself to lift the dumpster lid. *Please, God, I'm begging you.* In my line of work, I've seen everything.

The back door of the diner opens, and Chad pokes his head out. "What are you looking for?"

Ignoring Chad and my roiling stomach, I force myself to look inside the dumpster. If her body is in here, my life is over.

My eyes burn as I stare down at a couple of black plastic trash bags. Her phone is lying right on top. And there's nothing else.

Air rushes back into my lungs, and my knees nearly give out. I grasp the edge of the dumpster to keep from dropping to my ass on the pavement. My stomach drops as reality sinks in, and I feel sick.

Someone took her.

Braggart, that motherfucking dipshit of an asshole, took her!

"Sheriff?" Chad asks, frowning with concern. "You okay, man? You look like shit."

I scrub my hands over my face as I try to get my breathing under control. I need to remain calm. Otherwise, I can't help her. I estimate she's been missing for approximately ten minutes. There's still time to find her before he has a chance to hurt her.

I radio the station and instruct Darlene to have both Jace and

Ricky meet me at the Braggart ranch pronto. "Also, put out an APB on David Braggart, and issue a missing persons alert for Jennie Lopez."

"Shit, Chris," Darlene says. "Okay. I'm on it."

I get back in my cruiser, lights flashing, siren blaring, as I race toward the Braggart ranch.

I'm coming, Jennie. Just hang on, sweetheart. I'm coming.

26

Jennie

My head hurts. It's throbbing, and the pain is excruciating. I can't see a thing—it's pitch black. *Is it nighttime? Where am I?*

My heart starts pounding because I don't know. I can't remember a thing.

I try to sit up, but I can't. My limbs are tied down. I'm on something soft. *A bed maybe?*

I smell something—smoke. Like woodsmoke. A fireplace maybe? Or a woodstove?

"Who's there?" I ask. My voice is raw, and it hurts to speak.

No response.

"Who's there!" I yell. Or at least I try to. My words come out a garbled mess.

Heavy footsteps approach on a wooden floor, the boards creaking with age. I freeze, stealing myself for the unknown.

"You might as well save your breath, Jennie. No one can hear you out here."

That voice! I thrash, trying in vain to free myself, but the more I struggle, the more the ropes tighten on my wrists and ankles. Terror seizes me. He's not just a monster. He's insane. "Let me go, David!"

I'm having trouble breathing, and my mouth is dry. My head is killing me, and I can't think straight. The words tumble like pebbles from my lips. "You—can't—do—this."

"Of course I can," he says. "I can do anything I want. You underestimated me, Jennie-bean, for the last time."

"Chris will—"

"Your sheriff will never find you, I guarantee it."

Chris—Oh, God—Chris.

27

Chris

I pull up the drive at the Braggart ranch and park in front of the house. There's no visible sign of Braggart's car, an older model black BMW, but it could be parked in any one of the six garage bays. And of course there are several barns on the property. He could have hidden it anywhere.

As I'm getting out of my cruiser, two more police cars pull in behind me. Jace and Ricky get out of their vehicles and join me.

"I found her emergency pendant and cell phone back at the diner," I say. "My guess is Braggart grabbed her there as she was taking out the trash. We need to get inside this house to search for her. Jace, you search the garages and barns for Braggart's black BMW. Ricky and I will try to get into the house."

Ricky leads the way, striding up the walkway to the front door. He knocks loudly. "Sheriff's office! Open the door!" When there's no response, he beats his fist against the door.

The door finally opens, and the housekeeper, Marguerite, stands in the doorway. "Yes?" She spots me. "Hello, Sheriff. How can I help you?"

"Where's David?" I demand, my voice sharp.

Her eyes widen in surprise. "I don't know, sir. He left early this morning, and he hasn't returned."

Jace runs up, clearly out of breath "Found the BMW in one of the barns. There are trace amounts of blood on the front passenger seat and dashboard, and I found an open package of zip ties and a wet cloth on the floor. The cloth smells like chloroform."

That's enough probable cause to justify a warrantless search.

I step around Ricky and push my way into the house. The housekeeper cries out as she stumbles back. "Sheriff's office!" I yell. "Make yourself known! Come out with your hands on your head!"

"But there's no one here, Officer," the housekeeper cries. "Just me."

To the two deputies, I say, "Search every square inch of this house."

As we begin a systematic sweep of the residence, I yell, "Jennie! Are you in here?"

The housekeeper remains rooted to the spot, her hands covering her mouth.

"Have you seen a woman here this morning?" I ask her.

She shakes her head. "No, sir! Please, Mr. David would never hurt Mrs. Braggart. He loves her."

Mrs. Braggart? My blood starts to boil. "She's *not* his wife! Is she here? Have you seen her?"

Marguerite shakes her head. "No, sir. I haven't seen her. I swear to you." She makes the sign of a cross over her chest. "As God is my witness, I have not seen that poor woman."

* * *

Ricky and I search the entire house, going room by room. We look in every closet, every cupboard, hell even under every bed. We check behind every door, but we find no sign of David or Jennie.

We go outside to the barn to examine the BMW. Sure enough, just as Jace described, there are incriminating signs in the car, including drops of blood.

"Search all the barns," I say, and we spread out. We search every inch of the two story structures.

"All right," I say, thinking out loud. "He grabbed her at the diner, removed her panic button after she pushed it, and threw her phone in the dumpster. It looks like he might have zip tied her and knocked her out with chloroform before bringing her back here. But why here? They're not in the house, or garages, or in these barns."

"There are probably other outbuildings," Jace points out. "Or maybe a cellar?"

I radio the station and ask Darlene to send out three more officers to help in the search. There's a lot of ground to cover here, and time is of the essence. And the ranch itself is massive. I don't recall the total area, but it's hundreds of acres.

"Where would he take her," I say, "and how would they get there?"

"Chris, look at this!" Ricky says.

I join him where he's staring down at the dirty barn floor. There are spots of oil on the ground, and a tan canvas tarp is lying in a heap a couple of feet away. There's a toolkit on a wooden bench, and next to that is a flat tire propped against the barn wall.

"That's an all-terrain vehicle tire," Jace says. He crouches down beside it and runs his fingers between the treads. "See how thick the treads are? How chunky the tire is? See these deep grooves and the wide spacing? What if he moved her onto an ATV and took off with her?"

"Where? Into the woods?"

"I bet if the ground is soft enough, we'll find tracks on a nearby trail."

"But this property is huge," I say. "It would take days or weeks to search all of it. We need more boots on the ground." I call Hannah McIntyre and catch her up to speed. "I need the SAR team out here ASAP."

"You got it," Hannah says. "I'll put out a call."

"Make sure you bring Scout. He found Rosie. He can find Jennie, too."

28

Jennie

My wrists and ankles are hurting me, feeling like they're rubbed raw. My mouth is dry like a desert, and my throat feels raw. It hurts to swallow. I can barely move. There's a sleeping mask on my face, and I can't see anything. It's pitch black.

I turn my head to the side, and suddenly I can see a thin strip of light. I move my aching head from side to side, knocking the mask askew, until I can see enough to determine where I am.

Log walls. A stone hearth. A woodstove. *A cabin!*

A sofa and two chairs face the fireplace. There's a small kitchen in one corner of the room, and I'm lying on a large four-poster bed, my limbs secured to the posts with ropes. There's a large head of a buck hanging like a trophy over the fireplace mantel.

I know this place. I've been here before. But my mind is spinning, and I can't think.

My left wrist is rubbed raw where the rope is tied too tight. There's dried blood on my wrist and on the rope. The same is true for my other wrist.

I take stock of the fact my clothes are still on—blue jeans and my pink *Jennie's Diner* T-shirt. I've still got my white socks on. The only things missing are my sneakers. At least I can be grateful I'm still dressed.

Suddenly, the wooden door swings inward, and a man walks inside carrying an armload of split wood. "Oh, good," he says. "You're awake."

David.

"Where am I?"

"You don't remember this place? We spent some nights out here, babe. Surely you remember that bed." He smirks like it's an inside joke.

I think back to when we were married. His family has an old hunting cabin out in the woods, at least a good twenty-minute hike from the house.

"David, what have you done?" I'm horrified that he'd do something this crazy. "Kidnapping—is—a felony. You're going—to jail—for a long time." My throat feels like it's filled with glass shards.

He drops his armload of wood beside an iron rack, squats down, and starts adding the logs neatly to the existing stack. "I did what I had to do, Jennie-bean."

"Don't—call me—that."

"Come on, Jennie. What did you expect me to do? You wouldn't talk to me. You wouldn't listen. Then you went and got that asinine restraining order. It was the cop's idea, wasn't it? That smug bastard! Did you really think a restraining order could keep us apart?"

"Yes. That's what they're intended for."

He calmly finishes adding the new wood to the rack. Then he stands, brushes his hands off on his blue jeans, and then walks toward me.

I try to move away when he sits on the side of the bed, but the ropes don't have much give.

He reaches out, moving slowly, and lays his hand on my belly. "Don't be afraid of me, baby. You know I'd never hurt you."

"What do you call this?" I ask, my voice rising. "You drugged me, kidnapped me, and dragged me out here to the middle of nowhere. How is this not hurting me?"

He brushes my hair back. "How else could I get your undivided attention?"

"Certainly not this way!" I struggle against the ropes out of sheer frustration, but I only hurt myself in the process. My wrists are burning now from fresh abrasions.

"If you don't stop hurting yourself, I'll have to knock you out again for your own good. Is that what you want?"

Immediately, I stop. "No! Please, don't." I'll have zero chance of getting free if I'm unconscious.

He nods. "Good. If you behave, I won't have to."

I try another tactic. "Why did you bring me here?"

"To convince you to marry me again. Why else? We never should have gotten divorced in the first place. That was my fault for signing those damn papers. But we're going to fix this. We're getting married."

"Why do you want to marry me again?"

"It's the only way to claim what's mine. Everything you have should belong to me," he says matter-of-factly. "This is about fairness. You were my wife, and what's yours should be mine—your inheritance from your grandpa, the house, the diner. All of it."

"I already explained to you—Grandpa died after we got a divorce, so you're not entitled to that. And the house and diner legally belong to my grandmother."

"Yeah, but you'll inherit all that when she passes, which probably won't be long from now given the state of her health." He shoots to his feet and starts pacing beside the bed. "What you don't understand, Jennie, is that you *owe* me. Ever since the divorce, my life has gone to pot, and it's all your fault. My parents disowned me because of your stupid allegations in the divorce. I never *abused* you, and you know it."

"I'd say my bruises and broken bones proved otherwise."

"Those were all your fault, and you know it." He scowls at me. "After you humiliated me with your lies and accusations, I moved to Vegas for a fresh start, and what money I had left at the time, I lost. All of it. Not just in the casinos, but betting on everything from sports to car races to horses. I owe people money, Jennie. Powerful people who are going to hurt me if I don't repay them. And that's where you come in. You're going to marry me and sell everything—the house and the diner. All that money, plus your inheritance, will more than pay off my debts. And then you and I will go somewhere far away, where no one knows us—Mexico maybe, or Thailand—and we'll start over. Just the two of us. Newlyweds again."

He returns to sit on the side of the bed, seemingly more upbeat now. I think he just managed to convince himself that his plan is sane and rational.

He cups my face and brushes his thumb over my lips. "We're going to be happy, Jennie-bean, I promise." And when he leans down to kiss me, I turn my face away, and his lips end up glancing off my cheek.

He pats my thigh. "You'll come around, baby."

I glance past him, unable to stand looking at him, and notice a stockpile of weapons on the small kitchen table. I see what looks like semi-automatic rifles, handguns, and even hand grenades. There are boxes and boxes of ammo. He's prepared to wage war against anyone who tries to stop him.

He notices where my attention is. "Yeah, no one is coming between us again, baby. No one. Especially not that fucking cop of yours. If he comes near this cabin, he's a dead man. I'll blow his head right off his shoulders."

He gets up then and sits at the table to organize his stockpile of weapons. "You hungry, baby? I've got some protein bars around here somewhere."

His mood shifts are giving me whiplash.

He's truly insane.

When Chris comes, which he will—I know it!—I need to warn him. Not only is David dangerous because of his delusions, but he's well armed.

* * *

"Do you have any water?" I ask sometime later. I am loath to engage him in any type of conversation, but I'm desperate for some water to cool my burning throat.

"You're in luck," he says as he sets a metal bucket on the table. "When you were napping earlier, I walked down to the stream for water."

Napping? I was kidnapped and drugged, and he thinks I've been *napping?*

This is classic gaslighting. If only I'd understood the term narcissism before I agreed to marry him. I could have saved myself a lot of pain and suffering.

"Thank you," I say, forcing myself to smile at him. Showing him how I really feel won't win me any points. "I'm really thirsty."

"Sure, sure," he says as he grabs a ceramic mug from one of the open shelves in the kitchen area. He dips the cup in the bucket of water and brings it to me. "Here you go, Jennie-bean." He's smiling as if he's proud of himself. "Drink up."

I tilt my head up, and he holds the cup at my mouth. The cool water feels good against my raw throat, and yet it hurts to swallow. Still, I force myself to down the entire cup. I don't know how long this situation is going to go on, and I don't want to get dehydrated.

"That's my good girl," he says after I drain the cup. "You really are thirsty. Do you want more?"

"Yes, please." I do my best to sound grateful. One thing I remember about David is he loves being the hero.

I wonder if he'll untie me if I say I have to pee. If I remember correctly, there's no indoor toilet here, but there is an outhouse out back. He'd have to untie me to let me go outside to use the toilet. And if I can get outside, I might be able to make a run for it.

He returns to the table to fill the cup with more water and brings it back to the bed. As he holds it for me to drink, he says, "See how good we are together, baby? It's just like old times. Surely you haven't forgotten."

I remember nothing but torment for an entire year. My stomach churns as I force myself to smile up at him. "We were good together, weren't we?"

His entire face lights up after hearing those words. "Yes! We were." He reaches down to cup my face and brush his thumb over my lips. "God, you're so pretty. I've missed you, baby. I—"

"Actually, I am pretty hungry." I blurt out the words, hoping to derail his thoughts. "I haven't had anything to eat all day." That's not true, but he doesn't know that.

He frowns at the interruption. "Sure, I'll get you something."

He goes to the kitchen and searches through a box of supplies until he locates a bar of something. On his way back, he tears open the wrapper and holds it for me as I take a bite. It's a peanut butter granola bar.

"I can feed myself, you know, if you untie me."

He shakes his head. "Sorry, but no, baby. Not until I'm sure I can trust you."

"But you're going to have to let me get up eventually. After drinking all that water, I'll need to pee soon."

"I already thought of that." He nods to a back corner of the cabin, out of my line of sight. "I have a bucket you can use."

And just like that, my hopes for a quick escape are dashed.

29

Chris

The McIntyre Search and Rescue team shows up within twenty minutes of my call. That's pretty impressive considering they were scattered around town doing their day jobs—Hannah and Killian running the lodge, Micah at the auto repair shop, Owen most likely at home taking care of his baby daughter, John Burke tending the horses in the stable, Maya and Travis likely in the process of getting a group of visitors ready to go hiking or rock climbing. Even Ruth and Jack, who aren't officially part of the SAR team, come to join the search.

I've got two deputies scouring Bryce and the surrounding countryside looking for Braggart, in case he's not here and we're barking up the wrong tree. They're looking for Jennie, too.

But my gut feeling tells me they're both here on this property. This is where Braggart feels safest. He knows these acres like the back of his hand. This was his childhood playground. And that gives me an idea.

I call Ricky over—he was in the same grade as us in school. "Do you remember Braggart from school?"

"Yes."

"Do you remember who his friends were?"

"Honestly, the guy was an ass even back then. I don't think he had many friends."

"Was there anyone in particular he hung out with?"

Ricky racks his brain. "There was one kid, maybe. Someone as douchebaggy as Dave was. Clint Tolliver."

"I remember him. Doesn't he work in the hardware store here in town?"

Ricky nods. "That's the one. You want me to go talk to him?"

I nod. "Try to find out if he knows where Braggart would go to ground if he was in trouble. Is there a place on this property, or even elsewhere, he'd go?"

"Will do." Ricky gives me a salute as he turns and heads toward his cruiser.

* * *

We create a makeshift command center in the red barn. Hannah spreads a regional map out on an old wooden desk and weights the corners down with small stones. She pulls out her handy black marker.

"Here's the main house," she says as she circles an area. "And you've already searched it and found nothing?" she asks me.

I nod. "Yeah. You can scratch it off."

She draws a big *X* to mark the house as eliminated. She draws in the location of the barns, chicken coop, and other out buildings. "And these have all been searched thoroughly as well?"

"Yes."

Hannah sets a paper grocery sack on the table, opens it, and withdraws two garments—a pink camisole top and a pair of gray knit sleep shorts. I recognize them as the pajamas she wore to bed last night.

"I took the liberty of stopping at her house and taking these from Jennie's dirty laundry hamper. We'll use these to give Scout a scent to work with."

Scout, the dog in question, is lying underneath the desk, quiet but alert, his dark eyes darting back and forth. When Hannah says his name, the dog's head shoots up, and his ears perk sharply upright. But when no command follows, he relaxes and lays his head back down on his paws.

Hannah draws an outline around the entire Braggart property. "We're looking for a needle in a haystack. We need more intel to narrow the search."

I tell her about Ricky going to look for Clint Tolliver to see if he has any insight as to where Braggart might have gone to hide out.

"There's no point in sitting around on our asses and doing nothing," Killian says as he lays his hands on his wife's shoulders. "I say we start with the obvious trails."

"Agreed," Hannah says. "Let's survey the perimeter of the open space around the house and look for potential entry points into the woods. I imagine there are multiple trails that are passable by ATV. Maybe we'll get lucky and find fresh tire marks."

The carefully manicured yard surrounding the house is about two acres of pristinely mowed turf with a few well-placed mature trees. We spread out to examine the perimeter of the expansive yard, looking for breaks in the trees where an ATV might be able to slip through without leaving a lot of evidence behind—snapped branches and trampled undergrowth. We find tire marks at the beginning of two of the trails, so that approach isn't as helpful as we'd hoped.

"Three," Hannah says when we reconvene at the makeshift command center. "Three obvious trails wide enough for an ATV to pass through." She frowns. "I suppose it could be worse. Right now I propose we split into three groups and follow these trails as far as we can. Until we hear something different, this is the best we have to go on."

Scout is up on his feet now, a bit antsy. I suspect he knows something's up, that we're about to ask him to do something. This dog sure loves to be asked to do things.

Everyone splits into teams. I'm going with Hannah, Killian and Scout. Jace is going with Micah, Ruth, and Jack. Owen, John, and the rock climbers will take the last trail. One of my deputies is assigned to each team, so at least one member is armed. Most SAR volunteers aren't armed, but Hannah prefers at least one person on each team to carry a weapon. In this case, the officers are armed, of course. We're wearing full tactical outfits, including bulletproof vests. Hannah and Killian are armed, as are Owen and John.

After Scout is given an opportunity to thoroughly sniff Jennie's items of clothing, we set off.

Scout gets dibs on which trail he wants to explore. We take him to the first trail, but he's not too excited. Same for the middle trail. But when we take him to the third trail, he finally shows some enthusiasm. Tracking missing people can be a living saving event, but to Scout, it's all a game. And he loves to win.

"We'll take this one," Hannah says as she offers the dog Jennie's pajamas once more. "Everyone radio in if you find anything."

"Scout, go find!" Hannah says to her dog. "Go find!"

Scout takes off at a good clip, and Hannah, Killian, and I push ourselves to keep up with him. He stays mostly to the well-defined trail, occasionally veering off into the thick undergrowth. But each time he deviates from the path, he returns to the trail and continues forward, deeper into the woods.

I'm surprised to hear my phone chiming with an incoming text message. It's from Ricky.

Ricky: Spoke to Tolliver. He says the Braggarts have a rough hunting cabin deep in the woods on their property, near a stream. Dave used to hang out there with friends to smoke weed. That's the only place he could think of.

Well, at least we have something to focus on now.

"There's a hunting cabin somewhere on the property, near a

stream," I tell Hannah and Killian. "I think that's our best option."

Hannah radios the other two search teams with an update.

Micah radios back to say they have found a stream, and that they'll follow it in hopes it leads to the cabin.

At least we now have two potentially helpful leads to investigate.

I check the time. It's been almost ninety minutes since I received the alert from Jennie's pendant. In the wider scheme of things, that's not a whole lot of time. But in reality, Braggart could do a lot of damage to her in that amount of time. I figure he spent at least half that time transporting her to their destination, provided our assumptions are correct. That leaves forty-five minutes for him to terrorize her.

I'm trying desperately to keep a cool head, to treat this situation professionally, like I would in any case of a missing person. But this isn't just any case. *It's Jennie.* And my gut is in knots at the thought of her being frightened, or even worse—hurt.

I vow to myself here and now that if he has hurt her, he's a dead man. I don't care what it takes. I won't risk him possibly getting out on a technicality and threatening her again. My job, not as a sheriff, but as her boyfriend, is to ensure her safety, now and in the future.

* * *

We've been out here almost an hour on foot and moving at a good pace when we get our first inkling we might be on the right track.

I signal the team to stop. "I hear water."

Hannah and Killian come to a stop, and we all three listen. We can make out the sound of swiftly moving water off to our left.

We contemplate cutting through the trees to locate the stream, thinking we can follow it to the cabin. But Scout makes up our minds for us when he sprints ahead with a new sense of eagerness.

We keep pace with Scout, who's moving faster and faster as if he's zeroing in on his quarry. It's not long until we round a bend, and there ahead of us, in a small clearing, is a run-down log cabin that has definitely seen better days. The stream is close by, too. We can hear the rushing water.

The cabin is a single story log structure. It's a square building with a door in the center of the front wall, a window on each side. There's a wooden porch on the front with a sagging overhang. I spot an ATV parked alongside the building, partially covered with a filthy dark blue tarp.

Hannah calls Scout back to her, and we stay back, out of direct sight of the cabin. While Hannah radios her people with an update, I send out a message to my station, calling on all available officers to join me. I let them know where to rendezvous with us. We won't be able to make a move until I have a sufficient law enforcement presence on site.

Ricky and Jace are the first ones on the scene. The rest of the SAR team shows up, but I insist they pull way back out of the line of fire. They're search and rescue, not law enforcement. This is undoubtedly a volatile situation.

Jack Merchant walks up to me, looking as calm and deadly as a person can. "I can help." He's got a 9mm tucked into his hip holster.

I figure he can as he has an extensive background in military special ops.

Owen Ramsey joins him. "I can, too." He's armed as well.

The time spent waiting for more officers to show up is unbearable. I want to rush the cabin right now, guns blazing, and put an end to this, but of course I can't do that. I have no idea where Jennie is inside that cabin—assuming she's even in there—or if she is, what shape she's in. If I go in there half-cocked, I'd be putting her at risk.

So I do my best to tamp down my anxiety and focus on a positive outcome.

I pull Ricky aside. "I've got a plan. Listen carefully, and don't fuck this up."

"What kind of plan?" he asks, frowning at me. "You'd better not be planning something stupid."

"I'm going to do whatever it takes to rescue Jennie, and you're going to help me."

Hold on, Jennie. I'll get you out of there.

30

Jennie

Eventually, my bladder really is full, and I have no choice but to empty it before I pee myself. "David, I need to go to the outhouse."

He points to the corner of the room. "Use the bucket."

"I can't use a bucket. Be serious. At least let me use the outhouse. You can come with me, if you insist. You don't even have to untie my hands, just my feet so I can walk."

"You promise you won't try anything funny?"

For the first time since this ordeal began, I feel a surge of optimism. If I can get outside, I have a chance of escaping. "I promise."

He withdraws a serrated knife from a sheath strapped to his hip and cuts the ropes binding my wrists to the headboard posts.

Immediately, I wince as I sit up and cradle my ravaged wrists in my lap. The skin is rubbed raw, and the drying blood itches. "I don't suppose you have a first-aid kit, do you?"

"You don't need it. You're fine."

He proceeds to cut the ropes from my ankles, too. They're in about the same shape as my wrists. The sheet is splotched with blood.

I realize this place already looks like a crime scene, and it's likely to look a lot worse before it's over. All I care about is that the people I love don't get hurt.

"Can I please have my shoes?" I ask as I swing my feet to the wooden floorboards.

"No shoes."

"I'm not used to walking barefoot outside. The outhouse is in the trees, and I'll have to walk through the brambles."

"You'll be fine," he says dismissively. "Quit complaining and let's go. Or, piss in your pants. I don't care."

"Fine."

David drags me over to the kitchen table. He grabs a handgun, and then he directs me to the cabin door, opens it, and pushes me out onto the front porch. As he follows me outside, the door swings shut behind us. Half a dozen rifles poke out from the surrounding trees, pointed right at us.

"Freeze!" Chris yells. "Sheriff's office! You're surrounded, Braggart. It's over. Let her go."

David hauls me back against him and wraps one arm around my waist to hold me secure. He raises his other hand and points the muzzle of his handgun at my temple.

There's no cover near the cabin, so the officers are quite a ways back, camouflaged in the trees.

Time slows to a crawl as we stand here on the porch, out in the open, vulnerable from all angles.

"Let her go, Braggart!" Chris yells. "There are six of us, and only one of you. You don't have a chance."

"No, there are two of us!" David yells. He shoves the gun hard against my skull, making me cry out.

"Let her go, Dave," Chris says. "If you care about Jennie at all, you'll let her walk away."

"No, *you* walk away," David says. "She's mine. She's staying with me, so back off."

My heart is in my throat, and I don't think I've ever been so frightened in my life. I'm not scared for myself, but for Chris.

A moment later, Chris lays down his rifle and walks out from behind a tree, his arms held wide. He's wearing an armored vest, but he appears unarmed. "Let's talk about this, Dave," he says in a good-ol'-boy voice. "Just you and me, buddy. Let's talk it over."

David tenses, and his hand gripping the gun starts to shake.

"Chris, no!" I cry. The idiot's going to get himself killed trying to save me. "Please, Chris!" Hot tears burn my cheeks. "Don't do this!"

"Stop, or I'll shoot her," Dave warns. "I fucking mean it! Stop right there!"

Chris advances slowly, one step at a time as he heads right for us.

"I said stop!" David yells. "I mean it, Sheriff. Stop right there."

"Make me," Chris says with a taunting grin on his face. And then he flips David the bird.

"You asshole!" David screams. He aims his gun at Chris and pulls the trigger.

Chris recoils as the bullet strikes him, knocking him back onto the ground.

I scream.

Almost instantly, there's a deafening crack, and David topples backward, pulling me with him. Struggling to free myself from his grip, I roll over and stare at his head. There's a hole in the middle of his forehead, and his eyes are staring sightlessly up at the clear blue sky.

All hell breaks loose then. Officers come running out from the woods, along with Jack and Owen. Owen carries me several feet away from David's body before setting my bare feet down on the grass. Jack and Ricky check to make sure David's dead.

He's dead, all right. I could have told them that. When I looked into his eyes as he lay on the porch, I saw absolutely nothing looking back.

Meanwhile, three officers are huddled around Chris's body, kneeling beside him. One of them is checking to see if he has a pulse. One is checking to see if he's breathing. Micah comes racing out of the trees holding what looks like a medical bag. He drops to the ground beside his best friend. He goes to his knees as he frantically removes the body armor to expose Chris's chest. He rips open Chris's blood-soaked uniform shirt to expose his chest and shoulder.

When my knees buckle, Owen catches me. It takes me a second to regain my balance, and then I break free from Owen and run to Chris, falling on the ground beside him. "Chris!"

But of course there's no answer. He's unconscious.

Chris, my love, what have you done?

I realize there are a pair of strong hands clutching my shoulders. I glance back to see Ruth crouching behind me, tears streaming down her cheeks.

Several people crowd around Chris. Killian applies pressure to Chris's right shoulder as Micah bandages the wound.

"He's going to be all right, isn't he?" I ask through a throat clogged with tears. But no one answers me. I grab one of Chris's hands, which feels unusually cold. "Please tell me he's going to be all right." Because I can't live with the alternative.

I glance around at everyone standing in the clearing. Their expressions are glum as they watch Micah administer first aid. He's a former Army medic. If anyone can help Chris, he can.

My heart is shredded. *Chris!* He's my best friend, my lover, *my everything.* He can't leave me now, not when we've come so far. We're supposed to have a future together. It's not fair.

"It should have been me," I murmur, although I don't think anyone is paying me any attention. "It should have been me."

Ruth pulls me into her arms and rocks me. "Shush, honey." She strokes my hair. "Shush."

She doesn't even lie and tell me everything's going to be okay.

31

Jennie

Time slows to a crawl as I watch Micah work on Chris. There's a loud ringing in my ears, and I'm so cold my muscles are shivering.

"We need to get him to a hospital," Micah says. "God, I wish I had my chopper here."

"We called for a medevac," Jace says as he stands watching the grim proceedings. "But we're going to have to move him to the main house. There's not enough clearance to land a chopper here."

Killian pulls up in an ATV. "It's not the safest mode of transportation, but it's our only option."

Micah stands. "We don't have a choice. He's losing too much blood."

"The idiot," Jace says affectionately, and everyone nods. "God love him."

It's decided that Killian will drive the ATV back to the house. Micah will ride with him, and they'll sandwich Chris between them.

"It's going to be rough going," Killian says. "This machine wasn't designed to carry the weight of three grown men. It's going to be off balance and liable to tip. We're going to have to take it slow."

"We don't have time for slow," Micah says.

Ruth sits with me on the grass as the men arrange themselves on the black vinyl seat of the vehicle. Chris is still unconscious, so they use ropes to strap him to Killian's back. Micah takes up the rear, barely managing to fit on the seat. He does his best to hold Chris steady.

"Try to take it easy," Micah says to Killian. "The rest of you follow on foot."

"Wait!" I race up to the vehicle. Chris's head is resting on Killian's back, his eyes closed. "I'm so sorry," I whisper to him. I lean in and kiss his blood-splattered lips. My heart is pounding. There are so many things I need to tell him, but there's no time. There may never be time. "I love you, Chris."

Ruth gently pulls me back. "Honey, they need to go."

Hannah kisses Killian as he revs the engine. "Good luck," she says.

Killian nods at his wife, and then the ATV moves forward. Slowly at first, as Killian tries to balance the machine. A few moments later, they pick up speed, and suddenly they're around the bend and out of sight.

Immediately, I turn and race for the cabin. I shoot up the porch steps and rush past David's body, which is covered with a blanket as two officers stand beside it.

Ruth follows me into the cabin. "What are you doing?"

"I've got to get my shoes." I hunt around frantically for my sneakers. I find them under the bed and quickly put them on. I grab Ruth's hand and tug her with me toward the door. "We have to hurry!"

"Jennie." Ruth pulls me gently to a stop. "There's no way we can keep up with them. They'll make it back to the house long before we can, and they won't waste a second transporting Chris to the hospital. They won't be able to wait for us."

As I turn back to face her, all the energy leaches out of me. I'm running on sheer adrenaline now, and that's waning quickly as the stress of today catches up with me. "But I won't get to see him al— again." The unspoken word—*alive*—hangs in the air between us.

Ruth's smile is sad. "You'll see him at the hospital, sweetie. Jack and I will drive you straight there as soon as we reach the house."

"We still have to hurry," I say as I rush down the porch steps and head in the direction of the main house. "Every second counts."

Ruth and Jack are right on my heels.

"You guys go," Hannah says, waving us off. "We'll secure the scene here and be right behind you."

* * *

When we make it back to the house, there's no sign of Chris and the others. There's also no helicopter. The ATV is parked in the circular drive in front of the house, abandoned.

A middle-aged Latina comes out, waving her arms excitedly. "A helicopter took them away!" She glances at us. "Where is Mr. David?"

"He's not coming," Jack tells the woman.

Ruth leads me to her vehicle while Jack quickly explains to the woman everything that happened at the cabin. As she wails loudly and starts muttering in Spanish, Jack joins us. He gets behind the wheel and drives, while Ruth sits beside me in the back seat.

I lean numbly against her as she wraps an arm around me. I've lost all steam now. I'm shaking and numb, and I feel broken inside.

Chris.

He risked his life to save me. After everything that's happened, I don't deserve him.

"I can't lose him," I murmur. "I only just got him."

Ruth tightens her hold on me. "I know, sweetie. I know."

I hear Jack on the radio as he tries to reach Killian, but he has no luck. He glances back at us. "There's probably interference from the helicopter."

We drive the rest of the way to the hospital in silence.

There's not much to say. I don't know what Chris's condition is.

It might already be too late.

I told him I was sorry and that I loved him. But the one thing I didn't get to do was say goodbye.

* * *

When we near the hospital, Jack gets a phone call from Killian. After listening for a moment, he puts the call on speakerphone so Ruth and I can hear, too.

"He's in surgery now," Killian says. "He's stable at least. Jennie, how are you holding up?"

"I'm okay," I say absently. I really don't care about myself or how I'm doing. All I care about is Chris. I can't stop thinking about how he risked his life for me. He intentionally put himself in harm's way to distract David so Officer Stephens could take a shot.

When we arrive at the hospital, we make our way to the surgery waiting room, where Killian and Micah are. Soon the others arrive—Maya, Travis, Hannah, Owen, and John. The deputies come as well.

We sit for what seems like hours before a nurse comes out to give an update on Chris's status.

"He's out of surgery now and in Recovery," she says. "Is someone here his next of kin?"

Everyone looks at me. "I am! I'm his fiancée." Technically, it's a lie, but I don't feel one bit guilty for saying it. If I have my way, I *will* be his fiancée.

She takes down my name. "We'll come get you as soon as he's moved to a room."

Sometime later, the same nurse returns with an update. She says the surgery went well, and he's stable.

Upon hearing those words, I burst into tears.

Micah pulls me into his arms. "It's okay, Jen. He's going to be okay."

Micah goes with me to his room. We're silent as we step inside the dimly lit space.

The room is quiet, except for all the beeping and wheezing equipment. Chris lies on the bed, white as a sheet, dressed in a hospital gown. There are wires attached to his chest and an IV in his left arm. There's a blood pressure cuff on his left arm. His upper right arm and shoulder are wrapped in fresh bandages.

We stand beside his bed—the left side—so I can reach down and squeeze his hand. "We're here, Chris. Micah and I are here."

He doesn't respond. Clearly, he's still out of it.

Micah pulls a chair up to the side of the bed. "Here, Jen. Sit down before you fall down."

He pulls a second chair up beside mine, and we both sit there, holding a vigil as we wait for our best friend to wake up.

32

Chris

The light hurts my eyes, and I have to blink several times to focus on the white tiled ceiling above me. Machines are beeping. The place smells like antiseptic cleaner. My right shoulder is on fire, and the sling is back on.

Damn it! I'm in the hospital again.

"Jennie?" Her name comes out as a garbled croak.

I look frantically around until I spot her curled up sound asleep in a chair beside my bed. My entire body sags in relief—and damn it, that hurts! *She's okay.*

I guess I got shot. I honestly didn't expect that to happen because I figured Dave Braggart is a lousy shot. But I guess everyone gets lucky sometime.

The important thing is Jennie's here. She's okay. She's *safe*. Yeah, she looks tired, haggard even, but that's not surprising given the nightmare of a day she had. But at least she's in one piece. It looks like we both are.

"Jennie?" I try again, attempting to generate some volume this time. I'm a selfish bastard, and I want her attention. I want to see her eyes. I want to hear her voice. "Sweetheart?"

Her dark eyes fly open, and she sits upright in the chair, her feet falling to the floor. "Chris!" She jumps up and leans close, cupping my face as she gazes deeply into my eyes. She gently brushes my hair back. "Are you okay? How do you feel? I was so scared when David shot you."

"I'm okay," I say, surprised by how raspy my voice sounds.

She places a gentle kiss on my forehead. "I love you so much, but if you ever do something like that again, I will kill you myself."

I muster a smile. I don't mind getting shot if this is the reception I get. "I'll try not to."

She smiles at me, relief evident in her face. "We have to stop meeting like this."

"Yeah. I've had enough of hospitals to last me a while." My smile falters when I think about what happened today. "Are you okay? Did he hurt you?"

She drops back down onto her chair as if all her energy has been expended. "I'm okay. Really."

I notice the bandages around both of her wrists. "What happened to your arms?"

"It's nothing serious. Just some abrasions."

"What caused them?"

She looks away. "Ropes."

"He *tied* you up?"

She nods. "He tied me to a bed."

"Where else are you hurt?"

"My ankles. Same reason. Other than that, I'm fine."

My gut knots as I imagine her tied to a bed. *My God, if he touched her!* "Jennie, did he—"

"No," she says emphatically. "He didn't." She gives my hand a reassuring squeeze.

"Jennie." I slip into my cop interrogation voice.

"No, really. Other than tying me up, he didn't hurt me."

I scrub my left hand down my face. "Please tell me he's no longer a threat." Ricky had his instructions.

"He's dead, Chris. Ricky shot David right after David shot you."

I nod, satisfied.

"You don't seem surprised," she adds.

"I'm not. He was a threat to your life as well as to others. There were a lot of civilians there at the scene. He needed to be neutralized."

Jennie moves to sit on the side of my bed and reaches for my left hand, cradling it in hers. "You risked your life for me." Tears spring into her eyes. "You could have been killed."

"I had body armor on. I calculated the odds he'd manage to hit my head or a major artery, and decided they were in my favor.

Braggart's not a good shot. He was lucky he managed to hit my shoulder instead of my vest. I determined it was a risk worth taking because, at that moment, he was holding a handgun to your *head.* And that was unacceptable."

She leans closer, cupping the side of my face. "You saved me."

I swallow hard. "I couldn't let him hurt you."

She presses her soft lips to mine, and it's like being kissed by an angel. "Chris, I—"

There's a knock on my door. "Is this a good time?"

No, it's a terrible time! But I can't say that because it's Micah. "Sure, man. Come on in."

Micah walks into the room, right up to my bed, and offers a fist bump to my left hand. "How are you holding up?"

"I'll be right as rain in a few days. I'm just sore."

Micah nods. "Sure. But no more heroics, okay?" He glances at Jennie, understanding written all over his face. "I don't think Jennie can take it."

"I had everything under control. Ricky and I worked it out. The plan was, I would draw Braggart's attention, and once his gun was pointed at me and not at Jennie, Ricky would take his shot. Ricky's a damn fine shot. I knew he could take out Braggart without hurting Jennie, or I never would have suggested it."

Micah grips Jennie's shoulders. "Thanks for taking care of our girl."

"So, how did you guys get me out of there?" I ask. "When I woke up, I was here in the hospital."

Micah grins. "Killian and I drove you back to the main house on an ATV. That's where the chopper picked you up to bring you here."

"Three of us on an ATV? That must have been a tight squeeze. We're lucky we didn't topple over."

"It was tricky going," he says, "especially with you being out cold. Killian did some pretty fancy driving. I had the easy job—to hold onto you and keep you, and myself, from falling off."

A hospital employee pushes a cart into my room. "How are you feeling?" she asks. "Would you like some ice water and maybe some gelatin?"

"That depends. Is it strawberry?"

The nurse glances at the small container. "Actually, you're in luck. It is."

Micah raises the head of my bed so I'm sitting up. Jennie holds the giant tumbler of iced water so I can take a sip. I wince when I swallow. "Man, that hurts."

"That's from the intubation during surgery. The discomfort should ease up soon."

Jennie opens the container of gelatin and scoops some out with a spoon. "Open up," she says, grinning as she feeds me.

Throughout the evening, more visitors stop by to say hello—the SAR team members, several of my deputies, and Darlene.

Ricky finally shows up after his shift ends. The first words out of his mouth are, "You sure took one hell of a risk."

"It was worth it, man. And I knew you could take him out." Ricky was a sharpshooter in the Marines before he joined law enforcement.

"Yeah, well don't do that to me again, boss. Jennie's head was six inches away from my target. I about shit my pants."

I raise my left fist. "I owe you."

Grinning, Ricky gives me a gentle fist bump. "It looks like you'll be out on sick leave for a while. You can pay me back by making me the interim boss. Then I can really piss Jace off."

"It's a deal," I say.

Jennie dozed off in her chair around seven. She's awakened when her phone rings. "It's Dawn," she says as she takes the call. "Hi, Dawn. How's everything going?"

She listens for a while, then glances my way. "Are you sure?" She listens. "She does? Where does she think we went?" Jennie smiles. "Really?" She listens. "Okay, if you're sure. Thank you."

Jennie ends the call. "That was Dawn. She offered to spend the night with Granny so I can spend the night here with you." She laughs softly. "Apparently, Granny thinks you and I are on our honeymoon."

"Really?"

She nods. "And guess where she thinks we went on our honeymoon?"

"Where?"

"Hawaii."

"You're kidding me," I say.

"Yeah. I don't know where she got that crazy idea. I've never mentioned Hawaii to her before in my life."

"Actually, it's not that crazy," I say. "I have an aunt and uncle who live in Hawaii. My mom's younger sister, Cassandra, and her husband live in Maui. I think they've got three or four kids."

"You have family?" Jennie sits upright in her chair. "I didn't know that. You never mentioned them."

"Mom and her sister were estranged—no surprise there. Cassandra used to send me birthday and Christmas money when I was a kid, but my mom would always confiscate it. So then my aunt started sending me toys, and Mom would sell them on eBay. I eventually told my aunt to stop sending anything. God, I haven't talked to her since I graduated college. She actually helped me pay for school. She paid half my tuition, and I worked to pay the other half."

"I'd really like to meet your aunt one day," Jennie says. "I thought you had no family."

Jennie spends the night with me in my room. There's a recliner in the room that lays flat to make a guest bed. A nurse provides her with a pillow, sheet, and a blanket.

Her makeshift bed is close enough to my bed that we can reach out and hold hands as we fall asleep.

* * *

A couple of days later, I'm released in the afternoon after being examined one last time by my surgeon. Micah comes to the hospital in Robyn's car to drive us back to Jennie's house. There's no way I could climb in and out of Micah's truck.

"Looks like I'll be staying with you a while longer," I say as Jennie helps me out of the car.

"I should say so," she replies as she and Micah help me up the steps and into the kitchen.

They take me straight to Jennie's room. She puts me in her bed and fusses over me to make sure I'm comfortable enough.

"How was Hawaii?" Rosie asks from the doorway.

God, I love that woman. "It was fantastic," I tell her.

Rosie nods to Jennie. "See? I told you. This one's a keeper." Then she frowns. "I hope we won't be seeing any more of the bad one."

"I guarantee you won't be seeing any more of him," I say as Pumpkin jumps up in bed with me, purring like a squeaky chainsaw as he butts his head against my chin.

"Good," Rosie says. "I'm going to hold you to that." Then she looks at Jennie. "Are we having supper soon? I'm hungry."

Jennie hugs her grandma. "Yes, Granny. I'll get on dinner right away."

33

Jennie

Six months later

It's been an absolutely crazy day. The search and rescue team has been searching all day for a dad and his eight-year-old daughter who went on a one-hour hike this morning at 9 AM and haven't been heard from since. The wife is frantic, of course.

The McIntyre SAR team is out in full force, and Micah is on stand-by with the chopper in case the missing people can be extricated by air. We've got another SAR team out of Estes Park here, as well as local volunteers. There are over thirty people searching for this dad and his daughter.

My contribution to the effort is providing free meals and drinks to the volunteers. Right now, Michelle, Chad, and I are packing up a second shipment of boxed meals to take to the headquarters at the trail head. It's a chilly day in November, and the searchers need to keep up their strength. In addition to the food, we're bringing bottles of water and soft drinks, as well as coffee and hot chocolate to replenish the large stainless steel dispensers.

It's been so busy at the diner today I had to call in two of our part-time servers and an extra cook to help us manage the workload so Michelle and Chad could come with me to the trail head to help me set up.

When I pull the diner's catering van into the congested parking lot, I spot Chris standing at the hood of his SUV, talking with team leads as they refer to the map. He glances my way and smiles. It's so good to see him back in his element again after so many months of physical therapy and training after he was shot. He had to pass a thorough evaluation to be fully reinstated.

Seeing him in uniform and a brown leather bomber jacket does something for me. He's a handsome guy, but in his uniform, well, he's over the top. I get tingles just looking at him.

After I park the van near the hospitality tent, Michelle and Chad start unloading the boxed meals—deli sandwiches, homemade potato chips, apples, and chocolate chip cookies—and setting them on a folding table. For sandwiches, we brought got turkey and cheese, roast beef, and vegetarian and vegan options. For drinks, Maggie donated bottles of fruit juice, water, and soft drinks in ice-filled coolers.

While they're putting out the meals, I replenish the stainless steel dispensers with coffee and hot chocolate.

Volunteers who are currently on break waste no time coming to the catering station and helping themselves to the food and beverages.

Once the catering tent is organized, I finally get a chance to go see Chris. Right now he's meeting with Killian and a woman I don't recognize. I assume she's from the other SAR team participating in this search.

I walk up beside Chris and slip my hand in his back pocket. "Fresh food and drink for everyone is in the tent. Any luck?" I know it's wishful thinking on my part. If they'd found the man and his daughter, we'd all know by now.

"Thanks for the food. I really appreciate it. Everyone does. As for the two we're looking for, nothing yet."

It goes without saying that because it's already dark, and the night temperature is dropping, the risk of exposure to the two missing persons increases dramatically. The fact no one has heard from them in eight hours indicates that something significant has happened. Or else they'd be back at the lodge right now sitting in front of a fire and sipping hot chocolate.

"Do you need anything?" I ask Chris. "Food or coffee?" He's been at this since early morning, and I doubt he's had anything to eat or drink.

He shakes his head. "No, I'm fine." He reaches out to squeeze my hand. "But thanks for asking."

One thing I've learned about Chris is when he's in work mode, he's so focused he's impervious to discomfort.

Killian's radio squawks as his team members begin to report in as scheduled. Hannah, Maya, and Travis report in first. Then Owen and John.

Nothing.

I notice a woman seated off to the side on a folding lawn chair. She's got a blanket wrapped around her, and a cup of something hot in her hands. She's obviously been crying.

"Is she the wife?" I ask Chris.

"Yeah. Her name is Lynn Atkins. The husband's name is Jeff, and the daughter is Isabella. Lynn has been beating herself up for not going on the hike with them. But she wasn't feeling well this morning—morning sickness, she's six months pregnant—and it was just supposed to be a short hike for the dad and daughter, so she decided to stay in their room at the Lodge and sleep in. But when they didn't return as scheduled, she called the office and reported them missing."

"She was right to stay in," I say. "She doesn't have any business out there. Not on this trail."

This particular trail is known for being rugged. There are a lot of sharp drop-offs, and sometimes the trail narrows quite a bit. One careless step could lead to disaster.

"I assume they don't have a sat phone with them?"

Chris nods. "The father has a cell phone with him. That's all."

"They're not going to get a signal out there," I say. "Did Hannah bring Scout?"

"Yes," Killian says. "I'm heading up there to join her now."

Suddenly, Killian's satellite phone rings. "It's Hannah," he says as he answers the call and puts it on speaker. "Go ahead, Hannah. You're on speaker. Chris is here with me."

"Scout is showing strong interest in a connector trail that leads over to Black Bear Trail," Hannah says.

"That would explain why we haven't found them," Killian says. "If they switched trails, we're looking in the wrong place."

"How far up the trail are you?" Killian asks Hannah.

"A little over one mile."

"All right. I'm coming. I'll join you as soon as I can. Maya and Travis are still with you, right?"

"Affirmative," Hannah says.

"Good. All right, I'm on my way. Over and out."

Killian pockets his sat phone. "Let the other teams know where we're going," he tells Chris. "If we spot anything, we'll call it in."

"Got it," Chris says as he makes a notation on the map. Suddenly, the search area has increased significantly. "Good luck."

After Killian leaves, I go to the catering tent to grab a box meal and a cup of coffee for Chris. I set the items on the hood of his SUV. "Please take a moment to eat and drink. Knowing you, you haven't had anything all afternoon."

He reaches for the coffee cup and takes a sip. "Thanks." He touches my cheek. "Thanks for everything you're doing. It really helps."

Now that Chris is finally eating something, I bring Mrs. Atkins a boxed meal and a bottle of water. "It's a turkey and cheese sandwich," I say. "I've got vegetarian and vegan options, too, if you'd prefer."

The woman shakes her head. "Thanks for the food, but I can't eat anything right now. My stomach is in knots."

I crouch down beside her. "You need to eat something. It won't do your husband or daughter any good if you make yourself sick. When they're found, you're going to need your strength."

Her eyes flood with tears. "I know. I'll try."

More volunteers come down from the trail to grab some food. Other volunteers take their places. Even from the trailhead, I can hear people calling for the missing hikers.

These mountains are beautiful, but they can also be dangerous.

When I return to Chris, he gives me a rueful smile. "I'm sorry our plans for this evening were ruined."

We had planned to go on a dinner date tonight in Estes Park. "It's okay." I step close beside him, lean into him, and lay my head on his shoulder. "We can reschedule."

"I know," he says. "It's just that I had special plans for tonight."

I realize I left my gloves in the catering tent, and my fingers are ice cold. I slip them into his jacket pocket to warm up. To my surprise, his pocket isn't empty. There's something in here—something small, square, and covered in velvet. It's a little box.

"What's this?" Without thinking, I pull it out. My eyes widen when I see it's a small dark blue velvet jewelry box, and my heart goes thump. "Oh, my God." I shove it back into his pocket. "I'm so sorry."

He laughs softly as he retrieves the jewelry box from his pocket.

"This was my special plan for tonight. I guess the cat's out of the bag now."

"Is that what I think it is?"

The corners of his brown eyes crinkle as he nods. "Yes."

"You were going to—" I can't even say the words.

"Ask you to marry me tonight? I was. During a romantic, candlelit dinner at Mama Rosa's. But, obviously, the universe had other plans for us tonight."

As I stare at that blue box, the significance of its contents hits me like a ton of bricks.

Chris wants to marry me.

I think about the dream I've had so many times—the one I thought was completely out of my grasp—and it's right here. Within reach. "Ask me," I say abruptly, my voice shaking.

"Right now?" He looks shocked. "In a parking lot? This is hardly the most romantic setting. Honey, are you sure?"

"Chris, I don't need a romantic candlelit dinner. All I need is you. Ask me, please."

He opens the box and shows me the contents—a gorgeous engagement ring with a lovely slim gold band and a perfect diamond solitaire.

"It's beautiful," I breathe.

To my surprise, he gets down on one knee, on a gravel parking lot, and says, "Jennifer Lopez, would you please make me the happiest man on the planet? I promise I'll do everything in my power to make you happy."

And I believe him. "Yes." I'm shaking so much I can barely utter an intelligible word. "Yes, of course." I reach down and pull him to his feet.

He takes the ring out of the box, slips it on my ring finger, and pulls me close for a kiss. The kiss goes on and on until we finally break apart to get air.

Just as Chris is about to say something, his sat phone rings. He grabs it and takes the call. "Nelson here, over."

"Chris!" It's Killian. "We found them on the connector trail. Other than having a broken leg, the man is stable. The child is borderline suffering from hypothermia, but she'll be all right once we get her warm. Micah is on his way with the chopper to extract the man. I'll take him up into the helicopter, and we'll take him to the hospital in Estes Park. The others will bring the girl down to you. Please radio for EMT."

"Roger that," Chris says. "Good work, guys. Who found them?"

"Who do you think?" Killian asks with a chuckle. "Scout did."

I waste no time racing over to Lynn Atkins to give her the good news. "Your husband and daughter have been found, and they're both in stable condition." She breaks down in tears and mutters a prayer under her breath.

While I do what I can to comfort the mom, my gaze keeps returning to my hand.

Lynn notices my ring. "That's a beautiful ring. How long have you been engaged?"

I smile. "About five minutes." I point to Chris. "To that man over there."

"The sheriff?"

"The one and only, my childhood sweetheart."

Epilogue

One month later...
Jennie

It's just like my dream, only this time, it's real. It's actually happening. I'm not going to wake up a blubbering mess in a few minutes. I'm tempted to pinch myself to double-check I'm not dreaming, but since a roomful of people just turned in their seats to watch me, I refrain. Instead, I focus on the sight in front of me—Chris Nelson at the head of the room standing between his best man, Micah, and Reverend Jones. Dressed in a black tuxedo, white dress shirt, magenta tie and cummerbund, Chris takes my breath away.

My Chris.

My best friend.

Now my lover.

And soon-to-be my husband.

As I meet Chris's gaze, I can't help thinking about that life-altering moment seven months ago when this man literally risked his life to save mine. I could have lost him that day, and my dream would have been permanently shattered. But fortune was on our side that day, and he survived a gunshot.

As Chris smiles at me, his eyes become suspiciously shiny as he inhales a deep breath. Micah pats his back as he murmurs something under his breath, and Chris nods repeatedly.

The three amigos. It's only fitting that the three of us share the stage today.

"You doin' all right, kid?" asks the tall, dark-haired man at my side.

Jack Merchant offered to give me away today, since my own father and grandfather aren't with us anymore. I guess it's fitting as he's almost old enough to be my dad.

When Chris and I told our friends we were getting married, Jack approached me in private and offered to walk me down the aisle. I sobbed like a baby. Since Ruth is the closest thing I have to a mom—well, she and Maggie both—I guess it makes sense that her partner, Jack, would stand in as my father figure today.

As we walk down the center aisle in the gathering room at The Lodge, I smile at my friends. It's a small gathering, just our closest friends, but it's perfect because these are the people I love. These are the ones who love me. But the one who loves me the most is standing right in front of me, his gaze locked on me.

Granny is sitting with Dawn in the front row on the left side of the aisle. I'm not too sure what to expect when I reach her row. Will this be too much for her? Will she understand what's happening?

Granny reaches out and snags my hand. "My dear girl, look how pretty you are!" Her hand trembles as she squeezes mine. "Your mama would be so proud of you."

A knot forms in my throat as I glance down at my dress. When Chris and I told Granny we were getting married, she ran to her closet and pulled out a garment bag containing my mom's wedding dress. I didn't even know she'd kept it all these years.

It's a simple, sleeveless, ivory V-neck dress. A sheer layer of ivory lace, decorated with tiny seed beads, lays over a solid ivory satin underskirt, which barely brushes the floor. My bridal bouquet is a mix of ivory, pink, and magenta roses.

Granny points at Chris, her finger shaking. "I told you this one is a keeper," she says, nodding decisively.

"Yes, you did, Granny. And I agree—he's most definitely a keeper."

She releases my hand and shoos me forward. "Well, what are you waiting for? Go marry that young man."

Jack walks me to the front of the room, where Chris takes my hand. His grip is firm, and his gaze never leaves my face—not for a second. He's waited for this moment just as long as I have.

My throat tightens when I think about the circuitous route we took to find each other. He left Bryce for Phoenix, and yet he returned. I married the wrong man, and yet here I am. And now we have our chance to be together for the rest of our lives. We finally get our HEA.

Reverend Jones starts reading the vows Chris and I modified to fit us better. Our vows are all about partnership and equality, loving and cherishing, loyalty and acceptance. And while I had reservations as I entered into my first marriage, I don't have any qualms this time around. Not a single one. Chris is a good man, and he'll be a great partner.

"Christopher Andrew Nelson, do you take this woman to be your lawfully wedded wife?" Reverend Jones asks.

"I do," Chris says, his voice loud and clear.

"Jennifer Rosalie Lopez, do you take this man to be your lawfully wedded husband?"

"I do," I say, smiling as I gaze into a pair of teary dark eyes.

Chris squeezes my hands with a sure and unflinching grip.

"I pronounce you husband and wife," the Reverend says. "You may now kiss."

Chris wraps his arms around me, dips me, and kisses me with more enthusiasm than is probably acceptable for a public gathering.

Our guests stand and cheer. And before we know it, we're surrounded by our friends—*our found family*—who hug us, pat us on the back, and kiss my cheek.

Once all the noise begins to die down, Hannah makes an announcement. "I'd like to invite all of the guests here today to join Mr. and Mrs. Chris and Jennie Nelson in the restaurant for a reception and dinner."

Hannah and Killian were kind enough to reserve the entire restaurant for our wedding reception. In appreciation, I offered all of the Lodge guests a free dinner at the diner. They also gifted us a night in the Lodge's honeymoon suite, a beautiful, spacious room overlooking the lake out back.

Chris offers me his arm. “May I escort you to the reception, wife?”

“Why, thank you, husband,” I say as I take his arm.

Dawn escorts Granny, who’s absolutely beaming.

When we enter the restaurant, we’re greeted with applause. Chris grins as he kisses me. “Every time they applaud, I have to kiss you. That’s the rule.”

“Really?” His good humor is contagious, and I can’t stop smiling.

He nods. “Yes, really.”

Tammy, the host at the podium, escorts us to the head of a very long table. The tables and chairs have been rearranged so that everyone is seated together. Granny is seated beside me, and Dawn is on her other side.

Servers bring out menus for everyone. They fill everyone’s water glass. Bottles of wine and champagne are passed around.

“Gabrielle, you’ve outdone yourself,” I tell her as she comes up to give me a hug. “The menu is amazing.”

There are four entrées to choose from, as well as multiple sides and salads. And the icing on the cake, as they say, is a three-tier wedding cake that was made by a caterer in Estes Park. The icing is ivory, and the cake is decorated with ivory and pink roses.

Dinner passes in a whirlwind, with lots of conversations floating around the table. It’s impossible to keep up with it all, so instead Chris and I eat holding hands and staring into each other’s eyes.

“So,” Maggie asks, interrupting our love fest. “Have you decided where you’re going for your honeymoon?”

“They’re going to Hawaii,” Granny says before she takes a sip of her champagne.

Maggie looks at me for confirmation.

I nod. "Our flight leaves in two days."

Chris raises his champagne glass to me, and we toast. "To Hawaii!" he says.

"I told you so," Granny says with a decisive nod.

* * *

Chris

As soon as everyone's done eating, the DJ strikes up the music. A large section of the restaurant has been cleared out to make room for dancing. I escort Jennie to the center of the floor as our chosen song starts—*Ordinary* by Alex Warren.

Every time I hear this song, I get choked up thinking about Jennie and what she means to me. I don't care if it sounds sappy, but she's everything to me. She always has been. I feel like my entire life has built up to this moment—when I can say to the world she's *mine*. She chose *me*.

After our dance ends, Jennie dances with Jack, and I dance with Granny.

"You take good care of my girl," Rosie says. "You hear me?"

"Yes, ma'am," I say with the conviction of a man who's finally found his place in the world. When I carefully twirl her on the dance floor, she blushes like a bride.

We all dance for a while, and then Jennie performs the bouquet toss. Maya catches it, and the look of sheer horror on her face makes the entire room burst into laughter.

We cut the cake—strawberry on the inside—and Jennie and I feed each other small bites.

Everything has been perfect today—the wedding, the reception, cutting the cake and all the pomp and circumstance that's expected at these kinds of events. It's all good, but honestly, I just want to be alone with my bride.

As the reception comes to an end, Dawn takes Granny back to the house. She's going to stay with us and take care of Granny for the ten days we'll be gone, and we thought it would ease the transition for Granny if Dawn started staying at our house a couple of days before we depart.

We say goodnight to Granny and Dawn as they prepare to leave.

Granny hugs us both goodbye. "You two are going to be very happy together," she says. "I just know it."

After they leave, Jennie and I head to our suite, where our overnight luggage awaits us. When we walk inside, she gasps when she sees the pink and white rose petals sprinkled on the king size bed. Little clusters of lit candles are arranged throughout the room.

"Oh, my God, it's beautiful!" she says as she takes it all in. "Who did this?"

"A little birdy told me your friends decorated the room especially for us."

"It's perfect." She walks up to me and turns, giving me her back. "Would you mind helping me out of this dress?"

My first thought is, *Does a bear shit in the woods?*

But that seems a bit crass on my wedding night, so I say, "Sure,

I'd love to."

I undress her then, very slowly, removing one silky piece of clothing at a time, until she's left wearing only her panties and bra—a super pale pink lacy set that her friends gave her at the bridal shower.

My chest tightens. "My God, you're beautiful," I say, my voice nearly cracking with emotion.

Her cheeks flush in response. "Now it's your turn," she says as she reaches for my tuxedo jacket.

Catching her hands, I shake my head. "I need a moment to just look at you." And then, for crying out loud, I embarrass myself by tearing up. But I can't help it. The realization that we're *here*, that we're *married*, is too much.

She reaches out and cups my face, her own eyes tearing up. "I can't believe this is real. I dreamed about this so many times, but I never thought it would come true. I love you, Chris. I always have."

She wraps her arms around my waist, and we stand here a moment, simply holding each other and gazing into each other's eyes.

I run my hands up and down her back, marveling at the silky soft feel of her skin. Her lush breasts, about to spill out of the cups of her pretty pink bra, are pressed against my chest, and suddenly I need my jacket and shirt *off*.

I release her and yank off my jacket and toss it aside. Then, before I can shred my shirt, she pushes my hands aside and unbuttons it for me, removing the tie and cummerbund in the process before I wreck them.

My shirt comes off, falling to the floor, followed by my undershirt. Then I pull her too me and feel her pressed up against my bare chest. I reach around her and unfasten her bra so that it slides off her. Now I have what I crave—her beautiful bare breasts pressed against my chest.

I suck in a breath. "You're going to be the death of me."

She laughs softly. "You survived a car wreck and a gunshot wound, Chris. I hardly think my breasts are going to take you out."

"That's what you think." I sweep her into my arms and carry her to our bed and lay her down. "If I don't get my mouth on you within the next thirty seconds, I'm a goner."

Jennie has a very contented smile on her face as I carefully work her panties off. And then I'm where I want to be. My mouth is on her, tasting, licking, stroking, teasing every tender and sensitive spot. My finger slides inside her and goes directly to that happy spot that sends her over the edge.

Her thighs are trembling, her fingers are in my hair, her nails digging into my scalp. I love the sounds she's making, and when she starts to get a little bit too loud—after all, we're not the only ones in the house—she holds a pillow over her face to muffle her cries.

I know exactly when her orgasm hits her. Her thigh muscles tense up, her body shakes, and she grips my head tightly. She cries my name as her pussy trembles against my tongue.

I stand and finish undressing quickly. After grabbing a condom packet from our suitcase, I crawl back onto the bed and kneel between her thighs. My hands are shaking as I tear open the packet and sheath myself. She has set the pillow aside, so now I can lean forward to kiss her as I work myself into her soft, wet opening.

I push in slowly, giving her body a chance to adjust, but it doesn't take long because she's so ready. I thrust the way she likes, slow and steady, for as long as I can, listening to her soft sighs and whispered words of love. Her fingers are in my hair one moment, and in the next, she's clutching my shoulders. When she digs her fingernails into my back, I close my eyes and relish the feeling. She's welcome to claw me all she wants.

When my climax hits me, I bury my face into the crook of her neck to muffle my hoarse cries. She holds me close, stroking my back, then my hair. She peppers the side of my face with kisses. I roll us onto our sides so I don't crush her.

We lie like this as long as possible, before I feel the condom in danger of slipping off. After disposing of it in the bathroom, I wash up and return to bed with a warm, wet washcloth to clean her up.

After she makes a trip to the bathroom to pee, we cuddle in bed. Both of us are wired, far too excited to sleep. We talk about our upcoming trip to Hawaii, talk about all the things we want to do while we're there. What we need to pack.

"I'd like to make a suggestion," I say as we start to wind down and get sleepy.

"What's that?" she murmurs.

"I was thinking, after we get back from our trip, you could hire an assistant manager for the diner, so you'd have someone to share the workload with. You work such long days. I'd love to see you have more time to relax and just enjoy life."

"Funny you should say that because I've been thinking about promoting Cara to assistant manager. Then, if he's interested, I can promote Chad to server and hire a new dishwasher."

"I think that's a great idea."

"If we have a child, I'll need to be at home a lot more."

I smile at the mention of kids. We've discussed it, and we both want them. The question is *when*. I pull her into my arms and picture her belly big and round with our child. I picture a little dark-haired baby with dark eyes. "I definitely think it's a great idea."

* * *

Thank you for reading Jennie and Chris's story. Their story was truly a wild ride. I'm so happy they found their HEA together.

I hope you are enjoying the *McIntyre Search and Rescue* series. Check out my list of books below for all my McIntyre stories in other series, starting with The McIntyre Security Bodyguard Series featuring the whole McIntyre family.

* * *

Do you want to keep up-to-date?

If you'd like to receive free exclusive bonus content, sign up for my newsletter on my website. You can also find information on upcoming releases, a reading order, and more.

www.aprilwilsonauthor.com

* * *

Want to Buy Directly from Me?

I have my own online store offering select e-books, signed paperbacks, audiobooks, and merchandise, all at discounted prices. You won't find better prices anywhere.
www.aprilwilsonshop.com

* * *

Would you like some bonus McIntyre content?

If you'd like to read bonus content, get updates on what I'm up to and books I'm working on, enjoy early access to book chapters as I write them, and listen to audiobook chapters, follow me on Patreon. I have both free and paid tiers, so there's something for everyone.
www.patreon.com/aprilwilson

* * *

Audiobooks by April Wilson

My audiobooks are available on Amazon, Audible, iTunes, and my own online shop. For the best prices on my audiobooks, visit my online shop. Audiobooks from my shop can be listened to on the free BookFunnel app.
www.aprilwilsonshop.com

* * *

Join Me on Facebook

I interact daily with readers in my Facebook reader group (Author April Wilson's Reader Group) where I post frequent updates and share weekly teasers for upcoming releases. Come join me!

* * *

Books by April Wilson

McIntyre Security Bodyguard Series:

Vulnerable
Fearless
Shane–a novella
Broken
Shattered
Imperfect
Ruined
Hostage
Redeemed
Marry Me–a novella
Snowbound–a novella
Regret
With This Ring–a novella
Collateral Damage
Special Delivery
Vanished–a novella

Baby Makes 3–a novella

The Engagement–a novella

Wrecked

Under His Protection

McIntyre Security Bodyguard Series Box Sets:

Box Set 1

Box Set 2

Box Set 3

Box Set 4

McIntyre Security Protectors:

Finding Layla

Damaged Goods

Freeing Ruby

McIntyre Search and Rescue:

Search and Rescue

Lost and Found

Tattered and Torn

Dark and Dangerous

Locked and Loaded

Serve and Protect

Tyler Jamison Novels:

Somebody to Love

Somebody to Hold

Somebody to Cherish

Daddy Detectives Series:

Daddy Detectives Episode 1

Daddy Detectives Episode 2

A British Billionaire Romance Series:

Charmed

Captivated

Miscellaneous Books:

Falling for His Bodyguard

* * *

Audiobooks:

To purchase my audiobooks at a great discount,
visit my online shop:
www.aprilwilsonshop.com

Made in the USA
Las Vegas, NV
03 December 2025

35669317R00177